Lord and Lady Chatham were blessed with five sons and only one daughter. But when it comes to Caroline, one is more than enough . . .

Caroline is about to embark on her third Season and her parents fear she'll be permanently on the shelf if she fails to make a match this time. Unfortunately for them, that is precisely what Caroline wants! Curious and adventuresome, Caroline longs for a life of travel, excitement, and perhaps even a touch of danger . . .

If only she can remain unmarried until she turns twenty-one, Caroline will inherit her grandmother's bequest and gain her freedom. It's not a staggering amount, but it's enough to fund her dreams without a husband's permission. She has her future all planned out—until Lawrence Sinclair appears on the scene . . .

Intense, intriguing, and handsome, the man reminds Caroline of a caged lion. In fact, the more she knows of him, the more questions she has. And when she learns how dangerous he really is, he may just become her new fascination—the one she can't resist . . .

Books by Mia Marlowe

Touch of a Thief
Touch of a Rogue
Touch of a Scoundrel
Plaid to the Bone (ebook novella)
Plaid Tidings
Once Upon a Plaid

The Singular Mr. Sinclair

Mia Marlowe

LYRICAL PRESS
Kensington Publishing Corp.
www.kensingtonbooks.com

Lyrical Press books are published by

Kensington Publishing Corp. 119 West 40th Street New York, NY 10018

All Kensington titles, imprints, and distributed lines are available at special quantity discounts for bulk purchases for sales promotion, premiums, fundraising, and educational or institutional use.

To the extent that the image or images on the cover of this book depict a person or persons, such person or persons are merely models, and are not intended to portray any character or characters featured in the book.

Special book excerpts or customized printings can also be created to fit specific needs. For details, write or phone the office of the Kensington Special Sales Manager:
Kensington Publishing Corp.
119 West 40th Street
New York, NY 10018
Attn. Special Sales Department. Phone: 1-800-221-2647.

Kensington and the K logo Reg. U.S. Pat. & TM Off.
LYRICAL PRESS Reg. U.S. Pat. & TM Off.
Lyrical Press and the L logo are trademarks of Kensington Publishing Corp.

First Electronic Edition: July 2018
eISBN-13: 978-1-5161-0596-0
eISBN-10: 1-5161-0596-6

First Print Edition: July 2018
ISBN-13: 978-1-5161-0597-7
ISBN-10: 1-5161-0597-4

Printed in the United States of America

Prologue

Ware Hall, Cumberland, 1796

By the time Lawrence Sinclair was ten years of age, he was certain of one thing in this world.

He would never make a scholar.

His tutor, Mr. Hazelton, despaired of Lawrence's ever amounting to anything in the classroom. To start with, even after years of practice, his penmanship remained a rough scrawl of chicken scratches and uneven lines.

"I cannot be held to account for it, Your Lordship," Mr. Hazelton explained to Lawrence's uncle, Lord Ware. "The boy persists in using his left hand unless I tie it behind his back."

Mr. Hazelton didn't tell the earl that he also routinely beat Lawrence's left knuckles with a ruler until they were red as poppies. Nothing worked. Lawrence remained stubbornly cack-handed.

Perhaps his struggle to write legibly bled over into other subjects, but he failed to excel in any area of Mr. Hazelton's tutelage. Lord Ware, however, was delighted with the progress of his son Ralph. Though a year younger than Lawrence, his cousin was already leagues ahead of him in grammar, rhetoric, and Latin. Ralph could do sums of long columns of numbers in his head and his French translations of John Donne poems were so beautiful the words still sang.

Lawrence's only flash of brilliance was that he sat a horse with distinction. He and his mount took leaps with ease, even ones from which older, more experienced riders might shy. He also learned that his tendency to use his left hand could be an advantage in fencing.

"Your foe willna ken how to come at ye," his old Scottish fencing master had told him. "But dinna let His Lordship know I let ye practice so. We must make sure ye can switch hands at will, aye?"

Still, a gentleman with no prospects couldn't rely on those talents alone to make his way in the world.

For make his own way he must.

Lawrence would inherit nothing. He and his mother lived under the begrudging care of Harcourt Sinclair, Lord Ware, because his father, the earl's younger brother by less than a minute, had died in a curricle accident a month before Lawrence was born. Lawrence regretted not having any memory of his sire, but he wondered if he should. When the adults in his life thought he wasn't attending, whispers of "just deserts" and "larking about with a Bird of Paradise" floated in conversations just over his head.

People also remarked how very different Lawrence's father had been from his brother, the earl. In appearance as well as temperament, Harcourt was a steady, plodding, draft horse. Lawrence's father Henry had been a flighty racer, lean and strong. Twins were like that sometimes, everyone said. The earl took after their mother's people, while Henry favored the Sinclairs' darkly handsome line.

Sometimes Lawrence stood before his father's portrait in the family gallery of Ware Hall, gazing up at the deep brown eyes that were so like his own, and puzzled over the man. He often imagined how different his life might have been if his father hadn't died while "larking about," with or without any sort of bird.

For one thing, Lawrence wouldn't be living under his stern uncle's roof. That would be a blessing beyond measure. Ware Hall was a fine, prosperous estate, with expansive grounds, but however well appointed, a cage was still a cage. Lord Ware's strictures were hard enough on Lawrence, but the earl ruled the whole family with a heavy hand.

Just once, Lawrence would have rejoiced to see his mother contradict his uncle on anything. But his mother was a quiet woman who seldom smiled, so docile and frail, Lawrence wondered if she cared about anything at all. Still, she surely would have been happier, he thought, if she'd been allowed to return to her own family in Wiltshire.

Lawrence had never met his mother's people. His grandfather on that side reportedly held a tidy baronetcy, but Lord Ware always said his brother had "married beneath himself, if that were possible." The daughter of a minor, late-made noble simply did not signify when weighed against the son of an earl.

Even a second son.

But Lord Ware wouldn't hear of Lawrence and his mother returning south. The earl might not like Lawrence overmuch—or his mother, either, come to that—but he was duty bound to provide for his nephew's upbringing. For if there was one thing the earl was certain of in this world, it was duty.

"The boy is my blood, demmit. He bears the Sinclair name. I'll not have him growing up wild as a thistle and ending up like his father. We don't need another foolish accident to blacken the house of Ware."

Then, mere days before Lawrence's eleventh birthday, another accident did happen. It might not have been accompanied by whispers of shame and disgrace, but it was so horrific, so unexpected, it was an affront to heaven and the natural order of things and surely the will of God Himself. It made his father's sins—including the "larking about" bit—seem small by comparison.

And Lawrence became certain of a second thing in this world.

His uncle wished him dead.

Is there a more alluring sight in all the world than the sun rising over an unknown sea?
—from the diary of Lady Caroline Lovell, only daughter of the Earl of Chatham, who has never in her life set foot on a watercraft larger than a rowboat.

Chapter 1

London, The Ides of March 1818

"And then, because Lord Ware arrived late," Horatia Englewood said, pausing for effect, "Lady Jersey ordered him to remove from the premises forthwith." When this bit of information was met with a shocked gasp from Frederica Tilbury, Horatia added, "Politely, of course."

The breath of minor scandal was almost enough to pull Caroline away from the parlor window and back into her friends' gossipy patter. But there were so many carriages moving past her family's town house in St. James Square, she couldn't look away. It was too delicious to imagine where they might be going.

Granted, most of the travelers were bound for parlors just like hers, where dainties would be offered, both in the form of petit fours and in juicy tidbits about the ton. It was the time of day reserved for calls, after all, and Polite Society lived to see and be seen.

But surely some of the carriages rolling by were headed for the docks. And perhaps a fortunate few of the passengers would board ships.

Bound for far off Zanzibar or Madagascar or . . . some other exotic place that ends in –ar. The colors are brighter there, I'll be bound, and even birdsong must sound deliciously mysterious. Best of all, when I went to the beach, I'd feel warm sand beneath my feet instead of horrid pebbles like those at Brighton.

Caroline sighed, wiggling her toes inside her slippers, daydreaming about how that foreign sand must feel. She squeezed her eyes shut and, for a heartbeat or two, she actually thought she felt a soft breeze drift past her. When she opened her eyes, the gossamer curtains were swaying a bit. One of the parlor windows had not been locked down tight when the maids dusted last.

Caroline sighed again, wishing it was a trade wind that caressed her cheek. Her imagination was always more interesting than what was actually happening around her.

However, her friend Frederica, who, it must be admitted, did not suffer from an abundance of imagination, was riveted by Horatia's story about Lord Ware. The girl giggled loudly over the tale, mostly out of nervousness. It was a bad habit from which Caroline was trying to wean her. Freddie was pretty enough, and her dowry several notches above adequate, but more than a few young bucks might scamper away from her giggle.

"Surely Lady Jersey never did such a thing," Frederica said, her words tumbling over each other instead of flowing gently in a calm, ladylike stream. It was yet another thing Caroline was trying to improve about her friend. The rapid delivery betrayed a lack of confidence, Caroline insisted. When she took time to think about it, Frederica was making some progress, but when excited, dear Freddie reverted to her jackrabbit manner of speaking. Now she rattled on. "Not even a Lady Patroness would dare turn Lord Ware away from Almack's. Indeed, she wouldn't. Surely."

"Oh, yes, indeed she did. Surely." Horatia straightened her spine to ramrod uprightness. Then she looked down her nose in a surprisingly good imitation of Lady Jersey at her imperious best. "She said, 'If we turned away the Duke of Wellington for neglecting to honor the rules of dress, do not think for one moment we will not refuse to admit you, Lord Ware, when you have the temerity to arrive late to supper.'"

"Not that supper at Almack's inspires punctuality," Caroline murmured. To call the meager refreshments served promptly at eleven *supper* was charitable in the extreme. The weak punch and thinly sliced bread were famous for their awfulness.

"Still," Frederica said with a shiver, "imagine having the courage to snub Lord Ware?"

"Oh, Freddie, you little goose. Lady Jersey doesn't need courage. She has the rules on her side." Horatia raised her teacup and sipped delicately, pinky properly out.

She was right. Lady Jersey had the power of revoking Lord Ware's voucher to Almack's permanently. It was acceptable not to have that coveted ticket because one had not applied for a voucher. It was quite another thing to have been awarded one and then have it stripped away for behavior judged to be common. No matter how wealthy, how influential, or how important the Earl of Ware might be in the House of Lords, Lady Jersey wielded an even heavier club in Polite Society.

Frederica shivered again.

Like a wren fluffing its feathers. There's another thing I need to correct before the Season starts in earnest.

Carriage traffic had dwindled, so Caroline left the window and rejoined her friends. She settled into the Sheridan chair opposite the settee and helped herself to a biscuit. "Horatia, tell me. Did you see this astonishing exchange between Lady Jersey and Lord Ware with your own eyes?"

Her friend's lips pursed into a disgruntled moue. "Well, no, but—"

"Then, may I ask how you happened upon this extraordinary bit of intelligence?"

"You see, my cousin Violet's bosom friend, Amelia, heard it from—"

"So neither your cousin nor her bosom friend witnessed Lord Ware's humiliation?"

"You didn't let me finish," Horatia complained. "Amelia got it straight from her Aunt Harriet, whom she swears is the soul of discretion. And Amelia's aunt heard about the incident from Miss Penelope Braithwaite, who was *there*."

"Penelope Braithwaite," Caroline cast about through the myriad of introductions she'd suffered through during the last two Seasons, trying to remember the young lady.

"I believe she sings," Freddie prompted. "Didn't we attend one of her recitals?"

Suffered through one almost escaped Caroline's lips, but she held it back. Her dear mother always warned that speaking ill of others was a prayer to the devil. Caroline wasn't sure she believed it, but it didn't do to take chances.

"Oh, yes, now I remember," Caroline said. "You and I have heard her perform, Freddie."

"As have I, but only once," Horatia said with a snicker. "She abused the Mozart 'Alleluia' with such gusto, one hearing was more than enough." Horatia shook her head. "And she fancies herself a lyric soprano."

"Why, yes, I believe she does," Freddie said agreeably.

Dear Freddie. If Horatia said Miss Braithwaite fancied herself a trained chimpanzee in a Parisian frock, you'd nod and agree.

Caroline recommitted herself to shepherding her suggestible friend through the coming Season. She had no doubt fair-haired Frederica would turn heads. She was as pale and dimpled as the prevailing standards of beauty required. But fashionably pretty girls possessed of large dowries and small imaginations might fall prey to all manner of deception.

It was no trouble for her to guard Frederica's interests. After all, this would be Caroline's third Season. She was plainly on the shelf and not likely to be plucked down from it. Not since she'd turned down half a dozen proposals and avoided a few more by tactfully discouraging her admirers.

Which upset her parents no end, but suited her just fine. The sooner they realized she was unmarriageable, the sooner she'd be on her way to being her own mistress. Once she reached the magical age of twenty-one, she'd have access to the minor fortune bequeathed to her by her grandmother. Alas! She lacked another year before she attained that great age.

Then Zanzibar, here I come! But for now, back to the question of Lord Ware and Lady Jersey . . .

"Do you really believe Lady Jersey would deliver a set down to Lord Ware with Penelope Braithwaite, however praiseworthy, respectable, and . . . musically inclined she may be, as the *only* witness to the event?" Caroline asked.

Horatia and Freddie gave each other searching looks, as if wondering why they had not asked themselves this very logical question.

"No, if Lady Jersey decides someone is in need of a reprimand, she never misses an opportunity to do so in as public a manner as possible," Caroline said. "I think we may safely disregard this information."

Horatia's shoulders slumped. "But it's the most scandalous thing I've heard all week."

"What a thing to say." Frederica rolled her soft blue eyes. "As if we wish to hear about scandal."

Caroline struggled to keep her face composed in a neutral expression. She loved both Freddie and Horatia, but they lived for scandal, relishing each morsel of gossip as much as the daintiest piece of cake. Caroline, on the other hand, only considered the hearing of such tales a means of gathering useful information.

Such as . . .

"Lord Ware's daughters were all suitably married years ago. To my knowledge, he has no niece for whom he's trying to arrange a match. Why would he be seeking admittance to Almack's at all?" she asked.

"Perhaps he likes playing cards," Freddie suggested.

Caroline shook her head. "No, men only play cards at Almack's when their women have dragged them there. They save the real games of chance for White's or Boodles."

She had no actual proof of this, never having been in either of those hallowed masculine enclaves, but it made sense.

The male of the species saves all the good things for itself. Those mysterious, exclusive clubs into which they disappear are but one example. A gentleman may vote, or serve in Parliament, or study at university as he pleases. And men most particularly reserve for themselves the freedom to travel—unescorted and unquestioned.

"Oh! I believe I know why Lord Ware was attempting to enter Almack's." Horatia scooted forward on the settee to lean toward Caroline. Then she suddenly clamped her lips shut, leaned back, and crossed her arms. "But I'm not saying another word until you promise not to worry me over where I heard it."

Frederica looked hopefully at Caroline. "Please, Caro."

Caroline sighed. "Very well."

But she reserved judgment on the veracity of what Horatia was about to say.

Her hazel eyes sparkling, Horatia lowered her voice. "The word about Town is that Lord Ware is looking for a wife for *himself.*"

"He's too old for that, surely. Hasn't he been a widower for simply ages? Why, he must be well over fifty," Frederica said, with the callousness of the young. A pair of lines scrunched across her forehead as she tried to puzzle out Lord Ware's age. "Perhaps nearer to sixty. Didn't his youngest daughter Martha just present him with twin grandsons?"

Horatia tapped the side of her nose, and then pointed at Frederica to indicate that she'd hit upon the crux of the problem. "If memory serves ..."

It always does in Horatia's case. She hoards more nuggets about the ton than a squirrel amasses nuts for winter.

"...Lord Ware's only son died in childhood and his wife passed a few years after that, trying in vain to give him another," Horatia recalled. "Grandsons His Lordship may have in abundance, but no son."

"Ah! Then he needs an heir," Caroline said.

"He already has one," Horatia countered. "His nephew, Mr. Lawrence Sinclair."

Caroline might cast doubt on most of Horatia's gossip, but she never tangled with her on who was who among the ton. Sometimes Caroline wondered if her friend had accidentally swallowed a copy of *Debrett's.*

She turned the name Lawrence Sinclair over in her mind but couldn't find a face to put with it. He obviously hadn't been in London for the past two Seasons or she'd have met him at some ball or recital or lecture or other. "If Lord Ware has an heir presumptive, why bother filling the nursery at his age?"

Horatia lifted her chin and cast them a superior look. "It is well known that Lord Ware despises his nephew."

"Why?" Frederica asked.

Horatia's chin dropped a bit. "The reason is less well known." Which meant she didn't know. "But suffice it to say that his nephew's shortcomings are appalling enough that Lord Ware will do anything to make sure he doesn't inherit. Including taking a wife at his advanced age."

"One can only imagine how horrid the nephew must be," Frederica observed with yet another shiver.

But Caroline's thoughts had traveled a different road and she couldn't find it in her to fret about Freddie's bad habits at the moment. "So only the young and presumably fertile need apply to become the next Lady Ware."

"Caro! Please." Freddie's cheeks flushed prettily. "A lady doesn't speak of such things."

"Why not? It's true, isn't it?"

New wives were expected to pop out babies at regular intervals, though it was rarely commented upon, and women who were increasing took pains to remove themselves from public view. The three girls had pooled their meager resources, trying to piece together how this popping out of infants was accomplished. As of yet, none of them were satisfied they had the complete story.

"Caro," Horatia said primly, "you've missed the main point."

"Pray, enlighten me."

"If any of us should happen upon Mr. Sinclair during the Season, we must remember one thing."

"That he must be horrid?" Frederica guessed.

"Well, yes, that. Perhaps there are two things," Horatia said. "Aside from his presumed horridness, what we must chiefly keep in mind is that he is neither fish nor fowl."

"Meaning?" Caroline cocked her head.

"Either Lawrence Sinclair stands to become the next Earl of Ware or he is a gentleman with no prospects at all," Horatia said. "I'd not chance it. No, indeed. Give me a thoroughly settled suitor with unambiguous expectations of his station in life. I for one am not willing to risk all, no matter how sparkling a countess's tiara may seem."

"Nor I," Frederica seconded, though she'd be equally likely to leap off the London Bridge if Horatia was also keen on it.

"At least risking all would be exciting," Caroline muttered. Such a mésalliance would have the added charm of upsetting her family no end. Perhaps if she pretended to a sudden romantic interest in the surely horrid Mr. Sinclair, her father would relent and allow her to set out on the program of travel and adventure she'd compiled for herself. Caroline hoped to emulate the excellent example of Mrs. Hester Birdwhistle. She had read every account of that intrepid lady traveler's exploits a dozen times over.

As told by the unconventional Mrs. Birdwhistle, the wide world beckoned. "Only the courageous soul answers when adventure knocks" was her credo.

Caroline was about to ring for a fresh pot of tea because their current one had gone cold, when there came a pounding at the front door.

Would adventure knock that loudly?

It was more likely the caller was frustrated by the lack of an answer to his or her polite rap and had resorted to pounding. Their flighty footman, Dudley, must have abandoned his post again, leaving Mr. Price, the Lovells' decidedly long-in-the-tooth butler, to answer.

Even so, Caroline wouldn't mention Dudley's lapse to her father. Her lady's maid, Alice, had conceived a tendresse for the footman. Caroline had far too much fun hearing about the budding below-stairs romance to put Dudley's position in jeopardy.

Then came a shouted "Hallo!" followed by the heavy stomp of masculine boots coming down the hall toward the parlor.

Caroline's eldest brother appeared in the doorway, his sandy hair tousled by wind, his cheeks tanned. He seemed broader, his shoulders more massive than she remembered. He dominated the space with his mere presence. Still, though it had been nearly three years since she'd seen him, she'd have known him anywhere.

Caro had been suffering through fittings for the wardrobe for her first Season when he'd left, off to see the world on his Grand Tour. Once the war with that hateful Bonaparte had ended, civilized young Englishmen had flocked to the Continent to complete their education by traveling to new places. Her brother and his friend, Lord Rowley, had sampled the wines of Paris, viewed the majesty of the Alps, and experienced the splendors of Rome.

All places of which I can only dream.

But she couldn't find a single shred of envy in her at the moment. It was enough that her favorite brother was finally home. And while the world might call him Lord Bredon, because as Lord Chatham's heir, he was allowed to take one of their father's lesser titles, to Caroline, he would always be simply . . .

"Teddy!" She flew across the room to enfold him in a hug. "Oh, dear, dear Edward, you've grown so tall. A couple of inches at least."

"That's what travel will do for a man," Edward said, his voice deeper than she remembered it. "When you stretch your legs, they're bound to grow a bit."

"Oh, I'm so longing to hear all about it. Come." She took his hands and started leading him into the room. "You must tell us simply everything."

"A wise man rarely tells a woman everything." A richer, more rumbling voice came from behind her brother.

For the first time, Caroline noticed another man was standing there. He was dressed in the same manner as Edward, perfectly correct buckskins topped with a white shirt, striped waistcoat, and dark jacket. From his artfully disheveled cravat to his spit-shined Hessians, his ensemble was all the crack.

But he didn't seem especially at ease in his fashionable clothes. There was a *tenseness* to the man.

He reminded Caroline of the lion she'd seen at the Royal Menagerie a scant week ago. She'd watched it for more than half an hour as it paced its small space, thick tail lashing its own ribs, powerful muscles twitching beneath its tawny fur. Such a magnificent creature didn't belong in a cage. It was born to roam the savannas of Africa, king of all other beasts.

She wondered where this man belonged.

"Where are my manners?" Edward said. "And here I owe this fellow a great debt to boot. We met in Rome, you see, where he got Rowley and me out of a rather tight spot. We've been friends and traveling companions ever since. May I introduce him to you?"

"Please." Caroline welcomed anyone whom her dear Teddy held in esteem. Especially a gentleman who reminded her of a brooding lion.

Edward turned to his friend. "It is my great honor to present my dear sister, Lady Caroline Lovell. She's my favorite sister, mind, so behave yourself," he warned the other man with a good-natured grin.

"Stop it, Teddy. I'm your only sister, so naming me your favorite is far less of a compliment than you imagine," she said with a laugh. But all the while she was thinking, *Goodness! How irregular. Why would Teddy need to warn his friend about his behavior?*

Then Edward beamed at Caroline. "May I introduce Lawrence Sinclair?"

The man gave her a quick, austerely correct bow from the neck. Caroline returned the required curtsy.

So this is the perfectly horrid Mr. Lawrence Sinclair.

She knew she ought to withdraw from someone who'd earned such a poor opinion from his own family. And a warning to behave himself from her own dear brother.

But all she could think when she met the man's piercing dark eyes was that he didn't look horrid at all.

God save me from respectable women.
—Lawrence Sinclair

Chapter 2

Lawrence had met precious few ladies in his life. Lord Ware had packed him off to boarding school as soon as he could, lying about Lawrence's age to get him into Harrow a year early. At first, Lawrence had been grateful. However, if living at Ware Hall was insufferable, being raised by wolves might have been preferable to his life at public school.

Until Lawrence had shown the ability to defend himself, and become indispensable on the cricket ground, the prefects had made living at Harrow a hell on earth. But with enough time, one can become accustomed even to hell. Lawrence was forced to remain at school during holidays, when the other lads returned home to parties and country balls. He had few opportunities to acquire any of the social graces required for congress with the fair sex.

He told himself it didn't matter. He'd never need that kind of polish. He was better off at school than at Ware in any case. At least he was out from under his uncle's thumb.

Lawrence used the weeks when the hallways echoed with emptiness to catch up with his classmates in academics. He did manage to finally matriculate, though without much distinction. Lawrence was neither at the head nor the foot of his class.

"Sort of a golden mean," he'd told his uncle.

"Trying to find virtue in mediocrity, I see," Lord Ware had countered.

Lawrence had no wish to read law. He hadn't longed for a deeper understanding of algebra or geometry. Without a burning desire for more schooling, there was no reason for Lawrence to attend university. Still, his uncle wouldn't countenance his returning to Ware Hall.

Instead, the earl had purchased a lieutenant's commission for Lawrence, and specifically requested for him to serve in the heavy horse. Since this branch of His Majesty's cavalry always bore the brunt of any major action, Lawrence had no illusions about the sentiment behind his uncle's graduation gift.

However, Lawrence found that military life suited him. His old fencing master's tutelage was put to good use. Because he was more at home with horses than people, becoming a dragoon was not without its benefits. Lawrence had found a place where he actually excelled. He could handle himself and his mount in pitched battle, acquit himself admirably in the action, and his semicontrolled aggression would save the horse and rider next to him as well, more often than not.

He strove to be ready for whatever the enemy threw at him.

But his time in His Majesty's service had done nothing to prepare him for his reaction to Lady Caroline Lovell's astonishing amber eyes.

His mouth went dry. There was a hitch in his breath, and he suddenly felt all elbows and knees, a gawky youth instead of the steady young man he thought himself.

Bredon's sister was a goddess, or as near to one as Lawrence could imagine. All that was graceful, all that was innocent and sensual at once, all that was *woman*, she was neatly packaged before him, wrapped in a few layers of chiffon and lace.

"Won't you join us for tea, Mr. Sinclair?" she asked. Low and musical, even her voice was the perfect blend of angel and seductress.

He could scarce believe his luck.

Then he noticed that the goddess had reinforcements. Two other young ladies, of a somewhat less divine variety, had risen from their places on the settee. Unlike the gracious Lady Caroline, who smiled sweetly at him, these two eyed Lawrence as if he were a particularly repugnant type of slug.

Introductions were made all around. More tea and a fresh tray of biscuits appeared. Lawrence had hoped to feel more at ease with something in his hands. He was never quite sure where to put them otherwise. But balancing a delicate china cup and saucer on one knee and a plate of biscuits on the other was not an improvement. When the young ladies on the settee continued to study him furtively, Lawrence wished he'd declined refreshment.

And longed for his early days at Harrow.

"Mr. Sinclair, where is your home?" the one named Horatia Englewood said.

"Yes," he choked out. Lawrence could hardly be expected to say more; he had just bitten into a sweetmeat the instant before she addressed him. Ware was home. Or he supposed it was as much home to him as any place, though it held no warm memories for him. It was mildly disconcerting to find this Miss Englewood had apparently ascertained he was from Ware. He knew nothing about her, save that she tightened her lips into a prim line each time she looked his way.

"Your home, sir. Where . . . is it?"

"It is," Lawrence confirmed, wondering why Miss Englewood was belaboring the point. He'd been born in Ware Hall. Of what conversational value could that information be? Was she angling for confirmation of the fact that, even as the earl's presumptive heir, he wasn't likely to be welcomed back there any time soon?

Miss Englewood gave a decidedly unladylike snort. "Well, if you've no wish to tell me…"

Bredon laughed then, and slapped him on the back. His friend seemed unaware that he was seriously endangering the Turkish carpet beneath their feet because Lawrence very nearly dumped his tea. "She's asking from whence you hail, Sinclair. Lud, man, I know it's been years since you were at school, but do you not recognize a homonym when you hear it?"

"A what?" Grammar had not been his strong suit.

"A homonym," the angelic Lady Caroline said. "Two words that sound alike but have different spellings and meanings. Where and Ware, you see?"

The two girls on the settee tittered like a pair of canaries.

"Honestly, ladies, you mustn't laugh over a silly misunderstanding. Mr. Sinclair is our guest," Lady Caroline scolded. Lawrence was impressed that her mild rebuke made the others duck their heads, to all appearances suitably chastised. "And besides, if my brother met Mr. Sinclair on the Continent, no doubt he's been living in places where no one speaks English. Perhaps for quite some time. I wager if we held this conversation in French, he'd be brilliant."

"Or Italian or Spanish," Bredon put in staunchly. "Lawrence has an ear for languages."

"Ah! Then he will no doubt be pleased to dazzle us with something delightfully foreign from his travels," Miss Englewood said. When Lawrence didn't respond immediately, she added dryly, "An ear for languages, perhaps, but not a tongue, apparently."

Miss Englewood was right. As much as Lawrence wished he could impress Lady Caroline with something suitable for the present company, all that came to mind at this moment were the words to a bawdy Spanish poem about a camp follower and an Italian drinking song.

Neither would do credit to Lady Caroline's very proper parlor.

Fortunately, the goddess herself took charge of the conversation and steered it toward her brother's travels. Bredon was used to holding court and soon had all three ladies hanging on his every word.

Lawrence was grateful. It allowed him to seem to participate without actually doing anything but keep from spilling his tea. The other four laughed together so easily. They exchanged news of friends they held in common. Witticisms were batted back and forth like a game of shuttlecock. Sitting in their shadow, Lawrence almost enjoyed himself.

But then Lady Caroline turned to him. "Now that you've returned from your time abroad, will you remain in London for the Season, Mr. Sinclair?"

Lawrence swallowed hard. He wasn't sure what he was going to do. He'd planned to seek temporary lodging, somewhere cheap, near Wapping Dock, perhaps, while he untangled this particular knot. He had a vague idea about contacting his mother. Perhaps he could persuade her to allow him to take her to Wiltshire to visit her family there.

"I have no plans to remain in London, Lady Caroline."

"Then you must make plans," she said with another dazzling smile. Her teeth were brighter than the cliffs of Dover at sunrise. "There will be balls and routs and musical evenings and oh! ever so many fascinating things to do."

Those fascinating things sounded like the worst sort of torture to Lawrence, but if she were there, he thought he might be able to bear them. "Well, I—"

"That settles it." Bredon slapped him on the back. "You'll stay with us, Sinclair."

"Perhaps this is something you might wish to discuss with Lord Chatham," Lawrence said.

"Father will be in perfect agreement. In any case, I have five brothers in total, and once the others arrive, he'll scarcely notice an extra gentleman at table," Lady Caroline said. "Besides, we've yet to hear about that sticky situation in Rome from which you extricated Teddy and Lord Rowley. There's a mystery I'm dying to unravel. Do tell us."

Lawrence cleared his throat. Twice. He had no idea how to sanitize a tale that involved a brothel, a scimitar-wielding debt collector, and a dead weasel. When his teacup chose that precise moment to tumble from his knee, he was relieved.

"I beg your pardon, Lady Caroline," he said, kneeling at once to sop up the stain with his handkerchief.

"Nonsense, man, do get up," Bredon said. "The maid will tend to that." Lawrence stood, suddenly aware that none of the others in the room would have stooped to such a menial task. Even as low as his position had been in Ware Hall, he'd still been the nephew of the earl. Even as a child, he wouldn't have been expected to mop up a spill. Evidently, he'd been away from gracious living so long, he no longer knew how to behave among the upper crust.

"Undoubtedly, you're fatigued from your travels, Mr. Sinclair. Perhaps you'd like to be shown to your room," Lady Caroline suggested as she rang the small bell on the table beside her.

Lawrence could have kissed her. It was yet another highly improper thing for him to do, but one with real appeal.

"Thank you, my lady." He wanted to say something else, something that might erase the bad impression he'd made thus far. All that came to mind was that Lady Caroline's hands were as white and graceful as a pair of doves. He didn't believe expressing that bit of sap would improve his situation. So instead, he bowed to all the ladies, nodded to Bredon, and followed the butler, Mr. Price, out of the room.

With gratitude.

* * * *

"Well, Lord Bredon, it appears you are about to present the ton with a good deal of entertainment in the form of your new friend," Horatia said once Mr. Sinclair had followed Price from the parlor. "Under what rock did you find such an awkward fellow?"

"Sheath your claws, Miss Cat." Edward's smile turned brittle. "You say Sinclair is my friend and you speak truly. Perhaps you'd like to amend your comment, lest I take serious offense."

Horatia's eyes widened in surprise.

Although Caroline's brother had teased her unmercifully as they were growing up, he'd usually been kind to her friends. But Caroline—and evidently Horatia as well—had forgotten that he could occasionally lord his status over others. Everyone knew Edward was bound to inherit the earldom from their father someday—God willing, many years in the future—however, it was not something he made much of with those who'd known him since childhood, as Horatia and Frederica had.

Unless he was seriously vexed with them.

Caroline put a conciliatory hand on her brother's forearm. "She doesn't mean anything by it, Teddy."

"Neither do I, Lord Bredon," Frederica said, though she'd not offered a word against Mr. Sinclair. Apparently, an unkind thought had been squatting on her tongue so heavily, she felt as guilty about thinking it as if she'd spoken it aloud.

"Still, Edward dear, you must admit your friend has—"

"Careful, Sister," he interrupted. "Remember what our mother says. Speaking ill of someone, even the singular Mr. Sinclair, is—"

"A prayer to the devil," Caroline finished for him. "Very well. To show our good will, we shall each say something nice about Mr. Sinclair, shan't we? I'll start. He has…" She cast about in her mind for the space of several heartbeats. The man was striking in appearance, handsome even, but he couldn't hold up his end of a conversation to save his soul. Caroline finally came up with, "The man has symmetrical features."

Then she turned expectantly to Horatia, who rolled her eyes. "Let Freddie go next. I need more time to think."

"Well, it seems to me that Mr. Sinclair, well, he…" Frederica glanced at Horatia for moral support before saying, "He seems very clean-natured."

"He does indeed. An admirable trait in a gentleman. Thank you, Freddie," Caroline said. "And now you, Horatia."

"Very well. The teacup incident demonstrated that your Mr. Sinclair has quick reflexes, my lord. He was on his knees in a trice."

Edward crossed his arms, looking unimpressed. "Symmetrical features, clean-natured, quick reflexes…I hope you're aware you have just described a house cat."

Horatia and Freddie giggled, but then stifled their laughter quickly once they realized Edward was not laughing with them.

"Come, Teddy, even you must admit Mr. Sinclair is not the sort of gentleman you usually befriend."

"You are not acquainted with all my friends."

"Oh! But we do know some of them," Horatia put in, as if she hadn't just been chastened by the future Earl of Chatham. "Lord Rowley, for example. He was always so jolly and must surely have been an excellent traveling companion for you. I trust your sojourn on the Continent with him has not changed his nature."

"No, Rowley never changes," Edward said cryptically.

"I'm relieved to hear it," Horatia said, whipping out her fan and waving the lace before her. "What a pity he didn't come with you this morning. Caro speaks so highly of him."

If Horatia had been closer, Caroline would have given her a swift kick to the shins. Before Edward had left for his Tour, her brother had relished every chance to tease Caroline about her mild infatuations, which included the always entertaining Oliver Rowley. It was easy to fancy herself in love with Oliver. He was handsome in a ruddy, young King David sort of way, glib and full of charm. Even her mother called him a lovable rogue. But Caroline had been ever so much younger then, and incredibly naïve. Now, if she experienced a brief flutter over a gentleman, she extinguished it immediately. She'd realized, through observation of the couples in her parents' circle and reading the *widowed* Mrs. Birdwhistle's excellent accounts, that when a woman married, she surrendered everything to her husband—be it fortune, friends, or freedom of movement.

An attachment to a gentleman, no matter how jolly he might be, would keep her from traveling the wide world. There could be no more infatuations. Not if she wished to control her own life.

Admittedly, it was an unusual goal. In truth, she was hesitant to share it even with Horatia or Freddie, her two best friends in the world. They'd think her odd in the extreme. However, she was certain she'd never be able to settle for a life filled with sewing infant clothing and consulting the cook about menus and the other minutiae that filled her mother's days.

Still, though the sort of life she envisioned for herself held no room for a man in it, Caroline wondered about Oliver Rowley. "Lord Rowley did return with you, didn't he?"

To her surprise, Edward didn't take the opportunity to tease her about his friend this time.

"Yes, but he has no time to spend clucking in a parlor with a bunch of hens. Rowley had an appointment to keep," he said gruffly, rising and making for the doorway. He paused at the threshold and turned back to face Caroline and her friends. For a fleeting moment, it seemed as if Edward were much older than his years.

It made Caroline wonder if all his traveling adventures had been happy ones.

"Sinclair is loyal and resourceful, and there's no one I'd rather have at my back in a fight, but as you saw, he's hopeless in a drawing room," Edward said. "The man has fine qualities, many of which may not be readily apparent to you, but they have most certainly been demonstrated to me."

"Of course we respect your judgment, Teddy, but—"

"But nothing. Sinclair has agreed to remain in London, so it behooves us all to assist his entry into Society. I'll see that he's admitted to White's.

But when it comes to...the feminine side of the Season, well, you three have it within your power to help or hinder him in that regard."

"What are you suggesting?" Caroline asked.

"That you smooth the way for him a bit. He's not had much experience in Town. Help him fit into conversations. Make him feel comfortable."

"Do you wish us to keep him from cleaning up after his own spills as well?" Horatia said waspishly.

Edward snorted. "Just see he gets on with people, will you?"

"Of course," Caroline said. "We'll do what we can."

"That's all I ask," Edward said, and was gone.

Horatia waited until the sound of his boots on the hardwood had faded to dull thuds. "Well, His Lordship doesn't ask much, does he?"

"No indeed," Frederica said, missing Horatia's sarcasm completely. "Only last week, I was reading in *The Complete History of Knights and Heraldry* that the lord of the manor could demand *anything* of his vassals." Her cheeks flushed rosily, and Caroline decided Freddie was thinking of the mysterious droit du seigneur. Between the three of them, they'd amassed just enough information about this old custom to decide that whatever it was, it must have been incredibly wicked. "If all Lord Bredon asks is that we help Mr. Sinclair, why, he's being terribly undemanding. By comparison to some, I mean."

Caroline rose and wandered back to the window. A coach rattled past with a large trunk strapped to its luggage platform.

Someone is going on a long journey. Someday, I swear that someone will be me.

"Honestly, Caro, I can see a plot in the making hovering above your head plain as day," Horatia said. "It's as if you were in one of Mr. Cruikshank's caricatures."

Frederica squinted in Caro's direction. "Really? I don't see a thing. Perhaps it's a trick of the light."

"I wasn't speaking literally, Freddie. You're such a goose sometimes. But a well-loved goose," she hastened to add when Frederica's blue eyes began to tear up. The squall passed as quickly as it had threatened, and Freddie beamed at her. Then Horatia turned back to Caroline. "What do you intend to do?"

"Do? Why, just as Edward says, of course," Caroline said. "I plan to make his friend extremely comfortable."

"But remember that Lord Ware is seeking a wife. If he marries—and honestly, what gentleman of wealth and title can fail in that endeavor?—then it is all but certain Ware will have a new heir in short order. Mr. Sinclair is, for all intents and purposes, a man of no prospects," Horatia reminded her. "You can't mean to waste the Season on him."

"It won't be wasted." Caroline flounced back over to her seat. "He's presentable enough, so long as he's not required to speak. Why not allow the ton to think I'm entertaining his suit?"

"Ah! I see what you're about." Horatia cast her a sly look. "If the daughter of an earl finds his company bearable—"

"Scintillating," Caroline corrected. "That's the word I'll use when I speak of him."

"That will raise Mr. Sinclair's standing out of all knowing," Horatia said with a nod.

It would cut up her parents' peace as well to see their only daughter keeping company with a gentleman so far beneath her touch. Caroline was all for helping Teddy's friend, but, if she were honest with herself, alarming her parents was the main benefit of this little gambit.

"But you'd need to be seen with him for people to notice you're...being seen with him," Frederica said. "I doubt anyone we know will invite him to a private soiree."

Freddie might make a cake of herself with regularity, but she did have her moments. This time, she had the right of it, squarely identifying the problem with Caroline's plan.

"Perhaps he could persuade one of the Lady Patronesses to permit him to purchase an Almack's voucher," Horatia suggested.

Caroline sighed. "Can you imagine him being interviewed by Lady Jersey?"

Horatia snorted. "She'd refuse him immediately, and that would be the end of Mr. Sinclair in London. He'd be forced to return to...by the way, where is Ware?"

Frederica groaned. "Oh, please, let's not start that up again."

"So, the plan is that Mr. Sinclair and I need to be seen together," Caroline said.

Her friends nodded in unison.

"But the problem is, there are so few places where—" She stopped abruptly. Inspiration snatched her up like an eagle and allowed her to view the rapidly developing scheme from a godlike vantage point. It was perfection. Caroline smiled at her friends. "I know exactly what we're going to do."

If one has a dream, one must throw one's heart after it.
And, if necessary, be willing to see it stomped to bits.
—from the diary of Lady Caroline Lovell, who, through no fault of her own,
dined on the hearts of her lovesick swains for breakfast, elevenses, and tea.

Chapter 3

"I hope you find these accommodations adequate, sir," Price said as he
held the chamber door open for Lawrence.

Adequate? The room was far more spacious and well-appointed than
anywhere he'd ever slept. A small blaze crackled in the fireplace, chasing
away the chill that early spring had not yet conquered.

In Ware Hall, his uncle had consigned him to a small chamber, not on
the second story, where the rest of the family slept, yet not quite on the
fourth, where the servants shivered in winter and sweltered in summer.
Instead, he was given a room on the third floor, near the one where his
cousin's nanny slept. She was the other person in the household who was
deemed not quite family, yet not precisely a servant either.

Except that Lawrence *was* family, whether his uncle wished it or not.

Then he realized the butler was waiting for some sort of comment from
him. "This will be fine, Mr. Price. Very nice."

The butler beamed. "Lord Bredon quietly informed me when the pair
of you arrived that he meant for you to be a guest at Lovell House for the
foreseeable future. So I took the liberty of unpacking the contents of your…
ahem…knapsack. I hope that is to your satisfaction."

Obviously, Price had decided there was no chance Lawrence might
decline the offer to stay.

"Thank you, Mr. Price."

Price waved away his thanks. "The waistcoat and jacket that were packed therein have been brushed and hung. The two shirts and trousers are being washed, though I cannot vouch for how well the trousers will fare in the laundry. Travel is rather hard on one's wardrobe, is it not, sir?" Without waiting for a response, Price went on. "Your other accoutrements are stored in the clothes press. Shall I send for the rest of your belongings?"

"That won't be necessary."

"Ah, of course. You'll have made those arrangements yourself, no doubt."

When Lawrence had surrendered his knapsack and greatcoat to Mr. Price at the town house door, the butler had no idea he was turning over all his worldly possessions. The leather bag was worn and scarred, which wasn't surprising because he'd carried it with him throughout the French campaign. A cavalry officer had to travel light. Even after he left the service, Lawrence had never broken himself of the habit. He carried what he needed. Nothing more.

Many possessions came with an equal number of cares, he told himself. Weighed down with an abundance of things, a man could never be quite certain whether he owned them or they owned him.

Of course, the real reason for his economical bent may have been because he'd lived on a barely adequate officer's pay for several years.

The suit of clothing he was now wearing was entirely new and was quite fine, which might account for why Lawrence felt so uncomfortable in it. It was supposed to have been Lord Bredon's, but he had insisted on taking Lawrence to his tailor as soon as they disembarked at Wapping Dock that morning. It seemed Lord Bredon had received word before they left France that a bespoke ensemble was waiting for him at Weston's in Old Bond Street.

Fortunately, Lawrence and he were of a size. The tailor pronounced the fit perfect and offered to dispose of what Lawrence had been wearing, "so the gentleman need not trouble himself with it."

Lawrence had refused, carefully rolling up the worn trousers, waistcoat, shirt, and jacket. Then, to the tailor's horror, he'd stowed them back in his knapsack. A similar ensemble, some smalls, spare stockings, and a shaving kit were all Price had to unpack.

No wonder he thought there must be more.

"There is a fully equipped escritoire near the window, sir," Mr. Price said. "If you wish to send a letter, I'll be happy to post it for you."

"I may do that."

"Very good, sir. Dinner is served at eight o'clock. I'll send Dudley round when the dressing gong sounds at seven to assist you. He's our first footman, you understand, and not a true valet, but I hope he—"

"That won't be necessary. I have nothing better to wear than this." Since he'd cashed out his commission, he was no longer permitted to wear his uniform and had sold it to help finance his travels.

"Ah! Your wardrobe will have been delayed in transit; I see. Travel does discommode one, doesn't it, sir? No matter. I'm sure we can find something of Lord Bredon's for you to wear until your own arrives."

That settled it. He was going to have to add to his possessions, no matter what cares they brought with them. He didn't want to embarrass his host. Bredon had been good to him. It would be poor repayment to shame him by being a shoddily turned-out guest.

As soon as Price withdrew, Lawrence settled at the desk and took out the writing implements and a sheaf of foolscap. The nib had been shaved for a right-hander, but Lawrence was accustomed to that. He slanted the paper in the wrong direction, because there was no longer an impatient tutor standing over him, and fisted the quill. His penmanship was still crabbed, and he had to struggle not to smudge what he'd written with the edge of his hand, but his script had improved a bit over the years. He doubted his uncle would recognize it now.

The Right Honorable, the Earl of Ware
My lord;
I write to inform you that I survived my service with His Majesty's 4th Dragoons, where I acquitted myself tolerably well.

In fact, Lawrence had served with distinction at Waterloo in the heavy cavalry and, for his valor, earned a medal along with two additional years' pay. Twice he'd earned field promotions, rising from the rank of lieutenant to major. All told, he'd given ten years of service to king and country. When orders came for him to take ship for the Spanish Peninsula to command a company of cavalry there, he'd decided he'd been away from England long enough. He'd resigned and sold his commission to the son of a newly made knight. The young man was eager for adventure and glory.

Lawrence had seen sufficient *adventure* on the battlefields of France to last a lifetime. Lest some of the ghastlier elements of that adventure rise up to bedevil him, he returned to his letter writing.

Be assured that I require nothing from you; I have sold my commission and manage quite well on the proceeds.

Lawrence chuckled ruefully. Even if he were reduced to beggary, he'd not receive another penny from Lord Ware. He doubted his uncle would deign to spit on him if he were set ablaze.

Besides, he didn't need the wealth of Ware. Plenty of military men lived in comfortable retirement solely on the sale of their commissions.

But comfortable was not fashionable, and if Lawrence was to take part in a London Season, he needed to fit in somehow. The easiest way was to make sure he looked the part. On the morrow, he'd go 'round to Weston's and arrange for an appropriate wardrobe. Something suitable for balls and routs and musical evenings and all the other means of torture he'd gladly endure if Bredon's sister was also there.

The new suit he was wearing at present, as well as the invitation to stay at Lovell House, was likely because Bredon still felt himself in Lawrence's debt. After Lawrence had come to Bredon and Rowley's aid in Rome, he'd assisted them out of other scrapes when they'd found themselves in less than salubrious situations. He'd tried to convince Bredon that his actions didn't require that sort of ledger keeping. Lord Bredon owed him nothing. He was his friend. That was reason enough for Lawrence to exercise his fighting skills.

More than enough, because Lawrence could count his friends on the fingers of one hand.

Yet his resources were not limitless. The expense of acquiring fashionable clothing worried him. Staying at Lovell House would stretch his funds. Even so, the last thing he wanted was to hang on Bredon's sleeve. He'd seek other accommodations soon, so as not to discommode his friend.

Or the charming Lady Caroline.

Lawrence stared into space, contemplating that lovely creature for so long, his nib dried up and he was forced to re-trim it before continuing with his letter.

While I neither need nor expect financial support from you, I earnestly request news of my mother. As she has not responded to my many letters, I must assume she has not received them.

He refused to believe she *wouldn't* answer. His uncle must have withheld the letters from her. It was the only explanation.

The only one Lawrence was willing to entertain.

His pen was motionless on the foolscap for too long, and a blob of ink blossomed beneath the nib. The final word in the sentence was rendered illegible. He could almost hear the earl's gruff voice inside his head.

Still can't manage something as simple as a demmed letter. The boy's worse than useless.

Lawrence wadded up the foolscap into a tight ball and hurled it into the fireplace. It curled in fiery agony before turning to gray ash and crumbling to dust.

The worst thing was that he couldn't be sure his uncle was wrong.

* * * *

Every morning since Lawrence had come to stay at Lovell House, Lord Bredon had insisted he accompany him on his daily jaunts. They went to White's for coffee and a chance to read a freshly ironed copy of the *Times*. Once, he and Bredon had blazed out of Town in His Lordship's curricle to a horse race where Lawrence's keen eye for horseflesh was put to good use. Bredon bet heavily on his recommendations and took home a fat purse, which he tried to share with Lawrence.

He would have none of it. He was already sleeping under Bredon's roof and eating at his board. The ledger of their friendship was tipping too far in his favor. Bredon laughed whenever Lawrence broached the subject.

"Ledger? There is no such thing between you and me," Bredon would say.

But for Lawrence, who'd had to earn every scrap of approbation he'd ever received, that sort of unconditional friendship seemed unlikely to last.

Balance. That's what's wanted.

Lawrence wasn't sure what he could do to level the scales.

Bredon saw to it that Lawrence was introduced to all his friends and acquaintances. When anyone asked which university Lawrence had attended, Bredon would save him from having to answer by jumping in and expounding on the fact that Lawrence had served with His Majesty's 4th Dragoons at Waterloo. The subject of higher learning went by the wayside. The upper crust—the male half of it, in any case—loved to welcome a hero to its ranks, especially one who was heir presumptive to one of England's great houses.

Of Rowley, the man in whose company they'd traveled the capitals of Europe, they saw no sign.

On this particular day, Dudley crept into Lawrence's chamber and tried to roust him from a heavy sleep.

"Is the house ablaze?" Lawrence covered his head with his pillow. "If not, leave me be until it is."

He and Bredon had stayed late at the Pugilistic Club the night before.

Correction: We stayed until it was extremely early.

The eastern sky was turning a yellowish gray by the time they returned to Lovell House. Or perhaps it was merely that he was peering through a gin-soaked haze.

"If you'd be taken for a man about town, you must be part of the sporting scene," Bredon had explained as they bet on one boxer after another. Or rather, Bredon had been doing the betting. Just as they'd done at the racetrack, Lawrence picked the fighters his friend should back. He had a knack for judging the degree of aggression in the boxers entering the ring. The set of the shoulders, the tick of a jaw muscle, a singularly steely-eyed glare—Lawrence could tell who was willing to do whatever was necessary to put his opponent down.

One brute recognizes another.

Now, Lawrence glared brutishly from under his pillow, striving to tamp down his growing aggression toward Dudley, the footman-turned-valet.

"Begging your pardon, sir, but His Lordship sent me to wake you," Dudley said as he opened the curtains, sending a bar of sunlight knifing across the room. It struck Lawrence full in the face.

"I intended to sleep later today," Lawrence said, stifling the urge to add a few choice curses.

"That you have, sir," Dudley said with a trace of wistfulness. Servants woke with the sun, or even earlier. "It's half three in the afternoon."

He could've sworn his head had just hit the pillow.

Dudley laid out one of his new suits of clothing, taking special care with the starched cravat. The tailor at Weston's had been quick to finish Lawrence's new wardrobe because he was Lord Bredon's particular friend.

While it was helpful to have the new suits ready in record time, Lawrence wasn't sure he liked having things done for him simply because of whom he'd befriended. At school, he'd scrabbled for himself. In the military, his own deeds earned his promotions. Shouldn't his coin have been enough to stir the tailor to timely service without having to rely on social connections to speed them along?

As Bredon was fond of saying, "You may well be the best natural fighter I've ever seen, but as far as understanding Polite Society, you are a book filled with blank pages, my friend. Never mind, Sinclair. You'll learn soon enough how this world works."

In the meantime, Dudley was trying to urge him from bed without seeming to do so.

"His Lordship is waiting," Dudley said, shifting his weight from one foot to the other. "Do you want I should—I mean, shall I assist you with a shave?"

As a footman, Dudley was fairly mute. As a valet, he had not yet mastered Mr. Price's ease of speech with the one he served.

"No, that's all right." Lawrence hauled himself naked from the bed and slipped into his waiting smalls—unassisted, thank you. Some things a man had to do for himself.

"Mr. Sinclair, the hot water is ready for your morning ab…ab…absolutions," Dudley finally managed.

"Ablutions," Lawrence corrected gently. "Absolution requires more than hot water and is much harder to come by."

Lawrence stropped his razor a time or two, soaped up his face with the badger-bristle brush, and made short work of the stubble on his cheeks and chin. Even so, he probably should have let Dudley shave him.

No doubt he needs the practice.

But Lawrence had done such things for himself for so long, it would have felt too strange. Besides, something within him rebelled against allowing another man, however well-meaning, to hold a naked blade to his unprotected throat.

He forced himself to stand still while Dudley assisted him with getting dressed. It made him realize again how different he was from the family with whom he was lodging. This sort of thing was as natural as breathing to Edward Lovell, Lord Bredon. It was as bizarre as a two-headed dog to him. Even though by the world's lights, Lawrence Sinclair was quite wellborn—presumptive heir to an earldom, no less—his uncle had made sure he'd never felt his position entitled him to any special treatment.

And while the ton might expect him to succeed his uncle, Lawrence knew Lord Ware would do everything he could to keep that from happening.

"Where is Lord Bredon?" Lawrence asked as Dudley tugged on his second boot. "The parlor?"

"No, sir. He's waiting for you in the stable."

A ride was worth getting up for. Lawrence flew down several flights of stairs, making sure to slip through the kitchen on his way out so he could pilfer a couple of buns. He didn't take time for tea. He wasn't about to keep Bredon waiting in a horse stall.

Behind the row of fine homes on this oh-so-fashionable street, there was a narrow alleyway. Just beyond that were the stables used by the residents of those fine homes. Most were only big enough to house a carriage and the matched pair that pulled it. The Chatham stable was roomy enough for three additional horse stalls as well.

"There you are, Sinclair," Bredon said as he tightened the girth on a bay gelding. "I thought I'd have to send a hunting party of housemaids and footmen to drag you back here."

"Dudley was sufficient."

"Caro and her friends have taken the carriage," Bredon explained. "We'll have to ride."

That suited Lawrence better than a hot cup of oolong. He didn't miss much from his cavalry career, but he did miss the dusty smell of horseflesh and the easy sense of oneness he felt with his steed. He checked the security of his tack and mounted in one smooth motion. The world seemed a much better place when viewed from the back of a Thoroughbred.

"Where are we bound?" he asked as they trotted down the alley.

"Somerset House. The Royal Academy of Arts' annual exhibition opens today."

Lawrence pulled a face. "You and Rowley dragged me to the Vatican, where we all got stiff necks staring at the ceiling. We trudged through the Louvre together because you said you couldn't face your mother if you didn't see the Moaning Lisa—"

"*Mona* Lisa, you barbaric lout."

"As you will," Lawrence conceded. For some reason, Bredon's insults didn't carry the same sting as the earl's had. "The point is, haven't we seen enough art for a lifetime?"

"Trust me, Sinclair. This is more about being seen near the art than actually seeing it," Bredon said as they turned onto the main thoroughfare and nudged their mounts into a trot. "Besides, since you stole my tailor, you've turned into a swell of the first stare. It's high time you were out and about."

"I've been out," he grumbled.

"Coffeehouses and cockfights do not signify, my untutored friend. Not for a gentleman who means to cut a wide swath through the Season."

Honestly, the only reason Lawrence had agreed to stay in London at all was the hope of getting to know Lady Caroline. But she rarely came down to breakfast before he and Bredon were out the door for the day. At supper, the Lovell family filled the table. The earl and his countess had brought as many of their sons from their country estate as possible. Edward's younger brothers, Benjamin, Charles, and Thomas, were like stair steps around the long table. All were possessed of the Lovell good looks and quick wit. The first two were reading law at Oxford, while Thomas had chosen to break with family tradition and attend Cambridge, which gave his brothers plenty of cause for good-natured teasing. After the Lent semester ended, young Harry, who was at Eton, would be joining the family in London as well.

No wonder Lady Caroline had said her parents would never notice an extra young man about the house.

But they had. Someone had arranged matters so that Lawrence was never seated near her at supper. He was never granted even a hint of private speech with her. Since that first disastrous day, Lawrence had not ventured anywhere close to the parlor, especially if he heard the shrill giggles of Lady Caroline's companions behind the sturdy oak door.

Who could blame him? He'd made a thorough ass of himself. Yet the kindness of Lady Caroline in the face of his poor showing and the possibility of seeing more of her kept him in a state of perpetual and, most likely, impossible hope.

"Will your sister and her friends be there?" he asked, keeping his tone carefully neutral.

"They will. In fact, on opening day, you'll find more beauties lining up to tour the Royal Academy of Arts than you'll find masterpieces on the walls," Bredon promised.

That was enough to make Lawrence forget his rumbling stomach, even though a bun or two wasn't nearly enough to break his fast. Instead, he wished he'd let Dudley spend more time making him presentable.

God knows I could use it. But no matter. This is my opportunity to undo Lady Caroline's initial opinion of me. By heaven, I will impress her this time.

So he squared his shoulders as the three-storied Somerset House came into view. A muscle in his cheek twitched, and it seemed as if his vision sharpened a bit.

If he could have seen himself at that moment, he'd have recognized the look. He was a man willing to do whatever was necessary. Seeing that level of determination, he'd have been willing to bet his own money that Lady Caroline didn't stand a chance.

"'Fortune favors the bold,' they say. Obviously, they have never met Lady Caroline Lovell."
—Lawrence Sinclair

Chapter 4

The main exhibition hall in Somerset House soared three stories to an ornate cove ceiling. It was ringed with clerestory windows, allowing a splash of sunlight to illuminate the myriad canvases that were hung from the floor to the ceiling. Their ornate frames butted up against one another, like seasick passengers on an overcrowded ship, jostling elbow-to-elbow along the rail. The tops of the uppermost paintings canted inward, so the works might still be viewed from the floor far below without too much distortion. The arrangement created the illusion that the very walls were leaning in toward the milling crowd.

There was such a press of bodies in the great hall, Lawrence despaired of catching the slightest glimpse of Lady Caroline. Elegantly garbed cits and dandies paid court to young ladies, who were flirting with their fans and making doe's eyes when they thought their chaperones weren't attending. Groups of young people wandered from one painting to the next, gave the canvases cursory glances, and then returned to their flirting. Several stout matrons, most probably the inattentive chaperones, had found seats on benches situated in the center of the hall. These ladies viewed the canvases hanging near the high ceiling through opera glasses, exclaiming to one another over the artistry in each work and praising the budding talent. All the while, they were oblivious to the romances budding a few feet from them.

"I see what you mean, Bredon," Lawrence said without looking back at his friend, who must have followed him in and was no doubt standing a little behind him. "There's very little afoot here that has to do with art." "Indeed. Then pray, sir, do tell me what you believe *is* afoot."

He turned to find Lady Caroline gazing at him, the corners of her pink lips turning up ever so slightly. Ears burning, he belatedly remembered his manners and whipped off his hat.

"Lady Caroline," he said as he gave her a sharp bow from the neck. "I am most pleased to see you here."

"Mr. Sinclair," she responded with a quick curtsy, her mildly amused expression still intact. "Now that we have established our identities, may I point out that you see me nearly every night at the supper table?"

"Yes, that's true. But it's not the same as...well, we've never had the opportunity to...what I mean is... you and I have exchanged precious few words...you see...since I became your brother's houseguest."

"Perhaps that's a good thing because words seem to be a sticking point for you." Her smile broadened, but he didn't sense any malice behind it. It was an indulgent sort of smile, a smile that said it was all right for him to take his time expressing himself.

He'd never had trouble speaking to women before, though he was never able to gather a crowd around himself as Bredon could. It made no sense that the mere presence of this one, the one he most wished to impress, should render him hopelessly tongue-tied. Yet, because of her smile, some of the tension drained from between his shoulder blades.

"When I came upon you, you seemed to be talking to yourself," she said. "Would you care to explain what you meant?"

"About?" For the life of him, he couldn't remember.

"Exactly," she said. "You implied that the exhibit wasn't about the art. What else would it be about? I ask you."

He couldn't very well say it was about elaborate mating dances that would put peacocks to shame. That wasn't an appropriate thing for a gentleman to say to a lady. Besides, he was as guilty as the other would-be lovemakers in the hall. He'd come with the intention of tracking this goddess before him as stealthily as any deer stalker. And then, he planned to...he planned...

Somehow, he had lost his train of thought, lost himself in those eyes of hers. The lovely whites showing beneath her warm irises seemed to be shaped like little canoes as she gazed up at him. Her pupils expanded, darkening their warm amber shade and pulling him farther into—

"Mr. Sinclair? Are you quite all right?"

"Yes. Yes, of course. I'm…I'm fine. I was merely…" He might be fine, but he sounded not quite bright, even to his own ears.

Lawrence had hoped fate would allow him a few moments of private speech with Lady Caroline so he could duly impress her. Now he was throwing away his chance because he couldn't corral his thoughts. He felt powerless to stop himself from floundering.

He wondered if this was how it would feel if he were to hurl himself from the topmost spire of Westminster Abbey. The rush of wind, the exhilaration of being airborne, the—

"Yes?" she prompted.

The abrupt smack when I hit the cobblestones.

Lawrence swallowed hard and gave one last try at making sense. "If the exhibition were strictly about the art, wouldn't all the works be displayed at eye level? I mean, how does one give adequate attention to the paintings situated higher on the walls?" he asked, finally coughing up a coherent thought.

As elegantly as a cat coughs up a hair ball.

"You have a point, Mr. Sinclair. It is a challenge to view all the paintings equally, given the way they are displayed," she acknowledged, "but there are so many worthy artists associated with the Academy, it would be unfair to deny any of them a showing."

He liked her sense of fairness, but he wondered if the artist whose work was hugging the ceiling would consider its showing equitable. Then, like a shaft of heavenly light parting the clouds, a good idea descended upon him.

"I would consider it a great honor if you would show me your favorite work, Lady Caroline."

She chuckled.

"Did I say something amusing?"

"No, you merely asked for the impossible. One can't have a favorite work of art," she said. "At least, not for very long."

"Why is that?"

"I believe it is because we bring something of ourselves to each canvas. If I'm feeling poorly, even the most wonderful work will find a dull reception in me. Conversely, if I'm in perfect charity with the world, every canvas I see holds a wealth of charm."

Perhaps Bredon is right. I am *a book filled with blank pages. At least, as far as his sister is concerned.* "Are you truly that changeable?"

"As a weathercock," she answered gaily. "Aren't you?"

"No," he said in all seriousness. "I know myself well enough to know what I like. And when I find what I like, that doesn't change."

He gave her a direct look that, surprisingly enough, seemed to unnerve her a bit. For the first time since he'd met her, color rose in her cheeks. She swept her gaze downward for the space of several heartbeats. He wondered if it were possible for someone like her to suffer occasional moments of awkwardness, too.

Then she raised her eyes to his and tipped her head to one side, as if she were trying to gain a fresh perspective on him.

Her pink tongue swept her lower lip.

Why does she do that? It doesn't seem particularly dry in here. And why in blue blazes am I looking at her lips in the first place?

It was considered the height of rudeness to fixate on a particular feature of a lady, but in all fairness, she was giving him a fixated look of her own. Then, apparently satisfied by her careful perusal of him, she lifted one of her delicate eyebrows.

"Well, then, my unchangeable Mr. Sinclair," Lady Caroline said, "perhaps I *will* show you my favorite work."

"At least, the one for today," he said, pleased that she had agreed because it would mean more time to speak with her.

However, he wasn't quite sure what had just happened. He'd undoubtedly been weighed on some sort of feminine scale and come out on the positive side.

Yet it was more than that. Somehow, there'd been a spark, a connection leaping between them. Surely she'd felt it, too. Why else would her cheeks have turned rosy like that?

He wondered if, like the exhibition, their conversation had not really been about art at all.

No matter. When she blessed him with another of her brilliant smiles, he decided not to question his luck further. They strolled side by side along the perimeter of the great hall.

Not touching, of course. Not so much as the sleeve of his jacket brushed against the thin shawl that draped over her shoulders and down her lithe arms.

But he was acutely aware of her nearness and fancied that if they were standing still, he'd feel the heat of her body radiating toward him. Warm as sunshine or a cheery blaze or—

Stow it, Sinclair, he ordered himself. It was just that sort of fanciful imagining that made him fumble his words and look a fool.

Lady Caroline stopped before a landscape near the corner farthest from the door through which he'd entered.

"Here it is," she said. "This one caught my fancy."

Lawrence tore his gaze from her and fixed it on the canvas before them. On it, a series of arches supported a bridge of three stories spanning a river. It was a realistic enough representation to suggest an actual locale.

"Oh!" Lawrence said. "I know this place. It's called Pont du Gard."

"You've been there, I see. Alas, I can only read about such things, or gaze at paintings of them," she said wistfully, but then her smile returned, and she went on excitedly. "Just imagine how clever the Romans must have been to build an aqueduct of such monumental size. And what's more, after nearly two thousand years, it still stands."

"The henges on the Salisbury plain are far older," he said, feeling the need to tout English cleverness as well.

"Fiddle-faddle! Those henges are half-tumbled-down collections of stones compared to this ancient wonder. And the Roman ruins had an actual purpose. Who knows what the henges were for?"

"Perhaps they were meant to be art. Does art have a purpose?"

"This one does. At least, it's quite clear what the artist intended to show." She waved a gloved hand toward the amazingly accurate depiction of Roman engineering. "And besides, just look at the fascinating countryside around the aqueduct. And that beautiful river."

"It's the Gardon River," Lawrence supplied. Helpfully, he thought.

"Of course, you'd know its name, too," she said with a huff and crossed her arms.

Now what had he done? She seemed vexed with him, and just when he thought he'd been bringing something of substance to their conversation.

"The south of France is lovely," he said, "but it's no lovelier than our English countryside."

"But you've missed my point. It's *French*. It's someplace else. Other. Than. Here." She separated the words to give them emphasis. "Because of that, the flora and fauna there must certainly be more…well, by rights, they ought to be…you know what I mean, different from…" One of her hands flailed a bit as she struggled to capture her thoughts.

Lawrence's chest burned in sympathy. He wasn't the only one who fought to get the right words out sometimes. Though during his brief association with her, Lady Caroline had never experienced difficulty expressing herself before.

It was too much to hope that he had the same disturbing effect on her that she did on him.

Of course, if neither of us can put together a cogent sentence, we'll have a great deal of difficulty getting on.

Sounding exasperated, she finally said, "Surely in your many travels you've been moved by the beauty around you."

Not as much as I'm moved by the beauty at my side, he thought but dared not say. A crowded exhibition hall was no venue for a declaration of that sort. She'd think him mad if he let such a thought slip from his lips.

"And not simply because it is beautiful," she went on, "but because it is not familiar, because of its...otherness."

"I think I understand," he said.

Otherness was the problem. She was Lady Caroline and would ever remain so. She was the epitome of otherness. If his uncle had his way, Lawrence would be Mr. Sinclair to his dying day, barely hanging on to the edge of Polite Society by his fingernails. He cast about for something to say that wouldn't widen the gulf between them.

Clearly, she didn't want to talk about art. The only reason she'd been drawn to this particular canvas was its foreign subject matter. Her eyes had danced when she spoke of distant places.

Perhaps it was time to take her to one.

"When I was in France, I saw some beautiful sights. Often in the most unexpected places. I remember early mornings," he said softly as he sank into his vivid memories. "My horse's breath ghosting the air, frost sparkling on the field, and each blade of grass doubled by its own sharp-edged shadow. Small things really, but of such beauty, they made my chest ache."

"My word, Mr. Sinclair. Who would have thought it?" she said, clearly astonished. "You have the soul of a poet."

He shook his head. "No, not really. I'm just one who's had a good deal of time to think."

"I've heard it said that memories of dramatic, even horrific events seem more intense than others," she said. "You're speaking of things you remember from your time in military service, I believe."

He nodded. "How could you tell?"

"Don't look so surprised. Teddy told me you served with great valor at the Battle of Waterloo and elsewhere. But a number of years have passed since then, and, I must say, the details you shared seem very fresh."

"I suppose they are. Going into an action has a way of focusing a man." Before a battle, his senses had seemed heightened. He'd been acutely aware of everything. Each little detail had seemed so terribly important as he drank them all in. The creak and jingle of his mount's tack seemed loud enough that surely his counterpart across the field must have heard it. The light was both softer and harsher, the colors so vibrant they hurt his eyes. His skin prickled at each sensation, thigh muscles flexing as he settled deeply into the saddle. The air was ripe with gun oil and leather, horseflesh and damp wool.

And beneath it all, an acrid, low note of fear.

As if she'd heard his thoughts, Lady Caroline asked, "Were you ever afraid?" Then she quickly shook her head. "How impertinent of me. I beg your pardon. I shouldn't have asked such a personal question."

"Why? Don't you want to know the answer?"

"Well…"

"Yes," he admitted. "The answer is yes."

Her brows drew toward each other. "My, that was quick. Do you not care that others may think you a coward?"

"I care that *you* may, but if you do, you'd be wrong," he said. Their conversation had veered so far away from art, he was sure it would never make it back, but he felt the need to explain himself, lest she think he bore a white feather and despise him for it. "Being afraid doesn't make one a coward. It only shows one has a bit of sense."

"I had not thought of it like that. You may be right." She lifted her shoulders in a shrug. "But if being afraid doesn't make one a coward, what does?"

"Running away," he said. "It's a question of what one *ought* to do. I had a duty. I owed it to my king, my commanding officer, and to my comrades in arms to give my best in every action. The men who served under me deserved an example of steadfastness. I strove to give them one. No matter my feelings, running away was never an option."

"So, do you always live up to this sense of…of oughtness, for want of a better word?"

"I endeavor to do so, yes, my lady."

She narrowed her extraordinary eyes at him. "Even if it runs counter to your own wishes?"

"I had taken an oath. My wishes did not signify."

Her lips tightened into a thin line, and he was reminded for a moment of her friend, Horatia Englewood. The thought was disturbing, but then she flicked out her little pink tongue again and swept her bottom lip. Any resemblance to Miss Englewood fled away.

"What if you *hadn't* taken an oath?" A determined line formed between her brows. "What if others merely expected certain things of you, things to which you had not expressly agreed? Would you feel honor bound to set your own will aside simply to please them?"

Any pretense of discussing the artwork before them had clearly flown out the high clerestory windows. This question was of obvious importance to her, but he had no idea why.

"I suppose," he said carefully, "it would depend on who was expecting something from me."

"Such as whom?"

He almost said *my family*, but because his had expected precious little of him, he feared the words wouldn't ring true.

"If the person was someone I valued, someone whose opinion mattered to me," Lawrence said in measured tones, "I would certainly do my best to see that I lived up to their hopes."

"At the expense of subjugating your own will?"

"If the person was important enough to me, yes. It seems the height of selfishness to think that my will should hold sway at all times."

A stricken expression passed over her features. His gut sank. His words had missed the mark somehow. He was about to apologize for causing her distress, but then the injured look disappeared, and she lifted her chin.

"Well, then, Mr. Sinclair. It appears you were sadly missing on the day the good Lord handed out spines. Good day, sir."

Lady Caroline bobbed a perfunctory curtsy, turned on her heel, and left him standing by the painting of Pont du Gard.

"Bredon was right," he muttered. "This was definitely not about art."

To live by one's own lights, this is true freedom.
—from Mrs. Hester Birdwhistle's *Tales of an Intrepid Lady Traveler* or
How to Confound One's Relations by Refusing Pattern Behavior in Favor
of a Gratifying Life

Chapter 5

Drat the man.

Caroline's cheeks were still burning as she and her friends climbed into the carriage emblazoned with the Chatham crest. She was so upset, she let Horatia and Frederica take the coveted forward-facing squab without a word of protest. Riding backward often gave her a sick headache, but now, riding forward would not improve her mood one jot.

Lawrence Sinclair had made her feel all hot and jittery inside. Shivery and warm at once.

She didn't like it one bit.

She usually enjoyed intense sensations, like the head-to-toe goose bumps she felt when one of her brothers scared her with a good-natured prank. Or the thrill that shimmered over her when the moon rose above the dome of St. Paul's, a perfect silver disc hovering in the inky sky.

This sensation, however, was not that sort of excitement. Neither could it be compared with hearing a new symphony or seeing a first-rate play on Drury Lane. It wasn't the pleasure of slipping into a new gown or trying on a fetching bonnet.

Instead, it was a prickly, irritated, thoroughly frustrated ball of something she feared might be guilt. The great lump scoured her insides. It was as if Lawrence Sinclair had rubbed a scratchy piece of wool over her soul.

Subjugate my will indeed.

Old Anna Creassy was hoisted into the conveyance after the girls by Sedgewick, Lord Chatham's equally ancient coachman. Anna had been Caroline's nurse when she was a child and was now her chaperone for outings such as this. Her job, as always, was to make sure Caroline behaved herself, and to report any infraction to her parents if she did not. The woman settled into the backward-facing squab next to Caroline and immediately closed her eyes.

However, Caroline knew from sad experience that closed eyes rarely meant Anna was asleep.

Her friends were evidently unaware of this fact. Frederica and Horatia nattered on like a pair of squirrels, heedless of the chaperone's listening ears. The conversation descended into the realm of gossip as usual, so Caroline offered nothing to the stew of sly innuendo and gasps of surprise over the foibles of others.

Besides, she couldn't have slipped in a word sideways. Both of her friends' cups were obviously overflowing. And in any case, she didn't feel like joining in.

Not while Lawrence Sinclair's dreadful sense of duty still gnawed away at her insides.

"Oh, I say, did you notice Penelope Braithwaite's cunning new frock?" Frederica gushed on, not waiting for a response. "It was the loveliest, palest of yellows with white Vandyke lace points at the throat and cuffs. There were even more around the hem. Don't you just love Vandykes? I adore them ever so much. I do think they're the most stylish of embellishments, don't you?" Frederica paused for a much-needed breath and then sighed. "Miss Braithwaite's gown was simply divine."

"It was also identical to mine, you little goose," Horatia said with a frown.

"Oh!" Frederica turned and gave Horatia's ensemble a quick perusal. "So it is. I hadn't noticed, but…I believe they aren't exactly the same, are they? While the color and fabric are very much alike, your gown has Belgian lace instead of the Vandykes."

"That's so small a difference as to be of no import," Horatia said testily. Caroline was certain her friend knew that because a machine had been invented to produce netting for appliquéd Brussels lace, it was a less expensive ornamentation than Vandyke points. Miss Braithwaite had undoubtedly paid more for her version of the frock. "Barring that very small detail, the gowns are as like as two peas."

"But…but…" Frederica said, searching about for words of consolation. "…the color is ever so much more becoming on you, Horatia dear."

"It is, isn't it?" Horatia preened a bit. "I do think someone should tell her she ought not to wear yellow. Truly, it would be a kindness. That particular shade casts a ghastly sallowness over her complexion, and in all honesty, if it were me, I'd want to know and would bless the name of the one who told me."

The same way she'd bless someone who pointed out a carbuncle on her nose.

"But really, the whole thing was such a nuisance. That gown ruined my entire afternoon." Horatia picked at a loose thread on one of her cuffs. If she weren't careful, she'd unravel the whole row of tiny knots. "As soon as I spotted Miss Braithwaite, I couldn't even look at another painting."

"Why was that?" Caroline asked, deciding she should try to seem interested. It was what her friends expected. Besides, doing the expected just this once might take her mind off the wretched Mr. Sinclair and his overdone sense of oughtness.

"I had to make sure my path didn't cross Penelope's, of course," Horatia explained. "I spent the whole time slipping from one group to another, trying to make sure Miss Braithwaite and I didn't end up standing next to each other." Horatia gave a long-suffering sigh. "I mean, what would people think if they saw us side by side?"

"That you give custom to the same mantua-maker?" Caroline suggested.

"Oh, you're right. One should lay blame where it's due. This debacle falls squarely at the feet of Madame Fournier. Mama and I shall definitely have words with her. If she thinks she can sew the same dress for two different ladies, she has another thing…"

Caroline stopped listening after that. Lawrence Sinclair's words were still tumbling around too loudly in her head.

"If the person was someone I valued, someone whose opinion mattered to me, I would certainly do my best to see that I lived up to their hopes."

Her parents had high hopes for her. And Mama and Papa were important to her. Caroline adored them. Perhaps that was the trouble. She didn't want to displease them. Not really.

But ever since she was a child, they'd tried to make her conform to their notions of what a young lady should be like. When she turned thirteen, her days of roaming about the garden collecting bees in jars or sneaking up onto the roof to gaze at the stars were abruptly over. She was expected to acquire a set of ladylike accomplishments. To that end, a number of specialized masters had been hired so that Caroline might be "finished."

"It is," her mother had explained, "a program to improve your deportment, poise, and generally equip you with all the graces required for your future."

Which meant the scheme should improve her chances of making a brilliant match, though this was never explicitly mentioned. It was simply understood that marriage, homemaking, and childbearing loomed in her future.

The finishing process involved, among other things, hour upon hour of fidgeting at the pianoforte. She'd learned the rudiments of the keyboard years before and could be relied upon to be more or less faithful to the musical score. But her new maestro expected more from her than merely plunking away. He expected her to make music.

"After several weeks with no appreciable improvement," he had regretfully reported to her parents, "Lady Caroline's playing is still abominable. One might describe it as a battering ram to the ears, but only if one were charitably inclined."

At that, Lord and Lady Chatham decided Caroline's musical abilities would only gain society's notice for all the wrong reasons. The long hours of squirming on a piano bench ended. By that time, she was considered too old to begin the violin.

For which both Caroline and her music master gave thanks. And Polite Society should, too. One less debutante of very little musical talent being trotted out and inflicted upon them could only be counted a blessing all around.

Then her mother undertook to teach Caroline the homely art of sewing. It was a womanly pastime, providing for creative expression as well as practical application. Mastering the craft in no way reflected poorly on a wellborn lady, provided she took no payment for her work.

However, *no one* would pay for Caroline's stitchery. It only resulted in crooked seams, pricked thumbs, and bloodied shirts. To save on the extra laundry and bandage expense, even embroidery lessons ceased.

But there were a few ladylike things at which Caroline excelled. She became fluent in French, and, thanks to Teddy's secret tutelage, read Latin tolerably well. She was a nimble dancer, but only because she enjoyed it. She could do a creditable job of serving a proper tea by the time she was fourteen.

When she turned sixteen, her parents appeared to give up on further improving curricula. All that could be done had been done. Caroline was deemed a pleasant young lady who was bound to marry well.

If her father had had his way, he'd have arranged a brilliant match for her by now. However, her mother had encouraged him to allow her a dazzling London Season. During the whirlwind of balls and dinners, Caroline would surely strike a love match with a suitable gentleman.

After all, a presentable earl's daughter with a jaw-dropping dowry would not last long on the marriage mart.

"So long as no one asks her to play the pianoforte," her father had said irritably before agreeing to allow his countess to have her way.

It all might have gone as they planned, if, shortly after Caroline was presented at court, she hadn't attended Mrs. Birdwhistle's lecture on the joys of independent travel. The freedom, the adventure, the idea of seeing the world as all her brothers would see it someday was so beguiling; nothing else could compete in Caroline's imagination.

It was as if her soul took wing that day. No one could coax it back into its cage.

"…with Mr. Sinclair, weren't you?" Horatia's mention of the horrid man's name pulled Caroline out of her wool-gathering. Both of her friends were looking at her expectantly, waiting for Caroline to give an account of her conversation with said horrid man.

"We exchanged greetings in passing."

"Excuse me, but it was much more than that," Horatia said, "The pair of you practically promenaded around the hall before you came to rest before a canvas in a corner for a cozy tête-à-tête."

Caroline frowned at her. "I thought you were keeping an eye on Penelope Braithwaite all afternoon."

"Whatever my personal troubles, what kind of friend would I be if I hadn't taken a moment or two to see to your welfare?" Horatia shot her a sly look. "Now, what did you and the decidedly uncommunicative Mr. Sinclair find to talk about for so long?"

"It wasn't that long."

"It was half an hour, at the least. I'm certain of it. I heard the nearby church bells chime the hour, the quarter, and the half before you and he parted company," Horatia said. "It was quite possibly longer because I didn't see how the two of you happened to meet. How *did* you meet?"

"We met in my father's parlor a couple of weeks ago," Caroline said. "As you well know, since the two of you were there."

Horatia rolled her hazel eyes. "I meant today at the exhibition. As *you* well know."

"Please, Caro. Mr. Sinclair looked ever so debonair as the two of you were walking side by side. Why, I thought you made quite an amiable-looking couple actually, and—" Freddie stopped suddenly. "Why are you frowning so?"

"Am I? It must be the sun." Caroline glanced sideways at her chaperone and noticed that Anna's eyes were open just a crack. This was definitely not the time to rehash her distressing conversation with Mr. Sinclair. *Make that the upright, poisonously good Mr. Sinclair.* Even as she thought it, she knew it wasn't a fair assessment. It wasn't that he was so good, but that he made her judge herself to be so bad.

"We're waiting, Caro," Horatia prompted. "Do tell us about Mr. Sinclair."

"Only if you need a nap. The fellow is no life of the party." It wasn't an entirely truthful statement. Caroline hadn't been at all bored while talking to Mr. Sinclair. When he was describing his time in France, she'd been terribly drawn to him. He was a sensitive soul in a warrior's body. As to the rest of the conversation, it was difficult to be bored and irritated at the same time. "But what about you, Freddie? How did you enjoy the exhibition?"

A smile dimpled Frederica's round cheeks. "Oh, I had just the most wonderful time. And you'll never guess who I happened to meet. No, never, never. Not if you guessed for a million years."

"Since we haven't that much time," Horatia said dryly, "perhaps it would be best if you just tell us."

"Very well. I was minding my own business, contemplating a really fine Reynolds. It was the new one, no, not new exactly. I mean the one that was recently discovered by his heirs," Frederica said, her words coming slowly at first. Then it was as if someone had shouted tally-ho! and she was off in a rush to get her thoughts out. "Isn't Sir Joshua just the finest English painter of the age? Of course, I mean the previous age, I suppose. He's been dead for some time now, more's the pity, but his paintings live on, don't they? And don't you love how the subjects in his portraits seem to look back at you? Why, I'd swear the eyes were following—"

"Freddie, you're waffling on," Horatia interrupted. "Who did you meet?"

Frederica looked at first one of them, then the other.

To be sure we're attending properly. Caroline sneaked a glance at Anna, who had opened her eyes and was hanging on Frederica's words as well.

"It was Lord Rowley," she announced with the same giddiness she'd have had if she'd met the prince regent in front of the wandering eyes of a Reynolds portrait.

"Really?" Even in that press of people, Caroline was surprised she'd not noticed Oliver was there. After all, she'd fancied her brother's friend when she was younger. But to be fair, after spending that half hour or so with Mr. Sinclair, she wasn't exactly seeing straight. "I didn't even know Rowley was in town. I believe Edward said he'd gone straight to his country estate after they parted company at Wapping Dock."

"I thought Lord Bredon said he had an appointment," Horatia countered.

"Perhaps the appointment was at his estate," Caroline said, still a little miffed that Oliver hadn't bothered to show himself at Lovell House once since he'd returned from his Grand Tour. He always told the most amusing stories, and ones set in Nice or Naples were bound to be even more engaging than his usual fare. "Now that his father's gone, Rowley does have obligations to the viscountcy, doesn't he?"

"Well, wherever he's been, he seems to be in Town now," Horatia said. "So tell us, Freddie, did Lord Rowley smile and tip his hat to you?"

"Oh, yes, indeed he did." Frederica nodded several times to emphasize her words. "Very proper it was, too, because we'd been introduced before, you see."

"Really?" Horatia gave her a slant-eyed gaze. "When?"

"It was before he and Lord Bredon left on their Tour. I was staying with Caro for a fortnight, you see, and Lord Rowley came to collect Lord Bredon so they could make their way to the ship and—"

"So he was polite enough to vaguely remember you in passing?" Horatia said.

"Oh, no." Frederica shook her head.

"Rowley wasn't polite to you?" Caroline demanded. Whether Oliver was a friend of Teddy's or not, whether her infatuation with him could truly be labeled a thing of the past or not, if Lord Rowley had disrespected her friend, she intended to give him a proper tongue-lashing the next time she saw him.

"No, no. He was a perfect gentleman," Frederica assured her, "but he wasn't at all vague. Lord Rowley knew exactly who I was, who my father is, and where we'd met. And our conversation wasn't just in passing, because then he…well, he asked me a question or two and we talked for oh! most of the afternoon. It must have been hours, because he didn't leave my side until I told him it was time for me to meet you and Horatia so we could ride home together."

"What on earth did you find to talk about all afternoon?" Caroline asked, not caring if their chaperone heard the juicy details as well. If Anna had been on point, she'd have already been aware that Freddie had spent a good deal of time with Lord Rowley in the exhibition hall.

"First, he offered to escort me around the hall and tell me about painting techniques and various schools and such. Mostly explaining things about the artwork I didn't understand."

"That *could* take hours," Horatia muttered crossly.

Frederica didn't seem aware of the snideness in her friend's remark and went on serenely. "Lord Rowley had seen so many wonderful museums during his travels, you see, and could name the artist simply by looking at the painting instead of having to read the placard. He's quite brilliant in that way."

"Rowley has always been clever," Caroline said, remembering the scrapes Oliver used to get Teddy into and how he usually managed to wiggle away scot-free. "How did he seem? Did you find him changed?"

"He's as handsome as ever, if that's what you're asking," Frederica said, then immediately clapped her hand over her mouth when she realized Anna was paying close attention to their conversation. "Of course, I didn't really have a close acquaintance with him before he left, so—"

"In fact, your previous acquaintance could be measured in the space of one or two heartbeats," Horatia said. Caroline glanced at her sharply, wondering if Horatia had harbored a secret *tendresse* for the dashing young viscount as well.

As if she had not been rudely interrupted, Frederica continued, placid as a duck on a pond. "I can't judge whether or not his character has changed from before his travels. But although Lord Rowley was very pleasant today, he did seem to be the melancholy, brooding sort. He'd look at a painting and just sigh. It was plain the art affected him deeply, which anyone would tell you means he has a great soul. And after seeing how tanned your brother and Mr. Sinclair were after their sojourn in the south, it surprised me to see Lord Rowley looking so pale."

"Oliver has always been fair-skinned," Caroline said. "It goes along with the Rowley red hair."

"Yes, but he was even paler than I remembered. Of course, perhaps he was simply careful to always wear a hat. Indeed, that must be it," Frederica said with a satisfied nod. "I have a cousin in Surrey who has red hair, and if she doesn't wear a bonnet every time she steps from the house, her skin turns the most frightful shade of scarlet. Then she blisters up and peels."

Caroline grimaced at that unpleasant thought. Then a worse one struck her. "Lud, let us hope that's the case with Oliver. They do say consumption makes a body pale. Surely he didn't contract the disease during his travels."

"But how marvelous if he has. It's all the crack now, you know," Horatia said. "Even Lord Byron says he'd like to die of the disease, suffering nobly and leaving gently but with deep sorrow."

"Noble or not, suffering doesn't sound very nice to me," Frederica observed.

"That's because you haven't a romantic bone in your body," Horatia said. "It's well known that suffering from consumption marks one as interesting and artistic and intelligent."

And dead, sooner rather than later, Caroline thought but didn't say. Far be it from her to contradict Byron.

"Well, there's more," Frederica said, turning pink from her rounded chin to the tips of her ears. "Before we parted, Lord Rowley asked if I was planning to attend Lord and Lady Frampton's ball."

"You are, aren't you?" Horatia asked.

"Yes, of course. We all are, Horatia," Caroline reminded her. "We have ball gowns on order at Madame Fournier's, remember?"

"Oh, yes, that's right. Our final fittings are scheduled for tomorrow." Horatia's eyes turned heavenward. "How on earth could I forget an event that requires a new gown?"

"Now who's being a goose?" Frederica said, scoring a point against Horatia for the first time since the girls had started wearing stays. Then, to soften the blow, she added sweetly, "The confusion with Penelope Braithwaite's gown must still have you flummoxed where Madame Fournier is concerned. At any rate, I've saved the most exciting news for last. Lord Rowley begged me to pencil in his name on my dance card. For the *supper* dance," she added with significance. "Isn't that too delicious?"

"My word," Caroline said, trying not to let her surprise show. In whatever company he found himself, Oliver had always been a flash of brilliance, drawing people to him with no effort at all. Frederica was very sweet and pleasing, but people tended to shy away from her in droves when she started on one of her verbal torrents. Before he'd left on Tour with her brother, Rowley had cut a wide swath through the ton, leaving a trail of broken hearts bobbing in his wake. For Freddie's sake, Caroline hoped Oliver had grown up while wandering about the Continent and had learned to have a care for others.

"Asking for the supper dance means Lord Rowley wants to spend the whole meal at your side," Horatia said in wonderment.

Frederica would be nervous because she was clearly excited over Rowley's attention. That meant she'd be chattering away from the white soup to the blancmange.

Caroline hoped Oliver's ears were up to the strain.

Using just my voice, I can settle a spooked horse. Obviously it takes more to settle a spooked lady.
—Lawrence Sinclair, who wishes he'd paid more attention when Lord Rowley regaled him with boasts of his amorous conquests.

Chapter 6

Lawrence watched Lady Caroline go. Her strides were so long, they tested the seams of her column dress. If his aim had been to upset her, he was bang up to the mark, but for the life of him, he had no idea how he'd offended.

Unfortunately, he had no time to puzzle it out. A hand clapped onto Lawrence's shoulder. Then a familiar voice said, "Looks like the lady is in a great hurry to quit your company, my friend."

"Kind of you to notice, Rowley." Lawrence didn't turn to look at him. He didn't want to lose sight of Lady Caroline until she disappeared into the press of people. Even then, he caught occasional glimpses of the feather bobbing above her blue bonnet until she slipped out the door to the exhibit hall.

"Unless I'm much mistaken," Rowley drawled, "the woman bolting madly from your presence was Lady Caroline Lovell."

Lawrence nodded.

Rowley chuckled. "Careful, man. You're reaching for the moon."

"There was no reaching," Lawrence said, though in truth he would have loved to reach out and take her hand. "We were just talking."

"Quite," Rowley said dryly. "In my experience, just talking always makes women run away."

Lawrence turned and started back down the long row of paintings. To his consternation, Rowley followed him.

"I thought you were spending some time in the country," Lawrence said. "I thought I was, too, but how many mornings can a man be roused from his bed by a cock crow without going stark raving mad?"

"There are worse ways to wake." The brisk tattoo of a trumpet sounding reveille came to mind. A rooster was nothing by comparison. In fact, the early waking sounds of Ware—the creak of the well pump in the yard below, the stir of the servants overhead in their tiny chambers, and yes, birdcalls as well as the cock crow—were pleasant childhood memories. But he had no wish to return to the country now. Not so long as Lady Caroline was in London. "You didn't enjoy being home?"

"Rowley End suffers by comparison to Paris. But you're right. I had planned to rusticate for a few months. However, I find the country air doesn't agree with me." He drew in a deep breath as they passed a gaggle of young ladies. "Give me the scent of a woman's perfume any day, even if it has to compete with the fustiness of London."

When Rowley turned back to Lawrence, he didn't so much smile as bare his teeth. "And so, my plans have changed."

Though Rowley was entitled to a seat in the House of Lords, he had little interest in politics. To Lawrence's knowledge, Rowley had no business interests. His entire fortune was tied up in the family estate. In contrast, Lawrence's uncle had a long reach. In addition to the income from the estate surrounding Ware Hall, the earl held controlling ownership of a shipping company, a bank, and at least one cotton mill. Lord Ware kept a close watch on all his holdings. Even after gadding about the Continent for so long, Rowley seemed content to leave the day-to-day running of his ancestral seat in the hands of his steward.

"What do you intend to do in Town?" Lawrence asked.

"As little as possible."

Another pair of debutantes, willowy and fresh-faced, wandered by them. Rowley nodded pleasantly to them but didn't speak. He'd obviously not been formally introduced to the young ladies and propriety kept him from striking up a conversation with them.

Lawrence hoped his former traveling companion would continue to be guided by convention now that they were back in England. Rowley had run more than a little wild during their travels, and Lawrence was tired of cleaning up the scandals that had dogged them on account of Rowley. Even Bredon, who'd been his friend since boyhood, was out of patience with him.

"It seemed a shame to miss the Season when there are so many lovely young buds just starting to bloom," Rowley said, his gaze following the debutantes' swaying gait.

"Just remember, you're not in an Italian brothel anymore," Lawrence warned. "Those are ladies of good family."

"Ladies of good family who are ready to become women, I'll warrant." Rowley looked across the hall and raised his hand in a gesture of farewell to someone. Lawrence followed his gaze to find one of Lady Caroline's friends, the kinder one, waggling her fingers at Rowley.

"Who am I to discourage them in their quest for womanhood?" Rowley turned back to Lawrence. "I say, Sinclair, would you happen to have a pound or two on you?"

"Why?"

"I find myself a bit light in the pockets, and—"

"And there's someone here to whom you owe a goodly sum," Lawrence finished for him. It was an all-too-familiar story.

"As a matter of fact, yes. We ought to hire you out as a fortune-teller. We'd be swimming in lard within a fortnight," Rowley said. "Do you see the very tall gentleman over by the John Constable landscape? No, don't look so boldly. Have a bit of discretion, will you?"

Lawrence glanced in the direction Rowley indicated without moving his head. The fellow in question cut an impressive figure. A fashionably dressed lady hung on his arm, and he used a walking stick with a gleaming silver handle. Obviously, a gentleman.

And one didn't fail to make good on a debt to a gentleman.

"So a pound or two will settle your debt?"

"No, I actually owe him about fifty quid, but I've got eight and with your two, I'll be able to give him ten today," Rowley said with a smile that didn't quite reach his eyes.

"I haven't said I'll lend to you."

"But you will. I know you, Sinclair. You can't resist the chance to help me out. It makes you feel smug and virtuous while you're doing it."

Lawrence crossed his arms over his chest. "Not this time."

Rowley's smile disappeared. "But you must."

"The only thing I *must* do is continue to breathe. And what I *shall* do is leave. Good day." Lawrence turned and began to walk away, but Rowley hurried after him, matching him stride for stride.

"No, wait." Rowley caught him by the arm.

Lawrence eyed the hand on his elbow and then glared at Rowley. There was enough warning in his gaze to make the viscount release him immediately.

Lawrence possessed a violent temper.

People who'd never seen it in action claimed Lawrence was very self-contained. But he only disciplined himself so because he knew what he was capable of. He was a powder keg. When sorely provoked, he'd explode. The trait had stood him in good stead in the military. Like a Viking berserker of old, he was a terror in a melee, but keeping the warrior within chained and hidden meant exercising a great deal of restraint in civilian life.

"Look, Sinclair, one hand washes the other. There must be something you want." Rowley's tone turned wheedling. "Something I can do for you."

Rowley must be in serious fear of that gentleman and his walking stick.

"Now that you mention it, there is something," Lawrence said. "That young lady you smiled at across the hall."

"You'll have to be more specific." Rowley shrugged. "I smile at a lot of women."

"The one I mean is Lady Caroline's particular friend."

Rowley nodded in recognition. "Ah, yes. That would be Miss Frederica Tilbury. Lovely girl. Monstrous dowry. Giggles too much, but one can't have everything."

"That's the one." Lawrence stepped closer and made Rowley meet his steady gaze. He'd been told once that the softer he spoke, the more menacing he sounded. So Lawrence dropped his voice to a husky near whisper. "I want you to leave her alone."

Rowley stepped back and snorted, but he averted his gaze. "Got your eye on that one as well as Bredon's sister?"

"No. I simply don't wish to see Miss Tilbury hurt." There was no point in denying his interest in Lady Caroline. His heart was firmly on his sleeve.

"I assure you, Sinclair," Rowley said, suddenly serious, "if I should approach Miss Tilbury at all, it will be with the most honorable of intentions."

"That means she's safe from your attentions, then. You wouldn't know an honorable intention if it bit you on the arse." Lawrence dug into his waistcoat pocket and fished out a couple of sovereigns. "Take them and be done. I'm tired of looking at you."

"It was a pleasure seeing you again, too, my friend." The glib charmer was back in full force. Rowley secreted the coins in his pocket and gave it a little pat. "This will buy the time I need to make good on my debt. And I *will* repay you."

Lawrence scoffed. "The day that happens will be a day of note indeed."

"You laugh, but I will. When have I not been a man of my word?"

"I cannot count that high."

Rowley laughed and slapped him on the back again, as if they were bosom friends. It was getting to be an annoying habit. Lawrence tolerated

Rowley for Bredon's sake. If they hadn't been in a public place, Lawrence would probably have laid him out good and proper. His fists had gotten Lord Rowley out of a number of tight spots in the past. Perhaps they could be put to better use teaching him some manners now.

Lawrence laid a hand on Rowley's shoulder and squeezed. To anyone passing by, the gesture looked like a fond farewell between friends. Unless they noticed how the viscount's lips drew into a pale line.

"I trust I may rely upon you to remember your promise," Lawrence said, so softly only Rowley would hear him.

"To repay you?" Rowley winced as Lawrence tightened his grip. "Surely. Without fail."

"Keep the money." Lawrence released him. "I mean your promise concerning Miss Tilbury."

Rowley's eyes narrowed. "I won't forget, Sinclair. On *that* you may rely."

* * * *

After Lawrence parted company with Rowley, he found Bredon loitering near the way out of the exhibition hall.

"What are you doing skulking about here?" Lawrence asked. "Is Somerset House so short of doormen they have to press visiting lords into service?"

"No. I just decided that if the main point of attending the opening of this exhibit is to be seen doing so, this is the best place to be," Bredon said. "Everyone goes through these doors sooner or later, and I don't have to engage in conversations about brush strokes or color palettes."

"And you couldn't be bothered to suggest this strategy to me?"

"Sorry, old son. In the case of art exhibitions, it's every man for himself," Bredon said. "If I never see another fussy portrait of some dead lord or another hazy landscape, it'll be too soon."

Lawrence understood. Museums and galleries were fine in their way, but they couldn't compare to real life. The bustle of so many souls intersecting, unruly and seething, couldn't be reduced to a flat canvas.

He and Bredon walked to the nearby stable where their mounts waited.

"I learned something new about you today, Sinclair."

"How is that possible? We traveled in each other's company for months. You already know me better than anyone ever has."

"And yet there's more to learn. For one thing, you have an uncanny ability to vex my sister."

"You spoke with Lady Caroline?"

"Briefly, in my role as doorkeeper," Bredon said with a grin. "As she swept by me, I asked if she'd seen you in the gallery."

"What did she say?"

"That she'd seen far too much of you. I swear there were little wisps of smoke coming from her ears. All in all, it's a good thing she was leaving."

"Why?"

"Don't want the whole exhibit going up in flames, do we?" Bredon chuckled. "What did you say to provoke her so?"

"I didn't provoke her." Lawrence ran their conversation through his mind. No; he could think of nothing in word or deed that ought to have caused offense. "I asked her to show me her favorite painting."

"Ah! That must have been it. Women just hate it when a man expresses an interest in their opinions." Bredon tipped the groom who'd minded their horses and the men mounted. "But don't fret, Sinclair. Remember your Virgil: 'A woman is an ever fickle and changeable thing.'"

Lawrence had read very little Virgil and had never felt the lack. Until now. He wished he had more of mankind's wisdom to draw upon, though it did seem as if the poet weren't making an earth-shattering observation. What wisdom was there in merely stating the obvious?

"Changeable." Lawrence tested the word on his tongue and found it apt. "She *did* describe herself as a weathercock."

"That's our Caro. She's like a spring storm. Her ire blows hard and fast. Then, in a little while, she'll be coming up flowers, bursting with charity for all. You must simply have struck a sore subject without realizing it," Bredon said as they made their way around waiting hansoms to the main thoroughfare. "No harm done. She'll have forgotten all about it by suppertime."

Lawrence wasn't so confident of that, but he'd upset one Lovell already this day. There was no need to offend another by arguing the point.

It did him good to ride for a bit. Time spent on horseback always helped him make sense of the world. Once they reached Lovell House, Bredon was all for a game of chess in the library. The groom would tend to their mounts.

"I'll tend to mine, if you don't mind." Lawrence always felt he owed a horse he'd ridden his personal attention.

"Suit yourself, but don't be long. I'll set up the board and ring for tea."

So Lawrence remained in the stable, picking hooves and brushing down his horse's strong back and flanks. As he curried the animal, it was almost as if he were brushing away the knots in his own soul. By the time he was done with the chore, he felt more optimistic about the world in general and Lady Caroline in particular.

Lawrence had returned to a state of hope.

It lasted until he met Mr. Price in the hallway near the base of the grand staircase.

"Ah, there you are, Mr. Sinclair." The butler carried a silver tray that bore a single creamy missive. It was sealed with a blob of red wax embossed with an important-looking crest. "This came while you were out, sir."

Lawrence thanked Mr. Price and accepted the note. He opened it and read:

Lord and Lady Frampton request the pleasure of Mr. Lawrence Sinclair's company at a ball held at their home on Thursday next. Dancing to begin ten o'clock p.m. Supper to follow. The favor of a reply is appreciated.

Lawrence groaned and leaned against the nearby wall. This was a disaster of biblical proportions.

"Do you wish to send a reply?" Price asked.

"I wouldn't know what to say," Lawrence said.

"Well, generally, sir, people send either their acceptance or their regrets."

"I know, Mr. Price," Lawrence said testily. Did even the help think him an imbecile? "I just wasn't expecting something like this to happen."

"I say, what's that you've got there?" Bredon called down from the landing above.

"An invitation to Lord Frampton's ball."

"Splendid." Bredon came down the steps, rubbing his hands together. "Did the messenger wait for a reply, Price?" When the butler nodded, Bredon went on, "Then send back Mr. Sinclair's compliments and an acceptance."

"Very good, my lord." The butler bowed and withdrew.

Lawrence had met Lord Frampton at White's and played a few hands of whist with him but didn't think he'd made that much of an impression on the gentleman. "Did you have something to do with this?"

Bredon shrugged. "I may have."

"I wish you hadn't."

"How could I not drop a word in the right ear on behalf of a friend?" Bredon said with a confused frown. "The whole family is going, even Mother and Father. It wouldn't have seemed right to leave you here alone, counting your toes."

"That would have been a kindness indeed."

"In heaven's name, why?"

"Because I..." Lawrence shook his head. It was no use. It made no difference that he was unfailingly polite, or that he knew which fork to use. At a ball, it wouldn't matter that he deferred to others, as was expected of him in Polite Society. The only fact that signified was that he had never acquired all the polish, the gentlemanly skills usually associated with the wellborn.

"Bredon," he said with a sigh, "I cannot dance."

My mother says being a lady means governing my behavior so that those around me will feel comfortable. That's a bit like saying I must lace my stays so tightly I cannot breathe lest I discommode the seams of my gown.
—from the diary of Lady Caroline Lovell

Chapter 7

"Come," Caroline called out when a soft rap sounded on her chamber door. She slipped the book that held her secret thoughts into the top drawer of her escritoire and locked it quickly. Then she looked up from her diary's hiding place in time to see her maid pop her head around the opened door. "We've an hour or so until the dressing gong sounds. What is it, Alice?"

"Beggin' your pardon, my lady." The maid gave a quick curtsy. Caroline had tried to break her of the habit, saying there was no need to stand on ceremony. With all the other work Alice did for her, why add superfluous bobbing that would eventually ruin her knees? However, before coming to the Lovell household, Alice had served a dowager marchioness, who was a stickler for the rules. Even though she was now under a less-demanding mistress, Alice refused to let go of the deferential habit. "His Lordship requests your presence on the fourth floor."

"How very odd."

"That's as may be, my lady, but he begs you to hurry."

Since her father had suffered a mild case of apoplexy a year ago, he no longer climbed that many stairs unless it was unavoidable. Caroline couldn't imagine why the earl would need to visit the cavernous space on the topmost floor of the town house. It was never used unless Lord Chatham hosted a soiree for more guests than would fit around his enormous dining table or on the rare occasions when Caroline's mother convinced him to hold a private ball.

That still didn't explain why her presence was so urgently required. However, Caroline rose immediately to do her father's bidding, with Alice on her heels. When she reached the upper story, she found only her brother Benjamin. A shock of dark hair was falling forward across his forehead. He'd been affecting this Byronesque look since he finished his most recent term at Oxford.

Caroline's fingers itched to smooth it back into place for him, but she knew this was his attempt to appear an artistic man of deep feeling. She'd often teased him about it, but now she wondered if Ben was having as much difficulty coming to grips with his lot in life as she. Being a spare heir meant he had to find a living for himself unless he wanted to hang on Bredon's sleeve all his days.

Benjamin didn't look up from tuning his violin.

"What's this?" Caroline asked. "I was told our father wished to see me here."

Ben's face screwed into a frown. "To my knowledge, the earl has nothing to do with this. In fact, if we can keep it that way, so much the better."

"Beggin' your pardon, my lady," Alice said, bobbing yet another quick curtsy. "I know I said His Lordship had need of you, but I ought to have made my meaning clearer. 'Twas not Lord Chatham who called you here. Lord Bredon, he's the one who sent me to fetch you."

"Teddy's the reason I'm here as well," Benjamin said as he executed a florid series of arpeggios and runs to warm up his fingers. While Caroline was sadly lacking as a musician, her brother Ben more than made up for her deficit. He'd been gifted in double portion. As the second son, he was likely bound for the Church, but until he finished his studies at Oxford and was ordained, Benjamin wasn't apt to be found studying a theological treatise. Not if he could lay his hands on a new violin concerto instead.

"I was told this was a pressing matter," Caroline said.

"And so it is." Teddy's voice floated up from the stairwell. Then he appeared at the top of the steps with Mr. Sinclair in tow. "We've only a bit more than a week."

"To do what?"

Teddy gave her one of his sun-laden smiles. It was a trap, but she couldn't help returning it. He was her favorite brother, after all. Then he said, "We have to teach Sinclair to dance before Lord Frampton's ball."

"That's not enough time." Caroline swallowed her surprise that someone who'd grown up in an earl's household could come of age without acquiring the skill. Then she crossed her arms over her chest. "It cannot be done."

"That's what I tried to tell him," Mr. Sinclair said, his arms similarly crossed.

"Then for once we find ourselves in complete accord, sir," Caroline grudgingly said to him. "A week will never do. It takes years to master dancing."

"He doesn't need to master it. He just needs to be able not to embarrass himself too badly. And you'll make a wonderful teacher. You, my dear, are one of the best dancers I've ever seen," Bredon said. "Surely—"

"Save your breath. I know when someone's trying to turn me up sweet, Teddy," Caroline said, slanting her brother a sidelong glare. "Besides, knowing how to do something and teaching someone else to do it are two very different things."

Teddy shook his head. "Caro, what's happened to you? I've never known you to shy away from a challenge."

"That's not fair, Bredon. This isn't a challenge," Mr. Sinclair said, charging to her defense. "In the military we'd have called it 'a forlorn hope.' An impossible task. I never should have agreed to try." He gave Caroline a quick bow from the neck. "Pray excuse me. I need to send Lord and Lady Frampton my regrets."

Caroline's irritation with him dissipated a little. The man was being sensible and chivalrous and disgustingly decent about the situation. She sighed. "If you refuse this invitation, you'll not be invited to another ball all Season."

"One can hope." Mr. Sinclair turned and headed toward the stairwell.

Originally, she'd intended to make use of her association with Mr. Sinclair to irritate her parents. Now that she knew he was more than capable of irritating *her* as well, it didn't seem so good a plan.

But if consorting with a completely unsuitable gentleman would convince Lord and Lady Chatham to give up on their dreams of a marriage in her future, perhaps the aggravation would be worth it. And Mr. Neither-Fish-Nor-Fowl Sinclair was singularly unsuitable.

"Wait," Caroline said.

He stopped and turned to face her.

"I cannot promise success," she said, "but I will try."

"One cannot ask for more than that." Then Mr. Sinclair gave her a genuine smile. The expression took her by surprise. She hadn't seen him do it before. It turned his dark eyes from piercing to warm and welcoming and changed his countenance out of all knowing.

The man should smile more often.

"I am yours to command, my lady."

"What woman doesn't live to hear those words?" she said with a laugh. A strange warmth bloomed in her chest, but she dismissed it. This was no time to become mawkish over a gentleman's pretty words. She was only doing a favor for Teddy. And herself, once news of the time she was spending with Mr. Sinclair reached her parents' ears.

"Come. Let us begin." Caroline straightened her spine and took a formal pose, toes turned out. "Fortunately, there are only a few steps you need to learn."

"That doesn't sound so hard."

Benjamin chuckled. "It's not. The trick comes when you have to remember the order in which to perform them."

* * * *

"There is no need to add any flourishes," Lady Caroline said, after they'd been at it for a while. "No extraneous gestures, if you please."

"Indeed not." Self-conscious, Lawrence forced himself to let his arms hang at his sides. They felt overlong, as if he could scratch his kneecap without bending over. "I was unaware that I added a flourish. I'm disinclined to anything that might draw attention to myself."

"Nor should you."

"The man's trying, Caro," Bredon said from his seat next to Benjamin, who was supplying a steady tune for the lesson.

Lawrence hurried to catch up to her in the intricate forward and back, side to side, turn and bow of the steps. "That extraneous gesture, as you call it, was only my attempt to keep my balance on that last turn."

"If you shorten your strides, your center of balance will remain over your own feet," Lady Caroline suggested. "Remember, this dance is performed in two parallel lines. There will be dancers on either side of you. Should you topple over, you'll likely knock down several others."

"Hmm…I had no idea dancing could be so aggressive."

"Until I met you, Mr. Sinclair, I would have said it was not. Timely and decorous steps, if you please. There's no need to tromp about. Imagine you are in a garden and don't wish to tread heavily on the daisies."

Instead of imagining a garden, the forward and back movements suddenly reminded Lawrence of his fencing lessons. Those required lightness of foot. He decided to pretend he carried a foil in his hand.

"Yes, that's it," Lady Caroline said. "Much better."

"I wish you didn't sound so astonished."

"And I wish you wouldn't start on the wrong foot—no, no, your other left—but we can't have everything, can we?"

After a rough start, in a surprisingly short while, Lady Caroline had taught him the difference between a chassé and an allemande. The traveling waltz step, with its up-up-up-down rhythm, had him befogged for a bit, but he began to make sense of it.

So long as he imagined he was fencing.

"Now, we must put these steps to use." She faced him about four feet in front of him. "Stop playing for a moment, Ben. We'll need to just count for a bit." Then to Lawrence, "Mirror my movements."

She chasséd to meet him in the middle with her palm lifted. "Palm-to-palm. That's it, and lightly go we round."

She murmured more bits of encouragement and direction, counting aloud when he seemed to lose his timing. Lawrence tried mightily to pay attention to her words as they circled each other, but the wonder of touching her hand made it deucedly difficult. Not her gloved hand either. Lady Caroline was at home, so her lovely fingers were perfectly bare.

Her hand was soft. Tiny compared to his.

Then she raised her voice a bit. "I had heard the Duke of Wellington required his officers to know how to dance. How is it that you do not?"

Now that their circle was complete, she dropped her hand and danced backward to her original position. Lawrence followed suit, though with far less grace.

"I confess, my lady, that whenever a regimental ball was in the offing, I made certain my duties required me to be elsewhere to avoid such social obligations."

"And you never learned to dance at home or at school?" she asked.

He shook his head.

"How lonely that must have been for you," she said, her eyes dark and compassionate, "not to be able to join in the fun."

"I wouldn't say it was lonely. One cannot miss what one has never had."

"Well, you're having it now. And you won't ever be able to get out of dancing again, Sinclair," Bredon said. "Be grateful you never had a sister. Caro's been pestering the lot of us to dance with her since she was wearing leading strings."

Bredon's voice came as a jarring reminder to Lawrence that he was not alone with Lady Caroline. When he danced forward to touch palms with her and they circled round each other again, gazes locked, it was easy to imagine the two of them were the only people in the world, let alone the room.

Steady on, Sinclair. It's just a dance. She means nothing by it.

"Play us a tune, Ben," Lady Caroline said. "I think Mr. Sinclair is ready to try a promenade."

He'd be ready to try flying backward if she asked him. Fortunately, the promenade was much easier. And it had the added charm of requiring Lady Caroline to rest her hand on his.

"My lady," he said, glad their speech would be covered by the tuneful melody coming from Benjamin's violin, "I offended you somehow at the Academy of Arts and I wish to apo—"

"No, no. Of the two of us, I'm the one who owes you an apology. I said something about you that is not true. Someone who tries to learn a skill for which he has no appreciable aptitude is certainly not spineless."

That made him feel both better and worse.

"Oh, no, that sounded terrible. And it's not what I meant to…it's just that you…" Lady Caroline floundered. "In truth, during our conversation at the gallery I was thinking about something else."

That definitely made him feel worse.

"And whatever it was you were thinking about caused you to be upset with me?"

"Not exactly," she said as they circled each other, gazes locked. "Your devotion to duty; it made me upset with *myself.*"

He gave her a puzzled frown. "I doubt you have done anything for which you should feel the need to castigate yourself."

"Oh, no. It's not what I've done. It's what I plan to do."

His brows shot up at that, but there was no time to question her further. The tempo of the music quickened.

"Up, up, up, down, Mr. Sinclair," she said softly. "Do try to keep time."

"I'd do better if you called me Lawrence," he said, too softly for her brothers to hear. When she looked up at him sharply, he wished he could take it back. Even though she'd kindly agreed to be his dancing tutor, she'd shown no interest at all in letting their acquaintance become more familiar.

Then a minor miracle occurred.

"If you think it will help," she whispered. "Lawrence."

While I sincerely hope to prove my worth to Lady Caroline, please, Lord, let that endeavor not involve shopping.
—Mr. Lawrence Sinclair

Chapter 8

"How can the man not know how to dance?" Horatia said as she turned this way and that, admiring herself in the long standing mirror.

Her new gown of ivory lustring was lovely, but if Horatia didn't stand still, Madame Fournier's poor apprentice, Mary Woodyard, would never be able to pin up the hem evenly. Frederica had stood, docile as a lamb, while the apprentice made alterations to her ball gown. Horatia couldn't be shepherded into submission no matter how often Mary coaxed her to be still. Her mouth full of pins, Mary made a small noise that might have been a low growl, if such a thing weren't too impertinent for one of her station.

"Imagine not knowing a gavotte from a quadrille." Horatia punctuated the remark with a little snort of derision. "I for one can scarcely credit it, Caro."

"You'll credit it well enough this evening." Caroline ran her fingertips over a bolt of pale blue tulle. Her chaperone, Anna, had escorted the girls to the dressmaker's shop and then left them there while she ducked into the bakery next door for tea and scones with her friend, Lady Dinwattle's housekeeper. It was a pleasant break for the old woman and a relief to Caroline to be out from under her watchful eyes.

"I don't expect Mr. Sinclair to become a polished dancer, of course," Caroline said. "He only needs to be able to make a decent showing at Lord Frampton's ball. I'm counting on you and Freddie to help. Come to supper and then stay the night, won't you? Together, we can put Mr. Sinclair through his paces."

Frederica looked up from the bolt of dotted Swiss she'd been admiring. "How will we do that without additional partners?" she said with unusual practicality.

"I've enlisted my brothers' help."

"Which ones?" Frederica asked.

"Charles and Thomas. Of the five of them, they're the best dancers. Benjamin will play for us, so we'll have music."

"Bredon won't be involved?" Horatia asked, all innocence. Caroline had long suspected her friend of being sweet on Teddy but knew there was no chance he'd return her affection. Horatia's gossipy tongue had always tried his patience. He'd often told Caroline that only his devotion to her made him contain his irritation with her flighty friend.

And sometimes even that wasn't enough to keep him from vacating the room without explanation while Horatia was tittering her on-dits. Horatia was bewildered by his behavior, but Caroline knew Teddy was trying to spare her.

"Involved? Of course Teddy will be involved. It was his idea that I teach Mr. Sinclair to dance, after all. Throughout the evening, Teddy will be coming in and out and sending one of my other brothers down to take his place," Caro explained. "Someone has to play piquet with Mother in the parlor if we don't want her to discover we're playing caper masters on the fourth floor."

"Your parents won't notice anything strange if the three of us never appear in the parlor?" Horatia stopped batting her eyes at her own reflection long enough to ask.

"Mama knows we'd rather talk than play cards. She'll assume we're in my chamber," Caroline explained. "And once my father sticks his nose in a book, he wouldn't notice if an anvil fell from the sky and crashed through the roof."

"Is everything to the lady's satisfaction?" Madame Fournier came breezing in from the back room, a cunningly devised headdress in her hands.

Horatia squealed in delight when she saw it. "Yes, I think this will do quite nicely for Lord Frampton's ball."

When they'd first arrived at the shop, Horatia had given the dressmaker an earful about Penelope Braithwaite's yellow gown. Madame Fournier had seemed aghast at the news. She'd insisted, even swearing an oath on her mother's grave, that she would never make the same gown for two of her clients. It would be a grievous breach of trust.

"Perhaps one of my competitors, she has copied my style, mademoiselle," she had suggested. "It is—how you say?—an unhappy coincidence, nothing more."

Then, after Madame Fournier promised to make Horatia a coronet of embroidered muslin and tulle to match her new gown, all was forgiven. The dressmaker positioned the little cap on Horatia's head, realized it needed to be a bit bigger, and disappeared once again into the back room.

"So, will you two help me with Mr. Sinclair or not?" Caroline asked.

Frederica nodded. "Of course we will, won't we?"

"Why not?" Horatia turned sideways to view herself from that vantage. "It will be delicious fun to watch the man make a cake of himself."

"I have to give him high marks for persistence." That morning, Caroline had glanced down through the banister from the first-story landing and caught Mr. Sinclair practicing the traveling waltz step down the hall for a few beats as he followed Bredon out the door for their daily jaunt to White's. It was strangely endearing. Caroline had clamped a hand firmly over her mouth, lest she burst out laughing and embarrass him. "He *is* trying."

"Very trying, no doubt."

"Don't be unkind, Horatia," Frederica admonished.

"I wouldn't dream of it. But I do expect to be entertained. If your Mr. Sinclair is as awkward with his feet as he is with his tongue, this promises to be an amusing evening."

"He's not *my* Mr. Sinclair," Caroline protested, but her insides did a shivery little jig nonetheless. When she'd called him by his Christian name last evening, the look on his face was astonishing. He couldn't have been more pleased if she'd offered him a handful of diamonds and pearls.

"That insipid little smile of yours when you think we don't see begs to differ," Horatia said with a disgustingly knowing look. "Doesn't she look positively moonstruck, Freddie?"

"I am not." Caroline gave herself an inward shake. "Never mind about the dancing lessons. If you're intent on being hurtful, don't come."

"Hold a moment." Horatia abandoned the mirror, crossed the room to Caroline, and grasped one of her hands. "I was only teasing, Caro."

"I don't appreciate being teased."

"Then I won't do it. Besides, we know you're only spending time with Mr. Sinclair to please Lord Bredon. And I won't say a single unkind word to the man. I promise."

"Maybe you won't say them, but you think unkind things about him and…it makes me feel so very low when you do."

"Why, Caro," Frederica said, "if I didn't know better, I'd suspect you *are* harboring a tendresse for Mr. Sinclair."

"Don't be ridiculous."

"Oh, my stars and garters!" Horatia eyed her with such intensity, Caroline wondered if she could look directly into her heart. "Freddie's right."

"She is not. Not that you aren't right sometimes, Freddie dear," Caroline hastened to add when Frederica's face fell. It never failed to amaze her that her sensitive friend seemed to feel unintentional pricks from her more deeply than real jabs from Horatia. She pulled her hand away from Horatia, wondering, not for the first time, if their friendship, which had begun in childhood, had run its course. "Just because I don't wish Mr. Sinclair to become an object of ridicule, it does not follow that I am enamored with the man. I merely feel we ought not to mock someone whose life has been so very different from ours."

Caroline thought she heard the dressmaker's apprentice murmur "hear, hear" under her breath as she rose to her feet. Horatia had refused to stand still, so the woman was evidently giving up on pinning her hem.

"You've hit upon the very thing that puzzles me, Caro," Frederica said.

"When are you not puzzled, Freddie?" Horatia rolled her eyes and returned to the raised area in front of the mirror. Mary Woodyard dropped to her knees and went back to work on the hem with all the urgency of a squirrel gathering nuts for winter.

Undeterred by Horatia's remark, Frederica continued. "Why should Mr. Sinclair's life have been so different from ours? He was raised in Ware Hall. For pity's sake, the man is heir presumptive to an earldom—"

"Emphasis on presumptive," Horatia interrupted.

"At any rate," Frederica went on placidly, "it does seem odd that he shouldn't have learned how to dance...or converse...or manage his teacup...or—"

"Yes, I know. He's different, but I don't know *why* he is as he is," Caroline said in frustration. "The fact remains that Mr. Sinclair is a...a very singular gentleman."

"Singular," Horatia repeated meaningfully. "As in one."

"Oh! You're implying a deeper significance," Frederica said, happy to have followed her clever friend's train of thought. "You mean as in one and only?"

"Not at all," Caroline said testily, "and I'll thank you two hens not to entertain such faradiddles."

She was saved from further mortification when the dressmaker returned with a gown of pale pink silk in her arms. "Madame Fournier, is that mine?"

"*Oui, bien sûr.* This is the fine silk you have chosen, is it not?"

"Yes. Good. Then I shall go next." Caroline flounced away to the dressing room in the back, with Madame Fournier's apprentice following close behind her to carry the gown and assist while she changed into it. Caroline loved Freddie—and Horatia, too, when she didn't make Caroline the target of her barbed tongue—but she needed to be away from both of them. Immediately.

Unfortunately, the dressing room wasn't far enough.

As Mary Woodyard helped her strip down to her chemise, she could still hear Freddie say in a stage whisper, "My word, I believe we have offended her."

"If we have, it's only for speaking the truth. Our Caro is dangerously close to forming an unwanted liaison."

If Horatia was only trying to protect her from making a mistake, perhaps she was right to be a little cutting. Caroline's irritation at her friends began to fade.

"I believe you're wrong, Horatia. I don't think Mr. Sinclair is unwanted at all. I think she rather likes him."

No, I don't, Caroline almost shouted, but she held her tongue. As the only girl in a household filled with boys, she'd learned long ago that she might hear the most amazing things if others weren't aware she was listening.

"No, goose. I meant her attachment to him is unwise."

"But I've never known Caro to do anything unwise."

"Mark my words, she's close to it now." Horatia sighed expressively. "Honestly, one may see a puppy in the street and find it sweet, but one ought not to bring it home."

Frederica was silent so long, Caroline knew she was puzzling out the metaphor. Finally, she said, "Ah! I understand. Mr. Sinclair is the puppy. But…but Caro didn't bring Mr. Sinclair home. Lord Bredon did."

Horatia made an exasperated noise and then got distracted with giving Madame Fournier suggestions for more embellishments on the little coronet. In the meantime, Mary Woodyard used a special hook to fasten the row of tiny buttons that marched down Caroline's spine.

It was a gorgeous gown. Beautifully sewn, it was of the best quality silk. Seed pearls embellished the bodice and the fully lined train was long enough to do credit to a princess.

"If it not be impertinent," Mary said, "I shouldn't pay those two any mind were I you, my lady."

It was a little impertinent. Shopkeepers, like servants, were supposed to behave as if they didn't hear or see anything their customers said or did unless it was related to an ongoing transaction. Clearly, Miss Woodyard had chosen to ignore that unspoken code.

"They're my friends," Caroline said. "Why shouldn't I listen to their advice?"

"Because they aren't going to live your life for you, are they?" Mary stood and met Caroline's gaze. "You're the only one as can do that."

"That's true. You have some rather unexpected views. Have you, by chance, been attending the lectures of Mrs. Hester Birdwhistle?"

Just then, Madame Fournier called out to her apprentice, pronouncing her name as if it were Marie in the French style instead of plain English Mary. "Do not make to talk Lady Caroline to death. And hurry. *Vite, vite!*"

Mary smiled ruefully and whispered, "No, my lady. I've no time for lectures, save for those from my mistress."

"But your views are those of an enlightened mind." Caroline doubted she'd have thought about an independent life if she hadn't first listened to Mrs. Birdwhistle. "Whence do you hail?"

"Surrey, my lady," Mary said softly as she smoothed down Caroline's train. "And you may blame my enlightened mind on my father. He was a vicar who believed his daughters should be as well read as his sons."

Caroline remembered her struggle to learn Latin without her father's consent or knowledge. It would have been so much easier if she could have sat in on her brothers' sessions with their tutor instead of having Teddy deliver each new set of verbs for her to conjugate. "Huzzah for your father, the vicar."

"Indeed, my lady."

"Marie! Please to hurry. I need an extra pair of hands."

"Coming, Madame." But Mary didn't go immediately. Instead, she gathered up her sewing kit in one hand and Caroline's train in the other. Then she said, "About your Mr. Sinclair…"

"What about him?"

"The only one who knows what a person's life is like is the one who lives it. There are as many tragedies behind fine doors as there are in the ghetto around Seven Dials," Mary said. "If you want to know why he is as he is, discover his tragedy."

"And then I'll know the man?"

"Yes, my lady," Mary said as she trailed Caroline out of the back room. "But first, you must do the hard part."

"What might that be?"

"You have to make him trust you enough to tell you."

When Caroline rejoined her friends in the main part of the shop, to her great surprise, Mr. Sinclair was there, hat in hand. His jaw was clenched, his shoulders stiff. He looked as if he feared to move a muscle lest he upset the displays of ribbons and lace. But when he saw her, the tension drained from his face and his shoulders relaxed. His gaze swept her form with obvious appreciation.

"My lady," he said simply, followed by that quick nod of a bow of his. But the look on his face said, *my goddess.*

"May I take it you approve of my gown, Mr. Sinclair?" she asked, a ridiculously happy sensation heating her chest as she basked in his open admiration.

Caroline spread her arms and did a little spin, causing Mary Woodyard to drop her long train lest the gown tear. It was designed to be hooked up before the wearer launched into a dance figure, but Caroline had forgotten all about that. Unbound, the train turned into a flying whip at floor level. It caught on the bottom of the dressmaker's dummy displaying a new style of frock fresh from Paris. The dummy toppled over onto a large jar containing assorted buttons, frogs, and hooks and eyes. The jar spilled onto the floor and shattered to pieces, sending hundreds of small bits of horn and shell, woven cord and metal, scurrying around the shop like ants pouring from an upturned hill.

Madame Fournier shrieked. Then she lunged across the room, trying to collect the dearer fasteners off the floor, cursing in French at the top of her lungs. The dressmaker caught the hem of her gown under the toe of one of her shoes and she went tail over teakettle into the long row of upright bolts of fabric that ringed the room. They began to topple like dominoes. The last one smashed into a display of spangles. The small decorative leaves pattered to the hardwood like metallic raindrops.

Once the last tinkling sound died away, the shop went completely silent.

Mr. Sinclair cleared his throat. "Lady Caroline, I've come to assist you and your friends with your parcels whenever you are ready to leave."

"Oh, I think we're ready to leave right now," Horatia said, still perched on the raised dais before the long mirror, only now she was also clinging to Frederica. When the fiasco began, Frederica must have skittered over to join her there. The two of them were crowded onto that small buoy of safety above a sea of buttons and spangles, fallen lace and ripped muslin.

"But shouldn't Lady Caroline...and we, too, of course, help with..." Frederica began.

"No, mademoiselles," Madam Fournier said as she hauled herself from her sprawled position on the floor. "My poor shop, she could not bear so much as another thimbleful of Lady Caroline's help."

On a positive note, Madame Fournier has offered to come to Lovell House in the future for all my fittings and millinery purchases.
—from the diary of Lady Caroline Lovell, who suspects she may have been barred from the Fournier dress shop for life.

Chapter 9

Fortunately, the rest of Caroline's day went much more to plan than had her morning shopping. Mr. Sinclair served as an admirable bearer of parcels as he escorted the girls and old Anna back to the Lovell carriage. He even rode alongside the equipage, making conversation that was less stiff than usual with Caroline and her friends.

She began to hope he might yet find a place within Polite Society. Not that Lawrence would ever be high on the guest lists of the most fashionable houses. His prospects were too uncertain for that. And he didn't have the personal charm that made the bon ton embrace someone on the fringes of their society. Lawrence wasn't a bit like the remarkable Henry Luttrell, the illegitimate son of an earl. Without his wit, Luttrell would have been an outcast. Instead, his lively verse was celebrated among the ton.

Caroline didn't think Mr. Sinclair capable of rhyming a single couplet, but as she completed her most recent diary entry, his words describing the French countryside came back to her.

He noticed the small things. The often overlooked things. And by marking them, he made them meaningful.

My horse's breath ghosting the air, frost sparkling on the field, and each blade of grass doubled by its own sharp-edged shadow.

Not witty, but clearly effective, if the little tingle at the base of her spine was any indication. She could practically feel the cold kiss of that battlefield morning, its icy lips on her nape.

Mr. Sinclair would never hold court in a parlor, regaling the room with stories. His remembrances were too intimate for that.

But surely, she thought as she put away her diary, *there must be room in this world for an overlooked, genuinely decent man. Even if he is far too duty bound for his own good.*

Later that evening, Frederica and Horatia joined Caro's family and Mr. Sinclair for supper. Conversation with her brothers was stilted, which was a surprise; she and her friends had practically lived in one another's pockets since they were children. Then, when she caught Benjamin giving Frederica a sidelong glance, it occurred to her that this was the first meal they'd all shared since her friends had come out. Freddie and Horatia weren't children any longer. They were debutantes, and her brothers eyed them with the suspicion due such unfamiliar beings.

Then, fortunately, a near calamity ensued.

Frederica was wearing a new gown for the first time that bared more of her shoulders than usual. It fit admirably over her bosom, but the tabs in back hadn't been tied snugly and there was a bit of a gap beneath her bared nape. Dudley, the ham-handed first footman, accidentally dropped a serving spoon down the back of Freddie's gown. She squealed and leaped to her feet. Only Mr. Price's swift intervention stopped the footman from reaching in after it. Then Caroline's mother came to the rescue, took Freddie behind the chinoiserie screen in the corner, and retrieved the spoon. Everyone had a good laugh about the incident. The ice was broken, and they were all friends again.

Dudley, however, was relegated to the kitchen for the rest of the meal.

But while everyone else seemed to be enjoying themselves immensely, Caroline was mildly disappointed to find herself seated between Teddy and Thomas. She loved her brothers, and enjoyed teasing and being teased by them, but she couldn't help wondering how Mr. Sinclair came to be seated between Frederica and Horatia instead of beside her. When she considered it, she realized she hadn't been seated next to him once since he'd arrived at Lovell House, even when it was just her immediate family and he.

At the thought, she glanced at her mother sharply. But if Lady Chatham bore responsibility for the seating arrangements, she didn't betray any guilt over it. The countess was smiling and laughing along with the rest of the company.

After supper, Caroline's plan to educate Mr. Sinclair in the ways of the ballroom went swimmingly. Teddy came and went, sending one of her other brothers down to the parlor in turn to serve as his surrogate. Ben played as softly as he could, and everyone kept conversation to a minimum because Lawrence needed, first and foremost, to hear her instruction as they executed the dance figures. When neither of their parents climbed to the fourth floor to investigate their offspring's doings in the ballroom, Caroline could only conclude they had accomplished their caper mastering without Lord or Lady Chatham's detection.

After several hours, Benjamin ended the final reel with a flourish and the dancers all nearly collapsed, partly in relief that the strenuous dance was finished and partly in amazement that Mr. Sinclair had held his own. Sucking wind, Charles and Thomas both slapped him good-naturedly on the back and made approving masculine noises.

Why must men communicate by punching and grunting at each other?

"Very good, sir," Caroline said between panting breaths. She wished being a lady didn't mean she couldn't mop her brow with a handkerchief as her brothers were doing. She'd simply have to continue to *glisten*, as her mother called it. "I think it will be safe for you to join in the cotillion, the country dances, and the reel."

"But you might do well to offer to deliver punch to some of the elderly ladies seated around the room during the quadrille," Horatia said with a sniff. "My toes still hurt."

"Again, Miss Englewood, I'm terribly sorry for treading on them," Lawrence said.

Horatia waved away his apology. Just as she'd waved it away the last six times he'd offered it.

"And remember, it might be easier if you situate yourself and your partner at the bottom of the line," Frederica suggested. "That way you can refresh your memory by watching the other dancers go through the steps until it's your turn."

"But don't stare at their feet directly," Horatia warned. "It's considered rude."

Frederica drew her lips together in a tight line as she mulled over this problem. "Perhaps if Mr. Sinclair turned his eyes to follow the footwork but didn't turn his head?"

"People might still follow the direction of his gaze."

"No one but you will notice, Horatia. We must be practical, Mr. Sinclair." Caroline called him Mr. Sinclair for the sake of her brothers and her friends. Sometime between the trifles after supper and the end of the country dance, she'd begun thinking of him as simply Lawrence. "You have learned a great deal in a short amount of time. If I were your partner at a ball, I'd rather the steps were fresh in your mind. Should you need to, I see no harm in glancing discreetly at the dancers who are before you and following their steps."

"An excellent suggestion, Caro," Frederica said with a little clap, even though the idea had actually been hers.

If Caroline remembered correctly, Freddie herself had often sneaked a peek at the other dancers' feet when the three of them were just learning.

"But what if someone should catch him ogling my ank—" Horatia stopped herself before *ankles* spilled from her lips. Mentioning such an intimate body part in mixed company simply wasn't done.

"I assure you, Miss Englewood, I shall not ogle any part of your person," Lawrence said, faint amusement in his tone.

"Very well." Horatia sniffed. "I believe you'll do then, Mr. Sinclair."

He gave her a short bow from the neck. "It's gratifying to hear you say so."

"Come, Horatia," Frederica said, stifling a yawn. "It's getting late."

"If you think this is late, you'd best be sure you're caught up on your sleep before Lord Frampton's ball, Freddie," Ben said as he secured his violin in its case. "It's like to run till three in the morning."

"If it does," Frederica said, dimpling prettily, "you're like to find me curled up in a corner somewhere, fast asleep."

"And wouldn't you make an appealing little dormouse at that?" Ben chuckled. Then he clicked the violin case shut and tucked it under his arm. "Perhaps I should ask for a dance from you earlier in the evening, then. I prefer my partners to be awake."

Freddie turned pink to the roots of her hair. Her mouth opened and closed several times without a sound, making her look distressingly like a codfish. Then, clearly ruffled, she turned and scurried down the stairs. Horatia was after her in a trice, her furious whisper echoing up the well and circling the cavernous ballroom without revealing a single intelligible word. Charles and Thomas headed in the same direction, but their normally pitched conversation was about the upcoming cricket season. Far be it from them to trouble about anything as inconsequential to the masculine mind as a ball.

"Freddie is very tenderhearted," Caroline told Ben. "You shouldn't tease her so."

"Who says I was teasing?" Ben said testily. "Thomas and Charles got to dance with her all night. Even Teddy took a turn. My only choice was to claim a dance at the Framptons', where I won't be expected to be the invisible musician."

Caroline gaped at her brother, astonished that he wanted to dance at all, and even more that he wanted to dance with Freddie. Ben used to torment her friend by showing her his collection of insects when they were children. He loved watching her run off squealing over his six-legged beasties. "I'm sorry, Ben. I had no idea you would have liked a chance to dance."

He'd never shown any inclination toward it before now.

"Well, I would have," he said sullenly.

"I'll remember that in the future. Perhaps the next time we arrange for Mr. Sinclair to practice, we won't have to be so secretive. Now that he can hold his own, it won't seem so strange to our parents that the lot of us might want to do a bit of dancing. But we'd still need music." She tapped her temple. "Ah, I know! We might push back the furniture in the music room and I could play the piano."

Ben rolled his eyes at her. "Trust me, Sister. No one wants that."

"Brute." She swatted his shoulder. His expression had been so sullen when he talked about their brothers dancing with Frederica. Perhaps he was serious about wanting to spend some time on the ballroom floor with her. "To my knowledge, you may ask Freddie for any dance but the supper dance at Lord Frampton's. That one's spoken for."

Ben frowned. "By whom?"

"Lord Rowley."

Lawrence joined him in a frown. But before Caroline could ask why they both seemed disposed to dislike the idea of Rowley dancing with Frederica, Ben said his good nights and disappeared down the stairs.

Lawrence's rumbling voice stopped her when she started to follow her brother. "A moment, my lady."

"There's no need for such formality now that we know each other better, Lawrence. You may call me Caroline," she corrected gently. He'd done so well with this dance lesson, she was feeling in perfect charity with him. It was only fitting to give him a small reward. "If you wish me to call you familiarly when it is just us, you must use my Christian name as well."

"Caroline." There was that sunrise of a smile again. Then it disappeared as quickly as it had come and he was all seriousness. "You ought not to allow your friend to consent to the supper dance with Rowley."

"Why not?"

"Because he…" He made an odd sound, sort of a cross between a grunt and a snort. "I shouldn't like to say."

"Then how shall I convince Freddie to refuse him?"

"I don't know, but I hope you will try."

He looked so earnest, it seemed as if he could convince her of anything with nothing more than those dark eyes of his. She forced herself to look away.

"I'll consider it," she said. "But you should bear in mind that I've known Lord Rowley since we were children. It would take a great deal to change my good opinion of him."

"A great deal has happened since you were children."

"Yet if you cannot tell me what it is that concerns you about Rowley, how shall I know how to advise my friend?"

He stepped closer, and Caroline caught a whiff of his distinctly masculine scent, a mix of leather and bergamot and some other exotic spice she couldn't identify.

He smells like an adventure.

She hadn't thought about having adventures for the last day or so. It was passing strange that this man should remind her of her dearly held goal. Only somehow, this adventure didn't seem to involve traveling. It was more about sinking into his dark eyes. Caroline swallowed hard.

What were we talking about? Oh, that's right. Freddie and Oliver.

If Lawrence had thought his mere proximity would lend weight to his argument, he was right. Being near him made it harder for Caroline to remember they were talking about Freddie. But Lawrence didn't seem to be aware of her befuddlement.

"Miss Tilbury thinks the sun rises and sets on you," he said. "She'd attempt to swim the Channel if you advised her to give it a try."

There was a faint scar at his temple she'd never noticed before. How might that have hap—

Concentrate on Freddie, you goose.

She took a step back from him and felt a bit surer of herself for it. "If Freddie will do whatever I say, I bear even more responsibility for making sure I offer the proper guidance. To do that, I need the particulars."

Lawrence sighed. "I wish you would simply trust me."

She was tempted. There was such a straightforward goodness about the man, it was easy to trust Lawrence Sinclair. Perhaps too easy.

"I should go." She turned to do just that.

"Hold a moment." He put a hand on her arm, right at the place where her puff sleeve ended and her skin was exposed. The heat from his hand sent little tingles up to her shoulder. "Stay, Caroline. Please."

"Why?"

"There's still one dance you haven't taught me."

She cocked her head at him. "I agree with Horatia that the quadrille is beyond your grasp at present, but you have a rudimentary knowledge of the cotillion, country dances, and the reel. You'll do quite well at Lord Frampton's ball, I'll warrant."

"Yet there is one dance you've left off the list."

"Oh, the minuet, you mean. Well, to be perfectly honest, even I have difficulty with the minuet sometimes. In all honesty, that dance belongs to the last generation," Caroline said. "If a minuet is called at all at Lord and Lady Frampton's, it will be performed by a single couple as a demonstration."

"No, that's not the dance I mean," Lawrence said, giving her arm a slight squeeze. "I mean the waltz."

If a man is determined to reach for the moon, he needs to stretch toward it with all his might.
A thing is only impossible if I believe it so.
—Mr. Lawrence Sinclair, who'd never believed he could reach much of anything before now.

Chapter 10

The tingles running up and down her arm turned from pleasurable to panicky. Didn't he know what he was asking? Caroline pulled away from him and took a step back. It didn't make her feel one whit safer. "I couldn't possibly teach you to waltz."

"You don't know it?"

"Of course I do." The dance may have had a scandalous reputation at first, but once Countess Lieven introduced it to Almack's, all of Polite Society embraced it with a passion.

"Then if you know how to waltz, why not teach me? I shall try not to tread on your toes."

That was the least of her concerns. "It wasn't your fault you stepped on Horatia's foot. In truth, she fell behind the beat. Her foot was simply in the wrong place."

"Then what's to hinder you and me from waltzing?"

If they waltzed, his hand would be upon her waist. She'd rest her palm on his shoulder. They'd be gazing into each other's eyes for the whole dance while they dipped and turned around the room. They'd be so close to each other, she'd be able to feel him draw breath.

But Caroline couldn't say that. If she did, she'd have to explain why it would be difficult for her to be so tangled up with him.

Not that she was afraid of Mr. Sinclair. Not exactly. She was more afraid of the way her pulse jumped when she was around him.

So instead of telling him she couldn't possibly waltz with him for fear he'd realize how unsettling it would be to have him so near, she looked pointedly at the stairs down which Ben had just disappeared. "We've no music."

"We can manage without. I've no talent for singing," he said with a self-deprecating grin, "but I've been known to hum on occasion."

"That wouldn't help." Dear heaven, but there was something about the man that made her want to give in. She felt...soft all of a sudden. Soft in resolve, soft in body, soft in the head. It was not at all like her. Her will was usually iron, and she propped herself up with it now. "I couldn't teach you here. Not at this time, Mr. Sinclair."

"Lawrence," he corrected.

"Lawrence," she repeated. His name felt so right on her lips, but that still didn't mean she should give in to this request. "You know as well as I that we ought not to be alone like this."

"I ask your pardon. I did not mean to make you uncomfortable."

"No, of course not," she said, relieved that he understood. "I didn't think you did."

"And I would never disrespect you."

Caroline was certain that wasn't in his nature. "I doubt you're capable of being disrespectful."

"Just improper."

"No, I didn't mean to suggest that—"

He gave her a devastating, slightly crooked smile. "Then you don't believe I'm capable of having improper thoughts about you?"

"No. Yes. I mean...how should I know what you're thinking?" Caroline said, suddenly understanding why Freddie had left the room in such a flustered rush. "Besides, even if you do have improper thoughts, you're too fine a gentleman to act upon them."

"If you truly believe that, you've nothing to fear in continuing our dance lesson."

"But that's not the point."

"Ah!" he said. "Now I understand. You don't wish for us to be alone because *you* have improper thoughts about *me*."

"What? No," she said with force. He was far too near the mark. "Heavens no. Of course not."

"Why not?"

No one would blame her if she did. Lawrence Sinclair was handsome, possessed of fine sensibilities, and had far more determination than she would have credited him with. Who knew what other surprises she might discover? Even at first blush, there was plenty to like about the man.

But *she* couldn't like him.

Caroline fell back on the cutting wit that had scared off so many other would-be suitors. "Clearly you're so enamored of yourself, any admiration I might hold for you would pale by comparison."

Lawrence chuckled. "Of all the things I've been accused of, thinking too highly of myself has never been listed. But before we return to my original request, let us stipulate that neither of us harbors improper thoughts about the other."

"Agreed." Surprisingly enough, the idea that he *wasn't* having such thoughts about her rankled Caroline even more. But she couldn't very well say so.

He spread his arms in a fair approximation of a waltz hold. "Then where's the harm?"

"If someone should come—"

"They'd catch us engaged in a dance lesson, nothing more."

"That would be more than enough for most tongue-waggers."

"Do you honestly think your brothers or your friends are going to spread gossip about us?"

"No." She wasn't worried about Freddie, but Horatia might let something slip without evil intent. Whatever was rattling around her brain always seemed to find its way out of her mouth. Caroline edged closer to the head of the stairs. "But Freddie and Horatia are surely wondering why I haven't come down already."

"I've found most people are so concerned with their own small doings, they haven't time to spare for anyone else's."

Caroline scoffed. "Have you met Horatia? She lives for other people's doings."

"But surely a waltz lesson wouldn't take that long."

Her mother's voice rarely sounded in her mind, but Caroline heard her now, clear as a clarion call.

A reputation takes years to build. Seconds to destroy.

"I must go."

"Then if you must." As if to belie his words, he caught her by the wrist. "But know that you are only leaving because you're afraid."

"Of you?" She pulled her hand free before he could feel she was indeed trembling. "I assure you, sir, I am not."

"Then if it truly is only your friends' censure you fear, say you'll meet me for a waltz later."

"Later?"

"Yes. When the longcase clock chimes three, your friends will be asleep and I will be here."

"Then you'll be here alone."

"Nevertheless," he said, his gaze never leaving hers. "I shall be here."

She felt herself being drawn in, like a hooked perch on a line. Caroline broke away and made for the stairwell. Flying down the steps, she didn't stop until she closed her chamber door behind her. Then she sagged against it, her heart still hammering. She'd come so close to staying there in the empty ballroom with Lawrence—

No, no, no. It's Mr. Sinclair!

She had to start thinking of him that way again. It was beyond foolish not to keep the distance of formality between them. It was a thin shield, but it was all she had.

However, she'd worried needlessly that Frederica and Horatia would be concerned that she hadn't immediately followed them down to her chamber. Her friends didn't seem to realize anything was amiss.

They must have thought one or other of my brothers were still in the ballroom with me and Lawrence.

Unconcerned, Frederica and Horatia were chatting and giggling away, cooperating with, but mostly ignoring, the long-suffering Alice, who had assisted them out of their gowns and into their night rails.

"I do declare, this was ever such a jolly evening, Caro. Almost like a little house party," Freddie said as she climbed into the big bed Caroline usually slept in by herself.

Whenever her friends stayed the night, she always gave up the big four-poster and took the small daybed tucked under her broad windowsill. Horatia was known to kick in her sleep and Freddie occasionally snored. Consequently, Caroline never felt giving up her bed was much of a sacrifice. She slept better alone.

As alone as Mr. Sinclair will be at three o'clock.

"Well, I wouldn't have believed it if I hadn't seen it," Horatia said, "but Mr. Sinclair acquitted himself…"

"Quite well?" Frederica supplied hopefully.

"More or less adequately," Horatia finished. "In any case, Caro, your Mr. Sinclair will survive the ball."

"He's not my Mr. Sinclair."

He's my Lawrence. No, no, no!

She put a hand to her temple, as if that might drive the unwanted name from her mind. "Thank you for your help. The two of you made some real dancing practice possible."

"We were glad to do it, weren't we, Horatia?"

"You'd have been even gladder if you could've danced with Benjamin, I'll warrant," Horatia said slyly as she slid into her side of the bed and pulled up the coverlet. "Freddie's a bit sweet on your family's fiddle player, Caro. Always has been."

"Oh, pish. Nothing of the sort," Freddie said, the hot flush on her face giving the lie to her words. "I simply admire Ben's...talent on the violin. That's all there is to it."

"Then why did you behave like an addlepated goose when he asked you about dancing at Lord Frampton's?" Horatia said, a huge yawn distorting her voice.

"I'm not a goose. Am I, Caro?"

"Of course not, dear," Caroline said reflexively. "You're just high strung."

"Well, if I am, it's only because Benjamin is...well, he just...oh, dash it all! I'm simply not used to having so many invitations, you see," Freddie said. "First Lord Rowley and now Caro's brother."

Frederica wasn't bragging. There wasn't a vain bone in her body. She was truly befuddled by the male attention that had come her way since her debut. When Horatia said nothing, Caroline assumed she must be fuming a bit that, of the two of them, Freddie had received the most masculine interest since they'd both come out.

But when the silence stretched into half a minute, Caroline realized Horatia's breathing had turned slow and measured. She was already asleep.

"Good night, Freddie," Caroline said.

Frederica waggled her fingers in good night to avoid disturbing their friend's slumber. Then she tucked the coverlet up to her chin to join Horatia in sleep.

Alice pulled back the coverlet on the daybed and plumped the pillows for Caroline. "Did you have a fine evening then, my lady?"

"Yes, we did." Caroline couldn't very well tell her maid that she'd barely escaped the fine evening with her reputation intact.

"Well, you would have had a fine evening, wouldn't you, because you were with that Mr. Sinclair—"

"And my brothers," Caroline said, then added for good measure, "and my friends."

"Oh, yes, and a grand party you must have made of it, too. That's nice, then. My Dudley—you'll remember him, my lady—he's been first footman for ever so long, only now he's valet to young Mr. Sinclair since he came to Lovell House. Remember Dudley, do you?"

"Yes, of course." Who could forget a footman clumsy enough to drop a serving spoon down a guest's gown? Caroline was certain her father would have let Dudley go a long time ago if the young man hadn't been Price's nephew. Even her father didn't want to tangle with the butler over questions about the staff. Price was Lord Chatham's right hand in matters domestic. Lovell House would surely run aground without Mr. Price at the helm.

But the butler would do well to keep his nephew on a very short leash.

"In any case," Alice went on, "Dudley says as he'd like to be promoted to valet full time."

"There's no reason for a permanent promotion; Mr. Sinclair is only here as a temporary guest of Lord Bredon." Then again, after the spoon debacle, keeping Dudley far from the table was something devoutly to be wished.

"Still, Dudley says as he's never served such a fine, kindhearted gentleman as Mr. Sinclair," Alice said with persistence.

"Dudley's never been valet to anyone before, so that's hardly a ringing endorsement," Caroline said.

"That's true. Only it's just that when you're in service, well, you get a sense about people. How they are in their hearts, mind. There's those you serve because it's your job, and you try not to care when they treat you like a piece of furniture. Then there's those you serve because they appreciate what you do for 'em and it makes you feel your work means something. I know it may not seem like much, but for the likes of us, it makes a difference."

"A difference between dignity and drudgery," Caroline said thoughtfully. Lawrence, who noticed frost sparkling on the grass and his horse's breath ghosting the air, would be the sort to notice Dudley's efforts, even if they were less than skillful. "I hope I've never treated you like furniture."

"Oh, no. You're always kind, my lady. Not at all like some I could name." Alice rolled her eyes toward Horatia's sleeping form. Caroline smiled at that. Alice was always adept at speaking her mind, even when she didn't come right out and say it with words.

When her maid started to help her disrobe, Caroline waved her away. "I've already kept you up too late. When did you start work this morning?" Alice shrugged. "My days all start with the sun, my lady."

"Go on to bed then, Alice. Dancing keys me up. I believe I shall sit awhile." "But, my lady—"

"This gown is easy enough to remove. Just a tab or two to untie. Go. You've more than earned a rest."

The maid mumbled her thanks, curtsied, and left. Caroline turned down the lamp and settled into the small rocker by the fire. She hoped the hypnotic flames would soothe her, but something Mr. Sinclair had said kept tumbling around in her mind. Frederica wasn't snoring yet. Even at the risk of waking her friend, there was something Caroline needed to say.

"Freddie?"

"Hmmm?" From the drowsy tone, it was clear Frederica had been almost asleep.

"I wonder if it would be better *not* to accept Lord Rowley's request for the supper dance."

"Why?"

She couldn't very well tell her that Mr. Sinclair had urged her to convince Freddie to turn Rowley down. She'd only ask why again, and Caroline had no reason to give her.

Only the honest concern in Lawrence's eyes.

"By giving him the supper dance, you're granting him most of your evening," Caroline said. "What if you should meet someone at the ball you fancy spending time with more than Lord Rowley?"

"I doubt I'll do that."

Caroline hadn't expected meeting Lawrence would unsettle her plans either, but whether she wanted to admit it or not, it had. "What about Ben?"

"Before you came down, Horatia said Benjamin was just teasing me. She's probably right. She often is," Freddie said, as if trying to convince herself. "Ben has always teased me."

"That was when you were just a little girl. You're a young woman now," Caroline said. "Ben's a bit slow about noticing things, always caught up in his music or one of his other passions, but even he is aware of how you've blossomed."

"Well, perhaps," Frederica whispered.

"I wouldn't be surprised if my brother sent you some posies."

"I would. I fear he's just as likely to come at me with that foul insect collection of his again. Do you remember when he tossed a small black thing at my head and yelled 'Cricket'?"

"I'm sure Ben regrets that now."

"He should. I tore out a good deal of my hair before you calmed me down enough to show me it was only a bit of yarn." Frederica sounded more indignant than Caroline had ever heard her, but she suspected Horatia was right about one thing: Freddie wouldn't protest this much unless she was a little bit sweet on Ben.

"The cricket incident happened a long time ago. It's your Christian duty to forgive him," Caroline reminded her. "I know. Why don't you give Ben the supper dance at Lord Frampton's? It would be a lovely way to show that you aren't holding a grudge."

"I can't do that, Caro. I've already accepted Lord Rowley's request. I can't very well tell him no now, can I?"

"When did you accept him?"

"He sent around a lovely note the day after we spent that time together at the Academy of Arts. He repeated his request for the supper dance and told his man to wait for my reply. So I wrote him back on the moment," Frederica said. "Was that wrong?"

"No, I suppose not," Caroline said, wishing Mr. Sinclair hadn't put such doubts in her head. She knew Oliver much better than she knew Mr. Sinclair. Oliver's family and hers had been friends for generations; their country estates butted up against each other. It had only been a few weeks since Lawrence Sinclair first stepped into the Lovell House parlor. By those lights, she didn't know him at all.

Discover his tragedy, her dressmaker's apprentice had advised. *Then you'll know the man.*

Caroline crossed her arms over her chest. Maybe she didn't want to know him.

What little she did know cut up her peace quite enough, thank you very much. Mr. Sinclair made her stop thinking about the independent life she was sure she wanted. For days at a time, she'd forgotten about packing a trunk and sailing away and having adventures. She'd stopped pining for the foreign and unusual and found herself swamped in the everyday.

She couldn't allow that.

Besides, Rowley had only asked Frederica for a dance, only the pleasure of her company at the supper to follow. Where was the harm? Mr. Sinclair would simply have to get over it.

Just as he'll have to get over finding himself alone at three o'clock.

Making decisions is like a beach. I'm no fan of Brighton, but my choices of late aren't even as solid as the pebbles there.
—Lawrence Sinclair, who wished he were at a beach of any sort instead of trapped in the same house as Lady Caroline Lovell

Chapter 11

The longcase clock chimed a quarter past. When the last tone faded, all Lawrence could hear was the wind in the eaves and a few small creaks as the town house squatted a little deeper on its foundations for the night.

Then Lovell House went as silent as a churchyard.

She's not coming.

He sighed. There was no reason she should. He'd far overstepped himself. He really ought to take his leave in the morning and seek lodgings elsewhere. It had been beyond generous for Bredon to host him as long as he had. No matter what Bredon thought he owed him, the last thing Lawrence wanted was to wear out his welcome.

Besides, even while in residence at Lovell House, he'd not been allowed much time with Caroline. Passing her in the hallway or seeing her at the far end of the long dining table was becoming increasingly painful. The more time he spent with Bredon's family, the more aware he was of his own shortcomings. He had no polish, no great wit. He may have been wellborn, but his prospects were murky at best. Especially since he'd heard his uncle was still hale and hearty and in London seeking a young wife. He could so easily be displaced by an infant; he couldn't count on an heritance of any kind. He had nothing to offer a woman like Lady Caroline.

Lawrence felt a bit like Moses on the wrong side of the Jordan. He could see the Promised Land, but he could not cross over.

He still hoped she'd come.

After another quarter hour, he took his candle in hand and rose to trudge back down to his chamber. But as he neared the stairwell, light from another candle sent a shaft of brightness up to the ballroom. There came a soft tread on the steps and, against all expectation, Caroline appeared.

"You came," he said, his voice a scant whisper. His chest constricted strangely.

"Yes, well..." She seemed to have trouble meeting his gaze. "I expected you would have given up by now and gone on to bed."

"So you only came because you didn't think I'd be here?"

"No, I only thought you might be...I mean, I hoped you hadn't..." She set down her candle on a side table and moved into the center of the room. Lawrence followed suit. "That is to say, I was sure you would still be here, if you were serious."

"I'm nothing if not serious."

"About learning to waltz, I mean," she added hastily.

"Of course." She seemed a bit flustered. He didn't wish to cause her discomfort. Not for worlds. But the fact that his presence shook her usual poise did his heart good for some odd reason. "What else might I be serious about besides waltzing at present?"

"Indeed, Lord Frampton's upcoming ball is the only reason we're both here." She crossed her arms over her chest, as if daring him to dispute the matter. But from her tone, Lawrence guessed she was trying to convince herself and wasn't having much success. "If you asked me to join you because you were serious about anything else, meeting like this would be..."

"Improper?" he supplied. Helpfully, he thought.

"Quite." She nodded with vigor. "Above all else, we must not be improper."

"No, we won't be," he promised as he moved closer to her. She dropped her arms, but now her hands fiddled nervously with the diaphanous sides of her gown. "Being improper would be exceedingly bad form."

"We wouldn't want that." She stopped fiddling and finally met his gaze.

"No." He stepped closer, near enough that he heard a little hitch in her breathing. "We certainly..." *Closer.* "Wouldn't..." She tipped up her chin and her lips parted. "Want..." Her sweet breath feathered across his lips.

Her mouth was so near he could almost taste it. If he bent only a little, he'd close the distance between them. In all his life, he'd never seen anything as fine as Caroline Lovell. Just being near her made him feel stronger. And weaker. He didn't pretend to understand the paradox. He only knew it was so.

If he kissed her, everything would change. They could never go back to a time when they hadn't shared a single breath. He'd have a part of her always. If he could kiss Lady Caroline Lovell just once, his time on earth would not have been wasted.

Was it his imagination or did she raise herself up on tiptoe just a bit? Then, in the exact instant when he'd screwed his courage to take her mouth, she turned away and broke the spell.

"If we're going to do this, we must be quick about it," Caroline said, suddenly all business. "First, we must make a good frame."

Lawrence felt as if he'd been kicked in the gut.

By a draft horse.

He and Lady Caroline had teetered on the edge of something together, but she seemed determined to pretend that moment hadn't happened.

Perhaps for her it hadn't.

He drew a deep breath and spread his arms. "Once again, I am yours to command. I believe that's what you said all women want to hear, is it not?"

"Somehow I doubt you'd take my commands well."

He wanted to say, *Ask me to climb to the top of St. Paul's. Bid me swim the Thames all the way to the sea. Shall I run from here to Snowdon and back for you, my lady? Just say the word.*

Instead, he said, "I shall obey your wishes." Then he assumed the first dance position she'd taught him earlier that evening.

He wished he had the courage to give voice to his feelings. No one who'd served with Lawrence would ever name him cravenhearted. He was always first in, last out of any action. But when it came to Caroline Lovell, he bore a white feather.

If he could find the words to express what he felt and release them to her hearing, it would amount to a declaration. A declaration she was certain to stomp on.

Then it would be over.

Hope wasn't much, but it was all he had. As long as he kept everything bottled up, he could still hope.

"What do you wish me to do?" he asked.

Her brows tented in distress. "What if I ask you to leave Lovell House and never return?"

He had been gut-kicked again, and this time the kicking horse had brought along a friend. "Have I offended you?"

"No," she said with a sigh. "But you've put me at risk of public censure if we are found alone together. You made me toss out everything I've been taught. You cut up my peace so dreadfully that I couldn't sleep. You should never have demanded I meet you like this."

"It was hardly a demand." Besides, she'd made the decision to come. He'd only asked. She could have ignored his request.

"It was a dare, at the least." Even in the low light of the candles, her eyes flashed.

"And you can't resist a dare."

"Oh, but you knew that and used my very nature against me," she accused. "How could I rest, knowing you would think me a coward if I stayed away?"

"I'd never think you a coward. In fact, I doubt you fear anything."

"I'm not afraid of you, at least," she said with a firm nod. Then her certainty seemed to crumble. "Besides, even if I was, didn't you tell me that fear has nothing to do with cowardice?"

"I did." They may not have had many conversations, but she seemed to remember a good deal of what he'd said. "I could never work against you, and I am sorry to have disturbed your peace. My intentions toward you are only good."

Well, most of them.

"There is a place, they say, which is paved with good intentions," she said, pacing like a caged lynx, "but I've a feeling neither of us wish to summer there."

Actually, Lawrence already felt as if he had one foot in hell. He couldn't bear to be without this woman. And she couldn't seem to bear to be with him.

"My apologies. Because you wish it, I shall quit Lovell House immediately." He crossed the hardwood to retrieve his candle.

"No, wait."

He turned back to her.

"I…I didn't ask you to leave," she said, even more perturbed now. "I only said *what if* I asked you to."

He shook his head. "When you told me you were changeable as a weathercock, you certainly didn't lie. I'm out of my depth, Caroline. Which is it to be? Do I stay or go?"

"I want you to…" Her voice dropped to a whisper. "Don't go."

"Why?"

Bredon had warned him that women change their minds as often as their frocks, but Lawrence had thought he was exaggerating. He'd never doubt his friend again.

"Because I…because we haven't…" She lifted her hands and shrugged, as if she, too, were perplexed by her own behavior. "Because you don't know how to waltz yet."

"So far, my teacher seems less than willing."

"One lesson, then, as long as we're both awake and here and..." Again, she shrugged and sighed. "This is just so you can make a decent showing at Lord Frampton's, mind."

"Of course, my lady." He wouldn't dream of calling her Caroline now. She might take offense at that little intimacy, even though she'd allowed it before. "I thank you."

"And so should the toes of your future partners," she said, smiling for the first time since she'd joined him in the dim ballroom.

He grinned back at her. She might be the most vexing woman in the world, but he wouldn't change places with another soul on earth. It was enough simply to be in the same room with her. "How shall we begin?"

"Raise your left arm like so."

He mirrored her movement and slowly, she slipped her right hand into his left one. It was small and icy. He wished he could hold it close to his heart to warm it, but after narrowly escaping eviction, he decided his best course of action was to take no action that wasn't expressly dictated.

"Our joined hands complete one side of the frame. Now I rest my left hand on your shoulder," she said, as if captioning her motions somehow took the intimacy away from them.

"Where would you like my right hand?"

* * * *

Where indeed? Just holding his left hand made her insides quiver like a bowl of aspic. She'd waltzed with any number of men before, but never had just standing close to one made her breath hitch so. "Rest your hand gently at my waist."

Her column gown didn't have a clearly defined waist, so he made a guess. Unhurriedly, as if she were a mare who might spook at a sudden movement, he put his hand at the narrowest point of her body below her ribs.

"You're slenderer than I realized," he said softly.

"That is *not* an appropriate thing to say to your dance partner." Her cheeks heated. "But as long as we're saying inappropriate things, your hands are bigger than I thought as well."

Fashion dictated that a man's hands and feet be small and sensitive. A rough callus rested at the base of each of Lawrence's thick fingers. With hands like these, Lawrence might well pass for a dock worker in fancy dress.

"Is that a problem?" he asked.

"Not at all." Surprisingly, she rather liked the roughness. He'd worked with those hands. Fought with them. Lawrence was strength under tight control. "Once we begin, you will use your hands as points of contact to direct where we go, leading with your left hand and with a slight pressure from the right."

He squeezed her waist a bit.

"Yes, that will do to communicate your lead."

He pulled her closer until there wasn't a finger's width between them. "Like that?"

"Not exactly." She took a half step back. "We must keep some distance between us. Otherwise, our feet may become hopelessly entangled and we'll land on the floor together."

"And that would be bad, I take it."

"Very bad."

"Actually," he said with a grin, "I can think of far worse fates than having you tumble on top of me."

"Mr. Sinclair!" She pulled out of his embrace.

"Lawrence," he corrected evenly. "And I shall call you Caroline, because either we are friends or we're not. I grow weary of this back and forth. Friends should be able to say what's on their minds without fear of causing offense."

"Ordinarily I'd agree." She had been terrible to him actually, telling him to go one moment and ordering him to stay the next, but the man irritated her so. She'd never been so unsettled. "Friends *should* be able to share their thoughts, but what if what's on your mind is...well, if it's not really acceptable..."

"Then friends should be able to talk about that, too. But may I point out that *you* were the one who first raised the idea of our being tangled up on the floor together?"

"Oh, pish!" He was right. She had said something like that, without meaning anything untoward by it of course. And maybe he was right about the other thing, too. Friends should be able to talk about anything.

But the problem was, she didn't feel particularly friendly toward him. She wasn't sure how to name it, but she was certain this tingly, shivery sensation rolling around inside her had nothing to do with friendship.

He raised his arms in the approximation of a waltz hold. "Shall we continue the lesson?"

It was either that or she'd have to explain why she was being so touchy. She couldn't tell him he made a mess of her insides, so she stepped into his arms and began instructing him in the standard box step.

"Eyes up," she ordered. "Look at me, not your feet."

"With pleasure."

There was that smile of his again. She'd do anything for him if only he kept smiling at her. Caroline was grateful for the dimness of the candlelight. Based on the way her cheeks heated, she was blushing like a schoolgirl in the throes of her first crush.

She remembered what that was like. When she was a young girl, long before she'd decided to forsake convention and claim a life of adventure for herself, she'd had a bit of a crush on Rowley. She'd mooned over him during cricket matches. She frequently consented to play the part of damsel in distress so Rowley and her brothers could rescue her from an invisible dragon who'd trapped her in the haymow. Even then, she wasn't wild about the idea of needing rescue, but it allowed her to play with Rowley. Her diary from those days had several pages worth of *Lady Rowley, Lady Rowley, Lady Rowley* scribbled across them. Or, if she were feeling particularly syrupy about Oliver on a given day, *Caroline Rowley* might border her diary's pages, swimming in a sea of hearts and flowers.

But that kind of calf-love wasn't at all what she was feeling now. Along with frustration and jumbled-up confusion, a lump of something like tenderness glowed inside her.

For Lawrence Sinclair, of all people.

She didn't understand it, but that didn't make it less true. And it was a thing to be shunned with all her might or her plans for an adventurous life might well be upended for good.

"We've been stuck in this pattern for some time now," Lawrence said. "Is this all there is to a waltz?"

"No, of course not. This is just the basic step, which you seem to have more or less acquired."

"More or less, eh? Careful. Such praise will ruin me."

She swatted his shoulder. "You're doing well enough. Take the compliment. Now, you may take me around the room by pivoting a bit on the balls of your feet with each step. Ah! Just so."

Lawrence started humming the Sussex waltz as they circled the room.

"How do you know that tune if you've never attended a ball?"

"When I was in the military, I often volunteered for guard duty outside the dancing hall."

"As a way to avoid dancing itself," she surmised.

"Correct. In any case, I could not avoid hearing the music. This tune stuck in my mind."

It was just enough of a melody in three-quarter time to keep them together. Caroline showed him how to lead her in underarm turns and in the promenade hold that had them traveling around the room side by side. Lawrence even managed to remember the up-up-down dipping motion that helped them move in perfect harmony.

Her dance lesson was a success, but her real reason for venturing up to the dark ballroom alone had wilted along the side of the room like a sad wallflower. She was no closer to learning Lawrence's tragedy, and thereby knowing him better, than she had been when she arrived. He was dancing well enough now that a little conversation ought not to disrupt his steps.

"Did you lose many friends in the service?" she ventured, assuming that would be a natural point of tragedy.

"Yes."

Taciturn as always. Well, what else were you expecting? "And it affected you deeply?"

"How could it not?"

It was like trying to wring blood from a turnip. "Do you wish to talk about it?"

"Not particularly. It doesn't make pretty hearing." He began to hum a little louder.

"Because I'm a woman, you think I can't hear about such things?"

"No, because you're a human being with a sense of decency. Whatever else war is, it is rarely decent. What I did during my time in the military was for my king and country, and more particularly for the soldier fighting by my side. I've made my peace with it and have no need to dredge it up again." He led her through a couple of underarm turns in fairly quick succession, leaving her more than a little dizzy.

"Is it usual to pose such personal questions to your dance partner during a waltz?" he asked.

"No," she admitted. "In truth, it's not usual to ask such personal questions any time, but I wanted to understand you better."

"There's not much to understand. I'm a simple man, Caroline."

"I doubt that." Even though they continued to dip around the room, the ballroom faded a bit from her peripheral vision. All she could see was the man before her. "I've rarely met anyone as difficult to know as you."

"And you want to know me?"

"I do." Then, because that smacked far too much of a declaration of affection, she hastily added, "As...as a friend, of course."

"Then ask something else and I shall try to answer."

Because his military service didn't seem to qualify as a tragedy, Caroline was forced to look elsewhere. That left only his family.

"Why have you not gone home since you returned from the Continent?"

"Honestly?"

"There's no point to the question otherwise."

"Because *you* are in London," he said, not caring that he seemed to be making a declaration. "Since I first met you, I can't bear the thought of being where you are not."

The lump of tenderness inside her glowed even more warmly, but she tamped it down. "That's too bold for a friend."

His dark eyes said they were much more. Their waltz slowed to a stop, but they kept hold of each other, her fingers laced with his and his hand still heavy on her waist. "Perhaps you were mistaken when you called us friends."

"Perhaps I was." Silence stretched between them, and she feared if she didn't fill it soon, something dreadfully serious—she didn't know what exactly—was about to happen. Something she wouldn't be able to take back. "To be honest, I'm not sure what I feel about you. You are quite insufferable sometimes."

"So I've been told." He smiled as he said it, and the smile seemed to take the awful seriousness away.

"I only want to know you better, Lawrence." She'd asked Mr. Price if Lawrence had posted any letters bound for Ware, but the butler said Mr. Sinclair had failed to write any. It seemed beyond strange that he hadn't sent word to let his family know he was safely on English soil once again. "So in order to know you, I want to understand why you have not gone to Ware. Not even for a short visit."

He frowned, an implacable, grim expression. Caroline decided she wouldn't have wanted to be the French soldier who met him on a field of battle. "I didn't return to Ware because I wouldn't be welcome. Is that what you wanted to hear?"

She shook her head. Families weren't like that. No matter what, she knew with certainty that her parents loved her. Even when she disappointed them by refusing to accept one of the many proposals that came her way, she never doubted they cared about her.

"You must be wrong to be unsure of your reception at Ware Hall."

"Oh, I am sure," he said. "And I'm not wrong."

"Would you…I mean, sometimes it helps me to talk about difficult things. Perhaps if you tell me why your fam—"

"I'm sorry to have kept you from your rest, my lady." He released her hand and stepped back. "I thank you for teaching me to waltz. It would be inappropriate for me to see you to your chamber, so I shall wait here until you've had enough time to reach it on your own. Good night."

It was a blatant dismissal.

She'd been on the other end of such a rejection countless times. Sometimes, behavior bordering on boorishness had been the only way to rid herself of an unwanted suitor. But no man had ever dared to send her away like this.

None but Lawrence Sinclair.

"Yes, well, try not to tread on anyone's toes at Lord Frampton's ball," she said waspishly. "I shall make certain you have no opportunity to tread on mine."

Trying to put distance between you and your troubles never works. Wherever you go, you carry them with you. As soon as you pack your valise, thinking to leave them, your failures sneak into your pocket and come along for the journey. They sink in their talons and travel in your memories. They steal into your idle daydreams when you least expect them. Their ugly heads rise up in night terrors. And unfortunately, you can't misplace them or drop them off somewhere, as if they were an unwanted parcel.
They come home with you as well.
—Mr. Lawrence Sinclair, who wished he packed troubles as scantily as his personal effects.

Chapter 12

Lawrence and his mount flew across the freshly cut meadow. Crooning a few curses his uncle would have whipped him for, he leaned over the horse's neck. The forbidden words seemed to make the gelding stretch out and go even faster. Lawrence raised himself slightly in the stirrups, his knees bearing the jolting rhythm so that his body moved in perfect harmony with the galloping horse.

Ralph bumped along behind him on the crupper, clinging to Lawrence's waist, tight as a tick. The younger boy screamed at the top of his lungs.

His cousin wasn't afraid. Ralph always howled like that when he was excited. He said it was his Pictish battle cry. When Lawrence had asked what a Pict was, Ralph had explained that they were early Britons who defended the fair isle of Albion against Roman invaders. When Picts went to war, they dipped themselves in woad and screamed out their defiance.

Lawrence understood the battle cry part. Roaring as loudly as they could would give the Picts courage and scare the Romans silly. For the life of him, he had no idea why the Picts thought painting themselves blue would help, but Ralph was the history scholar. Lawrence believed him. If Ralph said they colored themselves with blue dye, it was so.

"Faster! Faster!" Ralph yelled. He wasn't a good enough horseman to handle this kind of speed on his own. But that didn't stop him from begging to fly across the field with Lawrence whenever the pair of them escaped the watchful eye of Ralph's father, the earl. "Now the jump. Do the jump!"

His uncle would kill him if he caught Lawrence at it.

But Ralph loved the thrill of flying over an obstacle. The harder the jump, the more he squealed for joy.

"Oh, fiend take it!" Lawrence cried and tossed caution to the wind. Riding neck or nothing, he headed for the nearest waist-high stone wall. The gelding's powerful haunches bunched under them and suddenly they were airborne. Ralph screamed again, a Pictish war cry if ever there was one.

The jolt of their hard landing knocked Lawrence awake. He must have been holding his breath in his sleep because he sucked in a noisy lungful. His heart hammered in his ears. He swallowed hard and sat up.

For a moment, he wasn't sure where he was. The dream had seemed so real, he half-expected the grassy smell of a freshly cut field and horse sweat to hang in the air. But he hadn't wakened in Ware Hall, eleven years old and shivering in his cold chamber. He was in as opulent a bedroom as he could imagine.

Then it all rushed back into him, the years of his life galloping by— the accident, the pack of wolves at the boarding school, serving with the dragoons, roaming the Continent alongside Bredon and Rowley, and, finally, running headlong into the original immovable object, Lady Caroline Lovell.

Beguiling, confusing, unattainable Caroline.

And with that sobering thought, he remembered what he needed to do that day. Judging by the light streaming in through his windows, breakfast was long past. He rose and dressed without ringing for Dudley to come help him. If he was going to live by his own means, the first thing he'd have to do without was a servant of any sort.

With regret, Lawrence didn't slip out the back of Lovell House and saddle one of Bredon's horses, even though his friend had told him often enough that any of the mounts in Lord Chatham's stable were at his disposal. A horse was another luxury he couldn't afford. Keeping one in London—never mind a carriage or a racy curricle—was a rich man's convenience. Lawrence was no pauper. He had enough to live comfortably, but he'd definitely have to cut back on some of the niceties he'd enjoyed in Lord Bredon's company.

It pained him to leave Lovell House, but he must. Caroline had decided to get to *know* him, of all things, and he couldn't have that. She was sure not to like what she saw. Leaving with her good opinion of him still intact was the best he could hope for.

So he set out across the city on shank's mare. In Leicester Square, he found a flat on the first floor of a respectable-looking house, located on a quiet street. The sameness of the house's surroundings ensured that he wouldn't waste much time looking out the small windows. There was a bakery on the corner, and a pub within easy walking distance where he could take his evening meals.

Best of all, his landlady had asked a modest sum that was well within his budget for the furnished flat. The three rooms were too humble for entertaining, but they were clean. Mrs. Abernathy even offered to come in weekly to tidy up and change the bed linens.

Lawrence decided it would suit him.

Of course there was no chance of seeing Caroline in this neighborhood, but he told himself that was a blessing. When he'd goaded her into meeting him in the ballroom last night, he had thought no farther than the joy of being alone with her. Of holding her in his arms. Maybe kissing her. But he'd pushed her too far.

Caroline had pushed back.

Why do women always think things are made better by talking about them?

He might have come round to sharing some of his war stories with her, but only if he sanitized the tales a great deal. He'd never tell her about how he came to be estranged from his family. He'd never told anyone.

He hadn't had a bite all day and the nearby church tolled three, so he decided to walk down to the bakery for a bun or two to tide him over until supper. But as he neared the corner, he noticed the carriage with the Chatham coat of arms emblazoned on the side. Old Sedgewick, the driver, nodded on his bench as usual, having slipped into the light sleep of age.

"What's this?" Lawrence asked him. "Where are your passengers?"

Sedgewick roused himself from his catnap with a shake and cleared his throat noisily. "My lady and her maid popped into that bakery yonder." He motioned toward the shop at the end of the block.

"The countess?" Lawrence doubted Lady Chatham had ever shopped for baked goods in her life.

"No, o' course not. Her Ladyship is at home receiving calls this time of day. It's the young lady of the house I'm meaning. Lady Caroline."

"Are there no bakeries near St. James Square? What's Lady Caroline doing in that one?"

"Buying scones and biscuits, near as I can guess." Sedgewick shrugged and scratched his balding head. "If you want my opinion, young sir, never try to figure out why a woman does anything. May as well ask the wind why it blows."

"That has the ring of truth and the sting of experience, my friend," Lawrence said, giving the draft horse a pat on the neck. "I shall take it under advisement."

Just then, the door to the bakery flew open. A lad with a disreputable-looking cap pulled down so the brim hid his face scrambled out of the shop, turned up the street, and disappeared down a narrow alley as if his knickers were ablaze.

"Help! Oh, help!" Alice appeared in the doorway of the shop. "Help, someone! Murder!"

Murder? Lawrence bolted across the street. "What's happened? Is Caroline all right?"

Alice lifted a brow at him. "*Lady* Caroline is fine," she said, correcting him with a withering tone for failing to use her mistress's title.

"But you cried murder."

"Well, maybe it wasn't murder, but that horrid boy stole my lady's reticule right enough. And half a dozen scones to boot."

"You're sure she's all right?"

"Yes, yes. She just took a fright," Alice said, shifting her weight from one foot to the other in nervousness. "Hurry! He's getting away."

"Wait here." Lawrence raced down the alley and spied the lad as he turned onto a cross street. Lawrence put on some speed and closed the distance, managing to keep the boy in sight as he dodged through a tangled rabbit warren of alleys and lanes. The youngster might have lost him in a sprint, but a half-starved urchin was no match for a well-fed man in his prime on a long run. Lawrence caught up to the lad, grabbed him by the collar, and swung him around, lifting his feet off the ground.

"What's this?" Lawrence demanded, an intense burst of energy still flooding his veins. But he decided to temper his tone when he saw the boy was even younger than he'd first thought. "Thievery in broad daylight." He made a tsking sound and lowered his captive until his feet touched the ground, but he didn't release his hold on the boy's collar. "A respectable footpad waits for night to cover his ill deeds."

"A bloke gets hungry in the daytime same as the night, don't he?"

"I expect you've the right of it there. Give me back the lady's purse. You can keep the scones."

The boy fished the small beaded reticule from his pocket. The laces had been cleanly slashed.

"Let me go, will ya?" The boy struggled, trying to free himself from Lawrence's grip to no avail. "Don't nobody despise a thief if he steals when he's hungry. Says so in the Bible."

"And what would you know about the Bible?"

"I sneaks into church sometimes. 'Specially if it's rainin'."

"And while you're there, no doubt you help yourself to the poor box when no one's looking."

The boy spread his arms wide. "Who's poorer than me, I asks ye?"

"I'll give you that, but you should go to the vicar if you're in need of alms."

The lad squirmed, trying to break free again with no success. "A thief I may be, but I ain't no beggar. I do for me and mine."

Against his better judgment, Lawrence felt a grudging admiration for the lad's twisted set of ethics. Not begging showed he still had a bit of dignity under that sorry excuse for a hat.

"You and yours, you say. Who is it you steal for?" Lawrence had heard there were gangs of street children run by thuggish types who took most of the boys' ill-gotten gains. Then they coerced the youngsters into stealing more in exchange for a roof over their heads and a few beans from a communal pot. If this boy was in thrall to a boss of some sort, Lawrence wouldn't rest until he gave the man responsible a good thrashing and hauled him before a magistrate. "Does someone force you to steal?"

"Don't nobody tell me what to do." The boy's lips settled in a tight line. "It's just…well, I got sort of a sister what I take care of by giving her a bit of coin when I can."

The boy's clothes were thin, but they were fairly clean for someone who lived on the street, and Lawrence noticed more than one neat patch in the boy's shirt. He ran a finger over the fine stitching on the boy's forearm.

"I suspect this 'sort of sister' takes care of you."

The boy sighed. "All right, then. She sees to a few of us what ain't got nobody else. You know, a loaf here and there. A bit of sewin' and scrubbin' when we needs it. She even gives me tuppence when she has it to spare. Lord knows, she's got little enough herself." The boy frowned. "I don't got no way to pay her back for all she does for us. But that don't mean I can't try to do somethin' nice for her once in a while, do it?"

"You stole so you could do something nice for someone. That's the most original moral code I've heard in a long time," Lawrence said. "Do you think this sister of yours would approve of your methods?"

He kicked at the cobbles. "No. Me methods don't work so well, do they? You got the purse and I got a handful of fingers."

Lawrence shook his head. "What I mean is someone who cares enough to mend your clothes might take offense at thievery done in her honor."

The boy pulled a face. "Well, when you put it like that, I s'pose she might take it wrong."

"Who is this sort of sister of yours?" Lawrence had in mind giving the lady a few quid to help with her street lads.

"Oh, no. You'll peach on me to her."

The boy hadn't begged Lawrence not to turn him over to the magistrate, but he definitely didn't want this sister to know he'd been lifting a lady's purse. That bit of shame saved him. Lawrence decided to help the lad.

"I won't tell your benefactress what you've been doing," he promised.

"My bene-what?"

"Your sort of sister. I will not tell her about this unfortunate incident," Lawrence said. "Now, you and I have a few more things to discuss. If I turn you loose, will you promise not to run again?"

The boy squinted at him. "Even if I did promise, who'd believe the likes of me?"

"I would," Lawrence assured him. "You'd be giving me your word, you see. And a man's word is sacred."

The boy stood straighter. "You have me word."

"Then I accept your parole," Lawrence said with the formal courtesy a military officer would give to a defeated foe. "And I'll also have the knife you used in your crime."

"Aw, gov'nor, not me knife," he whined. "I needs that."

"In order to steal more efficiently, I warrant."

"No, truly, kind sir. I needs it for protection," the boy insisted. "You don't know how rough it can be on the likes of me without I have a stinger in me pocket."

"Then will you give me your word you won't use the knife to slash the laces on another lady's purse?"

The boy nodded. "I swears."

"On the name of your sister."

"On me sister, Mary Woodyard, I—" The boy clapped a hand over his mouth when he realized Lawrence had tricked him into revealing her name.

"Ah, yes! Mary Woodyard. I believe I have met the young woman. She is apprenticed to Madame Fournier, is she not?"

Lawrence remembered the beleaguered dressmaker's apprentice from that unfortunate time when he'd come to collect Caroline and her friends at the shop. Madame Fournier's bugged-out eyes and tight lips had betrayed her quiet fury with her paying customers. Lawrence suspected her poor apprentice had suffered in their stead once the Quality Folk left the shop.

"Yes, Mary works in a dress shop, but don't you go peachin' on me, sir." The boy wrung his cap in his hands, as contrite as a puppy that had just piddled on the rug. "You promised you wouldn't."

"And I am a man of my word, too." Lawrence extended his hand. "Mr. Lawrence Sinclair. And you are?"

"Billy Two Toes." The boy shook his hand gravely.

"That's not your proper name."

"It's all the name I got."

"All right. Why Two Toes?"

"On account of I froze a couple off last winter, sir. That's when me mates started callin' me that."

Some mates. It made Lawrence even more determined to help the boy. "If you're willing to leave your life of crime, Mr. Two Toes, I should like to hire you."

The boy blinked in disbelief. "To do what?"

What indeed? Lawrence had already convinced himself he couldn't afford a servant. So far, young Billy had only shown an aptitude for petty crime. And a fondness for scones.

"Come to Rathbone Street off Oxford, second house on the left, around teatime."

The boy removed his cap and scratched a headful of carrot-colored hair. "When's that?"

"When the church bells ring five. I'm lodged at the home of Mrs. Abernathy. Ask to be shown to the first-floor apartment and I shall have a task for you by then." He planned to also have a plate or two of biscuits for the boy. Lawrence had no idea what sort of job he might offer Billy, but surely he'd think of something to occupy the boy besides lifting wallets. If he continued his career as a cutpurse, Billy was well on his way to Newgate. "Off you go now. And no more thievery. That is an unconditional requirement of your employment with me."

The boy sketched a deep, elaborate bow. "Right-o, your worshipfulness."

"Mr. Sinclair will do."

Billy gave him a gap-toothed grin. Lawrence hoped he was young enough to be missing his baby teeth but suspected they might have been knocked out. Life for a street urchin could be rough indeed.

Lawrence sprinted back toward the bakery, where he saw Caroline waiting at the door to the shop. By her side, a distraught Alice was still swaying and fidgeting with her hands.

Foot traffic in the neighborhood had picked up. Surrounded by folk of the middling sort going about their daily business, Lady Caroline was a goldfinch amid a flock of wrens. The Leicester Square neighborhood was perfectly respectable, but it might as well have been on a foreign continent compared to the rarified air of St. James. That was where she belonged, amid luxury and splendor.

And safety.

Lawrence, however, had to accept a place with the wrens. He was a gentleman of chancy prospects. She was the daughter of an earl. He had nothing to offer her.

Nothing but my very breath. Nothing but my heart's blood. Nothing but my adoration until I'm laid in the dust.

It was all he had, but it wasn't enough. He knew that now. It took getting out of Lovell House for him to see the world for what it was.

And his place in it. But he'd give ten years of his life if only he'd kissed her last night.

The Orient, the Gorgeous East, exotic islands…how shall I count my life well-spent unless I see them with my own eyes? I must concentrate on that which I want most of all. Trade winds, fragrant spices, dark eyes, a smoky baritone—dash it all! That man invades even the sanctum of my diary!
—from the diary of Lady Caroline Lovell

Chapter 13

"Here he comes, my lady. Looks like he got your reticule back, too," Alice said, giving a little clap. "I told you Mr. Sinclair would see to things."

"I'm more concerned he'll see that we've been following him since he left Lovell House this morning," Caroline hissed. It was one thing to trail Lawrence to see where he went. It was quite another to be caught doing it.

"Well, we can say you're shopping, but a lady such as yourself patronizing a bakery in this neighborhood might strike a body as odd, you must admit." Alice waved hugely to Lawrence as if he wasn't already headed their way.

"Stop that!" Caroline was feeling exposed enough. "You're making a spectacle of us."

Chastised, Alice dropped her hand. "Truth to tell, I didn't think old Sedgewick could make the carriage go so slowly or head down so many stray side lanes without us losing Mr. Sinclair entire."

Caroline had been afraid she'd already lost him. Once Lawrence disappeared into that house on Rathbone for better than half an hour, she realized she had pushed him away for good. He was doing as he'd said he would. He'd found other lodgings.

"My lady." Lawrence gave her one of his nodding bows as he drew near. "I trust you were unharmed during this unfortunate incident."

"I'm fine." She tried to keep her tone light, but that lump of tenderness inside her felt as if it weighed the earth. "Just surprised by the theft, I think."

"I understand perfectly. Such things don't happen in St. James Park."

"Well, no, they don't seem to," she admitted, not sure why that was important. "Thank you for your help, Mr. Sinclair."

He handed back her ruined reticule. "I regret that the laces have been cut, but the contents appear to be intact."

"No doubt Alice can mend it," she said, handing the bag to her maid. "See if you've a needle and thread in the carriage."

"My lady, I don't travel with—oh!" Alice's eyes widened as she belatedly realized Caroline wanted a word alone with Mr. Sinclair. "Yes. Now that I think on it, I might have brought a bit of something what would be useful. I'll see to it right away, my lady."

The coach was only a few yards distant, but it would give Caroline and Lawrence a bit of privacy to speak while maintaining perfect propriety.

"So, I gather you apprehended the thief?" she asked.

"I did."

"I hope you didn't hurt him. He was only a boy."

He cocked his head at her. "Do you really think I'm the sort to savage a child?"

"No, of course not." *Is the man looking for ways to be offended?* "I only meant, well, you let him go, didn't you?"

"I did. No doubt the magistrate's docket is full of criminals far more sinister than our young cutpurse." He clasped his hands behind him, assuming a rigid military stance. His hair had been blown back, and that thin scar at his hairline was exposed. Caroline's fingers itched to trace its length. "I hope you don't mind."

"No. I'm glad you showed the boy mercy." Caroline could use a little herself. She wished he'd smile. He looked so very stern when he didn't, and she feared he was still cross with her for prying into his past. "After all, the lad wasn't so very terrifying, even though Alice did scream blue murder when the knife flashed. It all happened so quickly, I didn't have time to be frightened."

"He intended for you not to realize your purse was gone until it was time to pay for your purchase. But the boy is not that good at his job."

"His job?"

"Thievery is how he feeds himself," Lawrence explained. "I don't think he's bad at heart. Only hungry."

"Then God be thanked, for I have never been that hungry."

"Amen. None of us knows what we might do if we were," Lawrence said. "But I have to ask, why are you here, my lady?"

"Even a lady can be mildly hungry from time to time." She waved vaguely toward the shop behind them. "I understand this is a very fine bakery."

"And you passed a dozen or more such establishments between here and Lovell House. If I didn't know better, I'd suspect you were following me."

Her first impulse was to deny it, but when she met his dark eyes, she knew only the truth would serve between them.

"Very well; if you want me to say it, I will. Yes, we were following you," she admitted. "But only because I feared you were leaving us."

"I told you I would."

Caroline sighed. The man was constantly dragging unladylike admissions from her. The words stuck in her teeth, but she had to say them. "I hoped to convince you not to."

"Why?"

Just knowing there was no chance she'd meet him on the stairs or see him across the supper table made her chest tighten. Already there was a hole in her life where he'd been. But she couldn't very well tell him that. "I…my…my brother…he'll be upset. Your friendship means a good deal to him, you know. Teddy will take it hard…your leaving, I mean." *Drat the man! What is it about him that makes it so difficult for me to construct a coherent sentence?* "Did you even tell Bredon good-bye?"

"I plan to drop him a note of thanks this afternoon and explain my new situation to him," Lawrence said. "Just because I am no longer enjoying your family's hospitality, it does not follow that Bredon and I will fail to spend time in each other's company."

It didn't seem to trouble him that he'd no longer spend any time in hers. "But…you didn't…I mean, if I hadn't been looking out the parlor window…" *Plague take the man! I may as well admit what's bothering me.* "You didn't say good-bye to me either."

"Yes, I did. Last night. After you so kindly instructed me in the waltz."

"That wasn't good-bye. It was…" *A dismissal. A set-down. If anyone had been watching, it was a cut direct of monumental proportion.* "You very nearly threw me out of my own ballroom."

"If I seemed discourteous, I apologize."

"You didn't seem so, you were so."

"If I'm such an unpleasant fellow, why are you following me?"

She didn't know. Her mind had never been so…untidy over a man before. She despised herself for it, but she couldn't seem to stop herself. Caroline had done so many ridiculous things over Lawrence. She'd have thoroughly castigated Freddie or Horatia if they'd even contemplated following a man through the streets of London in their family's carriage.

"I was concerned for you," she finally said to fill the uncomfortable silence that stretched between them.

He raised a skeptical brow.

"As far as I know, you have no family, no other acquaintances in Town with whom you might lodge. Why, for all I knew, you might have ended up in a dreadful neighborhood. There are parts of London where a decent person may not walk unmolested, you know," she explained, fearful she sounded just like Freddie when she started nattering on, but, like her friend, she was unable to muzzle herself. "As we discovered, even Leicester Square has its miscreants."

"I assure you, no one will slash my purse strings," he said dryly. "Is that the real reason you followed me?"

"Can't I be concerned about my brother's friend?"

That smile of his—how would she live without it?—lifted one corner of his mouth. "How did I ever manage to roam the Continent and find my way back to England without your concern?"

When he put it like that, she had to laugh. "Very well. You're right. No doubt you are capable of looking out for yourself."

"Thank you, my lady." His smile grew wider, reaching his eyes now.

"Caroline, please," she corrected. She loved the way he said her name and longed to hear it. When he called her Caroline, she was tempted to arch into the deep, rich sound, like a cat demanding a more thorough petting. "No one can hear if you use my Christian name now."

"I can hear." His smile faded. "And calling you *my lady* is what's right. I took too many liberties when I was at Lovell House."

She bit her lip. "I seem to recall one you did not take."

His voice turned even more husky. "No one regrets that more than I."

"What do you regret, Lawrence?" He might not call her Caroline, but his name passed her lips with such rightness, she wouldn't maintain formality with him.

"You know full well. Or if you do not, you are not as intelligent as I believe you to be." He inclined toward her by the smallest of degrees, but the heat in his gaze was so intense, she was reminded of her initial impression of him. A caged lion, with a predatory gleam in his eye. She was certain he wanted to kiss her. She'd never felt surer of anything. He'd been so close to it in the ballroom. Even now, he might have done so right there on the street, in front of God and everybody, but for his own strong will.

What a curse to a woman is a stubborn man!

Then he straightened to his full height and his cool military reserve was back in force. "My lady, I have more regrets than I wish to share or than you could bear to hear. But what I regret most of late is that I may have caused you pain."

She shook her head. "Frustration, yes. You've definitely left a good deal of excitement in your wake, and no end of confusion. But no pain." *At least, none but the strangely pleasurable ache of longing to have what one does not.* "Put your mind at ease, Mr. Sinclair. You have not injured me." *Not in a lasting way, in any case.* His refusal to act on his feelings still stung.

"Then I am gratified to have been of some small assistance to you today," he said. "Will you be needing an escort back to Lovell House?"

She was tempted to say yes, but once they rejoined Alice in the carriage, their conversation would become more horribly stilted than it already was.

"No, thank you," she said, determined to keep her tone bright. "However did I manage to find my way about London without your concern?"

"*Touché,* my lady. But perhaps you'll allow that I may be *concerned* for my friend's sister?"

That made her smile as he took his leave. Tall, lean, and possessed of a warrior's posture, the man was very fine to look upon, even when he was walking away.

Caroline sighed. She hadn't succeeded in convincing him to return to Lovell House as Teddy's guest. However, she viewed this unsatisfactory turn of events as but a momentary setback. She was more determined than ever to know the real Lawrence Sinclair.

Still waters run deep.

If just once she could see the lion uncaged and learn who Lawrence was under that deceptively calm exterior. If she could puzzle out why he held himself in such tight control, and help him loosen his grip, she'd count it a grand accomplishment.

Back when she first began to contemplate having adventures instead of living a pattern sort of life, she'd come across an account of one Antoine de Ville. In 1492, he'd been charged by the king of France with climbing Mount Aiguille. The mountain was said to be impossible to scale, but through great effort, M. de Ville did it, planting his king's flag on the peak.

Learning Lawrence Sinclair from the inside out would be an adventure without equal. Caroline was just the woman to conquer this man's inaccessible soul.

Then she'd see about whether she wanted to plant her flag.

Oh, what I'd give to be a mouse in Dudley's pocket!
—Caroline Lovell, upon discovering that Lawrence Sinclair has acquired
not one but two servants!

Chapter 14

"There you are, Teddy. I've been looking for you everywhere." The last place Caroline expected to find her brother Edward was in their father's study, poring over the earl's thick ledgers. He'd never been the sort for columns and sums. "What on earth are you doing?"

Lord Bredon ran a hand through his sandy hair without the slightest success in making it lie flat. Then he sighed and closed the heavy tome.

"Father said it's time I take on some extra duties. He wishes me to familiarize myself with the running of the estate. It seems the rest of the family can flit about entertaining themselves, but now that I'm done with my education, a multitude of responsibilities loom before me."

Teddy hadn't looked this oppressed since she'd caught him cramming for exams over his holiday break from Oxford, but she couldn't resist teasing him a bit.

"Ah, the perils of being heir apparent. How sad for you to look forward to becoming Lord Chatham. The peerage makes for such a long, weary lifetime when you consider all the wealth, honor, and prerogatives that go along with the title."

"The duties are as plentiful as the benefits, I'm discovering," Edward said.

"I rather doubt our brothers think their lots in life will be easier. After all, they'll have to make their own ways in the world."

"Not without a good deal of help from me," Teddy said testily. "Who do you think will see to it that Ben acquires a generous living as vicar in some charming country parish? Where will Thomas get the funds to purchase that infernal ship he's always talking about? And who knows what Charles and Harry will eventually decide to do with themselves? But whatever it is, the house of Lovell will be supporting them at every step while they do."

Life was ever thus. Men could follow their own interests and decide for themselves. They'd even have the family's support in their chosen endeavors. Once, Caroline would have railed at the unfairness of it all. Solely on account of being born a woman, she wouldn't be allowed to determine what to do with herself. But surprisingly, just now, she had other concerns that were more pressing. Somehow, without seeming to, she had to steer this conversation toward Lawrence.

"Yes, yes, you're a veritable rock, Teddy, and the family wouldn't be able to scrape by without you."

"If you're trying to turn me up sweet, you'll have to do better than that."

"Me? Never considered it for a moment." She batted her eyes in feigned innocence. "But have you ever considered what it would be like for our brothers if you and Father didn't support them? They'd be flailing about, left to their own devices, wouldn't they?"

Edward frowned. "I suppose so. Why are you so concerned about their futures all of a sudd—Oh, I see." He tapped a finger alongside his nose and slanted a knowing look at her. "You're thinking of Sinclair. His situation is much the same as our brothers'."

"You always did know me far too well for my comfort," she admitted. "And you're right this time, too. But Mr. Sinclair's case is much different from our brothers. His uncle hasn't given him the kind of support Ben and the others will receive from you, that much is certain."

The fact that Lawrence didn't feel welcome in his family's home made her chest ache. Caroline vexed her parents with regularity, but they wouldn't turn her away. She'd never feel the kind of rejection Lawrence had suffered.

"I wouldn't worry about Sinclair," Edward said, reopening the ledger before him and scowling down at it. "He's a very capable fellow."

"Capable of what, I wonder?" Caroline walked her fingertips along the edge of their father's massive mahogany desk, trying to seem nonchalant. "You never did tell me what he did to earn your undying gratitude and friendship, you know."

"And I won't now," Teddy said without looking up.

"Why not?"

"Because it involves a third party, and besides, it isn't my story to tell."

Oliver. "It has something to do with Rowley, doesn't it?"

"Caro, if you want to know so badly, why don't you ask Sinclair?"

"Why are you being so difficult?" She started a slow prowl around the perimeter of the room in frustration. "You know as well as I that it would be easier to flap my arms and fly to the moon than to get Lawrence Sinclair to talk about himself."

Edward laughed. "You've the right of it, Sister. He's not one to monopolize a conversation, is he? And even better than not waffling on about himself, Sinclair doesn't make a habit of gossiping about others either. A virtue I recommend we emulate."

"You should have been the vicar instead of Ben," she said, waving away his preachy suggestion. "Besides, you know Mr. Sinclair would never tell me, even if I asked. Which I wouldn't, of course. It would be the height of rudeness for me to ask him something so obviously personal."

"That's a very mature attitude. I commend you."

"And I you for protecting your friends' secrets," she said through clenched teeth. "But I hardly think it would be considered either gossip or rude if you should happen to tell your favorite sister what she wants to know."

"My favorite you may be," he said with a laugh at their shared standing joke, "but your logic is astonishingly absurd."

"How so?"

"You won't ask Sinclair anything personal, but it's not rude to harass me about it."

"You're my brother. Rudeness doesn't signify between you and me," she said, trying not to whine. "And in any case, it's not as if it could be considered gossip because anything you told me would go no further."

"No, Caro," he said with firmness. "Your wiles may work on Father, but I am immune."

She plopped into the leather wing chair near the cold fireplace. "Men are such vexing creatures."

Teddy studied her for a moment. "Are you harboring a tendresse for Sinclair?"

"What? No." She willed her cheeks not to heat, without much success. "Now *you're* being absurd."

"Am I? You were exceptionally keen on teaching him to dance."

"Only as a favor to you, chucklehead," she said, feeling quite out of charity with him, favorite brother or no. Teddy used to be far easier to manipulate. "I couldn't very well let your friend disgrace himself at Lord Frampton's ball, could I? And by the way, you're welcome."

He made a hmphing noise that sounded eerily like their father when he caught one of them in a faradiddle. "'The lady doth protest too much, methinks,'" he quoted.

"All right." Caroline decided a change of tactics was in order. "For the sake of argument, suppose you are correct and I am addlepated over Sinclair. Our parents have been waiting and watching with bated breath for the day when I become besotted with an eligible parti. Wouldn't *they* want you to tell me why you are indebted to him? After all, if Mr. Sinclair's actions aided my dear brother, it's something that would only increase my infatuation with the man."

"First of all, I doubt our parents think Sinclair is all that eligible."

"Why not? He *is* heir presumptive to an earldom."

"I wouldn't count on that," Edward said. "If the betting at White's is any indication, Lord Ware is about to announce his impending nuptials to a young lady from a notoriously fertile family."

"Who is it?"

Teddy shook his head. "I shouldn't have said anything, and I trust you not to repeat it. But suffice it to say that the ledger at White's is giving very long odds on Sinclair succeeding his uncle."

Caroline rose and resumed her nervous prowl about the room. "Oh, yes, by all means, let us consult the oracle of a betting book."

"In such matters it's rarely wrong," Teddy assured her. "Besides, as to your claim that the tale of how Sinclair and I met would redound to his credit, let me assure you, the reverse is true."

That stopped her in her tracks. "You cannot make that kind of statement and then keep mum. Now you've simply got to tell me. But no matter what you say, if Mr. Sinclair gave you aid, I would only rejoice in his actions."

"You didn't see the actions," he said softly.

"Oh, Teddy, you'll drive me to Bedlam." She leaned on the desk, bending down to meet his gaze. "You may as well get to it; you know you're going to tell me eventually."

"And why would I do that?"

"Because I'm your favorite sister. Because you know I won't give you any peace until you do. And because I can keep a secret," she said, ticking off the reasons on her fingers. When he rolled his eyes, she straightened her spine and played her trump card. "After all, I've never told Father who really wrecked his curricle that summer before you left for the Continent. At least, I haven't yet."

"You wouldn't."

She shrugged. "Father was very attached to that equipage. 'The finest, fastest in the shire,' he always said. Well, you'd know, wouldn't you? Because you and Rowley discovered exactly how fast it would go."

"Botheration! I should have learned from that episode not to blithely fall in with Oliver's plans."

"So, Rowley *was* involved in your meeting Lawrence—I mean Mr. Sinclair."

Edward leaned back in his chair. "Close the study door."

She obeyed quickly and returned to perch on the edge of the wing-chair seat.

"If ever I hear the slightest whiff of this story anywhere, I shall know who to blame," he said.

"Your secret dies with me. I'll swear on anything you like."

"Don't swear. It's not ladylike."

"Neither am I, half the time."

"Nevertheless," Edward said in an imitation of their father at his reproving best. Perhaps it was sitting behind Lord Chatham's desk that gave him a much graver demeanor than usual. "Your word should be enough, Caro."

"Very well. You have it." She folded her hands on her lap to still them, but her insides still jittered. She was finally going to learn something important about Lawrence. "Where did you first meet Mr. Sinclair?"

"In an Italian jail."

Caroline blinked hard. She'd heard that sometimes people paid to view the unfortunates at Bedlam, but she'd never understood the charm of it. "You were touring a jail?"

"No. I was incarcerated in one. We all were."

A pent-up breath whooshed out of her. "Why?"

"Trust me, there are any number of ways an Englishman can run afoul of the law in Italy. Rowley and I found several, I'm afraid, one of which would have been a capital offense had things gone badly for us at trial."

Caroline's belly roiled uncertainly. Punishment for crimes in England could be severe. If the boy who'd stolen her reticule were brought up on charges, he might well be hanged or deported to New South Wales. No doubt other countries were just as firm about enforcing their laws, but she never imagined such harsh punishment would be meted out to members of the aristocracy.

"What on earth did you do?" Surely they hadn't dabbled in thievery.

"It's not a tale fit for your ears, Caro. I shouldn't have told you this much."

Which meant her brother probably wouldn't tell her what offense Lawrence had committed to land him in the same jail.

"Thank heaven things didn't go badly for you at trial," she said softly.

"Only because we didn't make it to trial. We were being transferred to another prison closer to court when Sinclair, in shackles no less, overpowered the guards."

"Guards?" she repeated. "As in more than one?"

Edward nodded. "There were four of them, all goodly sized fellows, too. Honestly, I've never seen the like, Caro. Sinclair went from docile prisoner to Viking berserker between one heartbeat and the next. He laid them all out, with no help from me or Rowley, I regret to say. We were too astonished at the sudden change in him to move. His blows were methodical and ruthless and…" Edward met her gaze. "Such things aren't meant for feminine ears. I'm sorry if I've distressed you."

"I'd be more distressed at the thought of you languishing in a foreign prison," she said, only a bit ashamed of the little thrill that danced on her spine. She'd suspected Lawrence Sinclair could be dangerous, but instead of being repulsed, she wished she'd been there to see the lion uncaged. "Then what happened?"

"Then Sinclair grabbed the keys from the fallen guards and unshackled himself, and Rowley and me as well. The three of us took to our heels. We dodged through dark alleys and lanes down to the docks and jumped onto the first ship leaving that harbor. We didn't care where it was bound so long as it left quickly." Edward massaged the bridge of his nose, as if a headache were forming between his eyes. "Needless to say, we'll not be welcome in Rome again anytime soon."

"Well! I can certainly see why you feel you owe Mr. Sinclair a great debt." If she'd had a million guesses, she wouldn't have come up with that story. She still had more questions about Lawrence than answers, but it was a start. "It's obvious you won't tell me the exact nature of the offense that landed you and Rowley in jail, but why was Mr. Sinclair there?"

"Enough, Caro. You will have to ask him. I'm done with my quota of gossip for the month. Now, if you have nothing more—"

A smart rap sounded on the study door. Caroline sighed. If not for the interruption, she felt sure she could have wheedled more information out of her brother.

"Come," he ordered.

The door opened to reveal the inept footman Dudley, and, standing slightly behind him, the boy who'd recently stolen Caroline's purse. The lad doffed his deplorable hat and gawked openmouthed around the room at the myriad books and decorative statuary as if he'd entered a palace. Then he noticed Caroline. His eyes went round as an owl's when he recognized her, and he took a step back.

"Beggin' your pardon, my lord," Dudley said with a proper bow. "This… person bears a message for you and claims he has instructions from his employer to place it in your hands alone."

Lawrence wasn't the only one who could change personas in a heartbeat. Edward straightened his posture and went from Caroline's dear brother Teddy to the imperious Lord Bredon between one breath and the next. He motioned for the boy to come forward and took the carefully folded note from him. His gaze swept over the missive quickly.

"It's from Sinclair," he told Caroline. "He thanks me roundly for Lovell House's hospitality, but it seems he's found other accommodations."

Lord Bredon turned his attention to the footman. "Dudley, according to this letter, you are to pack Mr. Sinclair's effects and deliver them into this lad's keeping."

"Are you sure about that?" Caroline asked, eyeing the boy with suspicion. If he'd steal her purse, he might be brazen enough to try to steal Lawrence's belongings by trickery as well. "How do we know the note is genuine?"

"This is Sinclair's writing, no doubt." Teddy flashed the note at her. It was too quick for her to read anything, but the words slanted strangely across the page. "I'd know his cack-handed scrawl anywhere. So, boy, I assume you are in Mr. Sinclair's employ."

The lad nodded gravely and swallowed hard. He obviously couldn't trust his tongue at the moment.

Bredon shook his head. "He must see something in you, but frankly, your meager services cannot possibly be sufficient to meet a gentleman's needs. Therefore, Dudley, you will accompany this young man to Mr. Sinclair's new residence," Bredon said to the footman before turning his gaze back to the boy. "Your name, lad, if you please."

"It's B-Billy, your mightiness."

"Billy," Edward repeated, lips twitching as he stifled a smile. Caroline's brother was m'lorded from morning till night, but to her knowledge, no one had ever dubbed him *your mightiness* before. "Dudley will go with you to make sure Mr. Sinclair's effects reach his new abode in good order. You may wait in the hall while Dudley packs, and mind that you keep your hands in your own pockets."

"Aye, sir, I mean, your exceedingness, your fulsomeness, your—"

"Lord Bredon will do."

"Aye, Lord Bredon." Billy executed an awkward bow, then made a great show of shoving his fists into the deep pockets of his jacket as he slipped out the door.

"Dudley," Bredon said, turning his attention back to the footman, "did you enjoy serving as Mr. Sinclair's valet while he was in residence here?"

The footman-turned-temporary-valet straightened to his full gangly height. "Oh, yes, my lord. Mr. Sinclair is a fine gentleman. A pleasure to be of service to him, I'm sure. I was proud to be his valet."

"Good. Then you shall continue in that role."

"But, my lord, I don't..." Dudley said, clearly dismayed. "Does this mean you're releasing me from service? I'm more than happy to remain a footman here at Lovell House. Please, my lord—"

"No, no." Edward raised a hand to silence him. "Rest easy, Dudley. You're not being given the sack. You're being...promoted, as it were. Permanently. Nominally, you shall remain on the Lovell House staff, without any diminution in pay, but your duties will be performed elsewhere. Instead of being our footman, you'll serve as valet to my particular friend, Mr. Sinclair, in his new quarters."

"Then I'm to leave Lovell House?"

"A valet can't very well serve his master if he's across town from him, can he?" Edward said. "Mr. Sinclair will no doubt provide a place for you to stay near him. He has a number of engagements coming up and he'll need someone to assure that he has a sharp turn out for them. Since my friend is heir presumptive to an earldom, I don't need to tell you what a splendid opportunity this is for you."

Dudley was not the sharpest quill in the inkpot, but he was quick enough to realize a servant borrowed his standing in the world below stairs from the rank of those he served. Being valet to a possible future earl was several steps up from answering the front door and dropping silverware down diner's dresses at Lovell House.

"So tell me now," Edward said. "Are you the man for the job?"

"Oh, yes, my lord," Dudley said, but Caroline suspected he was about to gnaw through the inside of his cheek. The move was not all positive. Her maid Alice would be inconsolable when she heard about Dudley's new living arrangements.

"Good. I shall apprise Mr. Price of your new assignment. You may leave the study door open as you go."

"Very good, my lord. Thank you."

Once Dudley had gone, Caroline's shoulders slumped. "Well, it's official, then. Mr. Sinclair has truly taken his leave of us."

"Can't say I'm surprised. He's not the sort to be satisfied to hang on someone else's sleeve. When we were traveling, Rowley and I had a good deal more credit at our disposal, but Sinclair always insisted on paying his own way."

"Still, won't it be a problem, your sending Dudley off like that?" Caroline said. "Isn't Mr. Price supposed to be in charge of the staff?"

"Price will thank me. Truth to tell, he's been looking for a way to give walking papers to his nephew for weeks, but he feared angering his sister. Price says Dudley is too clumsy to serve at table, and he's doubtful further training will help." Teddy shook his head. "I'm sure his services as a valet leave a good deal to be desired, but Sinclair won't mind. I don't think he's had servants of his own since he left Ware Hall."

Lawrence had seemed uncomfortable each time he was waited upon by one of the Lovell House staff. "You may be right," Caroline said.

"His standards are a good bit lower in that regard, so Dudley will undoubtedly suit him well enough." Edward stood and stretched his arms wide. "That's a job well done. I found a way to rid Lovell House of a less-than-ideal footman and since Dudley will be of some use to Sinclair, I can continue to show appreciation to my friend by providing a valet for him. Two birds with one stone and all that."

"Yes, you're very clever, Teddy." When he looked away, Caroline scooped up the note from Lawrence that her brother had left on the edge of the desk. She was certain there was much more in the letter than he'd shared with her. She slipped it into the bodice of her dress. The gong sounded, signifying that the family had one hour to prepare for their evening meal. "I must be off. See you at supper."

Caroline scurried out before her brother had time to notice his note from Lawrence had disappeared. She nearly stumbled over young Billy, who was cooling his heels in the hall.

"Nice pull, my lady," the boy said with a grin. "When I peeped round the doorway, I seen you nick that note, slick as snot. Couldn't a done it better meself."

Caroline's mouth opened and closed twice, but she couldn't very well scold the lad over his cheeky attempt at a compliment. Billy was right. She'd just purloined something from her brother as surely as this boy had sliced the laces on her reticule earlier. So she settled for turning on her heel and forcing herself to walk sedately up the stairs to her chamber when everything in her wanted to fly up them.

Because the dressing gong had sounded, Alice was waiting for her, but Caroline wanted privacy, not primping. "Go at once to Mr. Sinclair's chamber. He's moved out and Dudley is packing his things for him. I'd like you to help him."

"Right away, my lady," Alice said with a wink and a breathless smile, jumping at the chance to work alongside her sweetheart. "Oh, but how will you manage without me?"

"I'll wear the sprigged muslin this evening." It was one of the few garments in Caroline's wardrobe that she could wiggle into by herself. "In a pinch, I can tie up those tabs, and with a good brushing and a fresh ribbon, my hair will be fine. Now, off you go."

Alice scurried away, humming to herself. Caroline felt a bit mean, sending her maid off to certain disappointment, but she wasn't ready to deal with the hysterics that were bound to come. She'd rather Alice heard about Dudley's supposed promotion and new living situation from him rather than her.

Besides, she needed Alice out of her chamber. She couldn't bear to wait another moment to read Lawrence's letter. She drew it from her bodice and unfolded it carefully. Her hands were surprisingly unsteady. If she were this pent up over a letter the man had written to someone else, she wasn't sure what she'd do if he ever screwed up his courage to write to her.

My dear Bredon,

No one has been a better friend to me than you. I'm more grateful than words can convey. The gracious hospitality of Lovell House has been far beyond what I deserve. I shall convey my thanks to the earl and his countess in a separate missive, but I wanted you to know the real reason I must remove myself from your family's home. I owe you that much.

It is because of your sister.

I love her.

There it was. Ungilded. Direct. True.

Plenty of gentlemen had offered Caroline flowery words and grandiose protestations. One had even composed the most dreadful verse of more than one hundred couplets praising, of all things, the slight upturn of her nose! But none of her previous suitors' words had reached anywhere near her heart. Lawrence's simple confession went straight to her soul.

"He loves me," she whispered. Caroline sank onto the foot of her bed because her knees would no longer support her weight. She felt warm all of a sudden, glowing as if a candle had been lit inside her.

The fault is not hers, she read on. *Lady Caroline has not encouraged me.*

"Oh really? You didn't find my meeting you in the dead of night for a waltz lesson encouraging? Honestly, men are so stupid sometimes."

She shook her head at his foolishness, feeling both tender and giddy about him at the same time. She didn't understand the strange mix of emotions swirling inside her. It was as if her stays had been too tightly laced. She couldn't make sense of her sudden urge to dance and laugh and weep all at the same time.

Only that it was so.

I understand that my attachment to Lady Caroline may cause awkwardness between us. I would not put you in that difficult position. My prospects alone make me an inadequate suitor for your sister's hand, and I will not insult her with less than she deserves.

"Perhaps you might let me be the judge of whether you are adequate, Mr. Sinclair," she said, wishing he were standing before her right then so she could scold him properly for thinking so poorly of himself.

But even laying that aside, you, of all people, know why I will not shackle Lady Caroline to one such as myself.

"Oh, for pity's sake." If this self-flagellation was about the incident in the Italian jail, she knew all about it now and felt more warmly toward him than ever. After all, he'd saved her dear Teddy from heaven knew what horrific end.

She turned back to the note.

I pray God to grant that she find someone respectable and worthy, who will love her as deeply as I.

"Oh, pish! Doesn't he imagine I might have something to say about this?" She'd started reading with a flutter in her chest and hope in her heart. Now she was angry.

What was wrong with the man? What good did it do for him to explain himself to her brother? Didn't he know that if she failed to buckle under pressure to conform from her parents, she certainly wasn't the sort to be *managed* by her male relatives?

When she heard the longcase clock chime the half hour, Caroline refolded the note and hid it in her diary before she began to dress herself for dinner.

"If the man has something to say *about* me, he'd better say it *to* me," she muttered as she struggled out of her morning dress and into the sprigged muslin for evening. Yes indeed. Lawrence Sinclair owed it to her to speak his heart plainly and let *her* choose what to do about it.

This was far too important a decision to leave solely in a man's keeping. Lawrence couldn't make it without her. And Teddy certainly could not.

She'd see to it that Lawrence made his declaration.

And there'd be no better time or place for it than at Lord Frampton's ball.

Women are always counseled to keep quiet and let men do the talking. This might be good advice under some circumstances. One can learn a great deal by allowing someone else to fill an uncomfortable silence. However, this strategy is woefully inadequate for dealing with the likes of Lawrence Sinclair. I swear, silence is his native state.
—from the diary of Lady Caroline Lovell

Chapter 15

Lord and Lady Frampton's home in Mayfair was not quite as grand as Lovell House. Caroline remembered from last Season that there was no dedicated entertaining space on their topmost story. Instead, the drawing room on the ground floor was transformed into a ballroom. All the furniture was removed, except for chairs and settees, which were pushed to the perimeter of the space to provide seating for those who did not dance but wished to watch those who did.

Lady Frampton's parlor was pressed into service as a card room for those who preferred games over "tripping the light fantastic toe." The spacious dining room was already being prepared for the upcoming midnight supper, and no doubt a first-story parlor had been transformed into a ladies' retiring room.

Upon arriving, Caroline planned to seek out that room. Anything to escape the watchful eye of her parents. She wished she could have accompanied her brothers later, when they came in the Chatham carriage's second trip. The Lovell boys always made for a jolly party. But Lady Chatham had insisted Caroline ride with her and Lord Chatham. This arrangement made it easier for Caroline's mother to pepper her with advice the whole time they bounced over the cobbles.

"Your posture has been sadly lacking of late. Stand up straight, but don't square your shoulders. A lady's should be delicately rounded."

"Yes, Mother." *I wonder what she'd have to say about my posture if I decided to stand on my head in the middle of the dance floor?*

"Don't meet anyone's gaze too boldly, but don't be unapproachable either."

"Yes, Mother." *Honestly, walking a tightrope would be easier than this narrow path.*

"Be sure to greet everyone. The last thing you should do is disappear into a corner with those simpering friends of yours."

"I happen to like my simpering friends." *And by the way, only I am allowed to call them simpering.*

"Your loyalty does you credit, but gossiping in the corner is never attractive."

"We don't gossip." *Not all the time.*

"The pool of eligible gentlemen is a bit slim this year. You need to show yourself to best advantage."

The rebellious thoughts that had been running through Caroline's head finally found their way out of her mouth. "Perhaps we ought to take out an advertisement in the *Times* listing my sterling qualities."

"Caroline," her father said gruffly. He seldom reproved her, so his tone was enough to leave her thoroughly chastised.

"I'm sorry," she murmured.

"Don't be sorry," her mother said. "Do better. This is likely your last Season, you know."

God be praised nearly sprang from her lips, but she was certain her father would recognize her pious outburst for the mutinous exclamation it was. So she merely nodded, grateful the carriage finally rolled to a stop before Lord and Lady Frampton's town house.

Once inside, her mother couldn't resist one last bit of instruction.

"The more time an unattached lady has to see and be seen before the festivities begin, the more likely her dance card will be full," her mother explained as the footman took their wraps at the door. The footman handed her a gilded dance card with her name at the top and the order of dances to be performed listed in ornate script.

"There seem to be no partners penciled in on my card," she told her mother.

"Ah! That's Lady Frampton for you. She prefers to allow the assembly to sort itself out instead of having partners preselected. She's always been a bit eccentric," her mother said, clearly wishing their hostess had left less to chance. "That's why we made sure you arrived before your brothers, you see. This way there's ample time for gentlemen to request a dance before the festivities begin."

"Indeed, Mother," Caroline said, softly enough that her father couldn't hear. "The bird that hangs most prominently in the butcher's window is always the first to be sold."

"Behave," her mother whispered and shot her a look of censure as Caroline's father headed for the card room.

"Oh, look. There's Lady Ackworth," her mother said. "No, don't look. She'll think we're talking about her."

"Perhaps because we are?"

"Lady Ackworth considers herself the final arbiter of propriety." Lady Chatham was careful to keep her voice soft. "If she gives you a black mark, it doesn't go away."

The obnoxious busybody divided the ton into two camps. One was either her sycophant or her target. Even Lady Chatham, the most proper of countesses, was terrified of finding herself in the vindictive witch's sights. Caroline's mother palmed her cheek.

"You see now why I admonish you to be on your best behavior. I'd walk through fire for you, sweeting, but even the most doting mother cannot protect her daughter from that old scold's tongue."

When her mother took that tone, Caroline felt a stab of guilt over her rebellious attitude. Not enough to change, of course, but she did regret causing her mother grief.

"I'll try, Mother," she promised. Trying wasn't always succeeding, so she didn't feel as if she'd fibbed. Given half a chance this evening, Caroline intended to misbehave in the extreme.

Then Lady Chatham spied a group of her friends near the punch bowl on the far side of the room and threaded her way through the press to them. Caroline made for the base of the broad staircase. Before ascending to seek the retiring room to make sure the gem-studded pins Alice had tucked into her coiffure had survived the carriage ride, Caroline stood still for a moment, searching the crowd.

Lawrence was nowhere to be seen.

Drat the man! He promised he'd be here.

Instead, Horatia, with Frederica at her side, caught Caroline's eye. Across the room, Horatia gesticulated wildly with her fan in Caroline's direction. Since her debut, Horatia had been studying what she called "the language of the fan." It was an arcane set of stylized movements, more suited to the previous generation's flirtations than theirs, but because it had fallen out of fashion, Horatia was convinced the three of them could use the gestures to communicate clandestinely when they were in public.

It might have worked if Freddie had possessed a better memory or Caroline had shown the least interest in learning the signals. So instead of conveying a secret message, Horatia looked as if she were being accosted by a cloud of midges.

When Caroline didn't respond in kind, Horatia and Frederica scurried across the room to her, nearly bowling her over when they reached her.

"Oh, Caroline, where've you been?" Horatia complained. "Well, no matter. You're here at last."

"We thought you were coming early, dear," Frederica explained.

"I thought I did."

"Never mind. You're here now," Horatia hissed. To the glittering assemblage, her friend presented a brittle smile. However, Caroline spotted real tears trembling on Horatia's lashes. "Perhaps you can think of a way to salvage the situation. I confess I'm at a loss."

"What's wrong?" she asked.

"It's a disaster, I tell you," Horatia said, still smiling bravely. "A total, unmitigated disaster."

"Indeed one might class it a disaster of biblical proportions," Frederica said agreeably. "Truly, how shall dear Horatia ever show her face again?"

"It's not my fault, you little goose. Why are you acting as if I'm to blame?"

Frederica blinked at Horatia with the innocence of a newborn lamb. "Well, whose fault is it, then?"

"Come now. Settle down, you two," Caroline said, pulling them off to a quiet spot. The rest of Lord and Lady Frampton's guests were milling about in clumps of twos and threes, so their conference in the corner should call no undue attention. Unless, of course, her mother should happen to spot her "gossiping with her simpering friends." In that case, Caroline would catch it later, but she'd deal with her mother's scolding then. Horatia was in real distress now. "Whatever it is, it can't be as bad as all that."

"Oh, yes, it can," Horatia said miserably. "Look." Setting the spangles on her headdress quivering, she jerked her head to the right, indicating where Caroline should direct her gaze.

Across the ballroom, Caroline spied Miss Penelope Braithwaite. She was decked out in an almost exact replica of Horatia's ensemble. If the gowns had been perfectly identical, Horatia might have been satisfied. Between the two of them, she easily had the more fashionable figure. Penelope's bosom was far too full to be stylish. But it was the *almost* exactness of their gowns that tipped the scales in Miss Braithwaite's favor.

The cut and style of the gowns were the same. The shade of ivory was like two matched pearls. But while Horatia's gown was of lustring, Miss Braithwaite's was fashioned of much costlier watered silk, covered with silver netting. The dear seed pearls and silver embroidery on Penelope's gown made Horatia's spangles seem tawdry and common by comparison. Their head dresses were also identical, save that Penelope's boasted a splendid ostrich feather. Its grand height made the headdress seem like an achievement of major architectural importance.

By contrast, Horatia's was a mud-speckled shack.

"How could this have happened again?" she almost wailed.

"Hush." Caroline grasped Horatia's hand and gave it a squeeze. "If you let others know you're bothered by this, it will be worse for you. Your gown is perfectly lovely." That would have been true had Penelope not been wearing the drastically improved version of it. "Chin up, my dear, and ignore her. Others will, too."

Penelope's laugh made their gazes swivel toward her and the older gentleman at her side.

As part of her "finishing," Caroline had been taught that a lady's laugh must be genteel. "An ethereal sound no more obtrusive than an angel's sigh," her deportment teacher had told her. Penelope's laugh was more like a demented cackle.

"How can we ignore that?" Frederica asked.

The older gentleman with Miss Braithwaite made a courtly obeisance over her gloved hand, then left her to make his way to the card room.

"Who was that with her?" Caroline asked.

"Lord Ware," Horatia said dully. "He's been hovering about Penelope like a bee around a flower since we got here."

Maybe that's why Lawrence hasn't come. He knew his uncle would be here.

"Have you seen anyone else we know?"

"Oh, my, yes," Frederica said excitedly. "We've encountered Miss Cowper and Lady Greenhalgh and those three sisters—I forget their names, but they're the ones who play wind instruments so…memorably."

"By memorably you mean wretchedly, dear. And they're the Misses Harewood—Letitia, Lavinia, and Lucinda," Horatia supplied. "I so pity the one who plays bassoon."

"It does sound rather like a gander with a head cold, doesn't it?" Freddie added.

"Forget how it sounds. The poor girl who has to play it must make sure her skirts are plain enough not to catch on the unwieldy thing. Imagine having to forget fashion for the sake of a musical instrument."

Forget fashion? The musical world will never forget the way the Harewood sisters desecrated that transcribed Boccherini trio last week, Caroline thought but didn't say. If speaking ill of others was a prayer to the devil, she didn't dare. How was Caroline to wrangle a declaration from Lawrence tonight if she didn't have help from every angel in the vicinity?

"Is there anyone *else* here I should know about?" she asked.

Frederica colored up prettily. "Lord Rowley has arrived. He smiled at me when he first came in."

"He smiles at everyone," Horatia said pettishly.

"Anyone else?"

"No, Caro. Your Mr. Sinclair has not shown his face yet," Frederica said.

Caroline blinked in surprise. Sometimes she underestimated Freddie's powers of observation. "Again, he's not *my* Mr. Sinclair."

"Not for lack of your trying," Horatia muttered.

Caroline glared at her.

"Oh, dear Caro, don't frown so." Frederica patted her forearm soothingly. "Your face might stay like that."

"Freddie, you sound like my mother. I shall frown if I please." Caroline pulled what she was sure must be a truly horrific expression. "And whatever face I end up with, I will deserve. At least it will be because of my own choices. For pity's sake, can I not have one evening without everyone trying to tell me what—"

"Lady Caroline, if that frown is any indication, you are still a damsel in distress." Oliver Rowley appeared before the three of them. He made a formal leg to the girls, a bow that would have been more at home in the ballroom of a generation past. Despite his actions, his grin was anything but proper. Frederica giggled nervously, but Rowley kept his focus on Caroline. "Judging from your dreadful scowl, there must yet be a dragon lurking in your haymow."

"No, just a rogue standing before me," she said, extending a hand for him to make a civilized obeisance over. She smiled back at him, remembering the boy he'd been. "Rowley, it is good to see you. You've been such a stranger since you and Teddy came home."

"Yes, well, there were a number of matters that required my attention upon our return." His gaze swiveled to Frederica. "Miss Tilbury, how enchanting you are this evening. I look forward to sharing the supper dance with you later, but now I must beg Lady Caroline for the minuet."

A string quartet was beginning to tune up in an alcove adjoining the drawing room. Judging from the purity of their scales and singing tone, this ensemble would far exceed the musical endeavors of the Harewood sisters.

"Surely the dance master has already designated a couple," Caroline said. Few dancers knew the minuet and even fewer could do justice to its intricate steps. It was often skipped over when the lady of the house called the order of dances. If the minuet was performed at all, it was done only as an exhibition. The dance was spritely and elegant, and Caroline's toes tapped inside her slippers, itching to try it. "I shouldn't wish to push myself forward."

"You're not," Rowley assured her. "I've already done the pushing for you. I know what a brilliant dancer you are, so I brought you to the attention of the dancing master."

"Thank heaven the master didn't catch you making that horrible face," Frederica said.

"Quite," Rowley agreed. "In any case, the master remembered your dancing from other fêtes and suggested we pair up for the minuet. Say you will." Then he drew himself up to his full height to issue the formal invitation. "Lady Caroline, may I have the honor of this dance?"

Caroline often railed against the lack of choices in a lady's life and indeed, she had none now. So long as she knew the gentleman who asked her to dance, a lady was required to accept his invitation or remain a wallflower for the rest of the evening.

Lawrence had been adamant that Freddie should turn Rowley down for the supper dance. Since then, Caroline had suffered a number of niggling reservations about her old friend.

But she had no reservations whatsoever about dancing the minuet with him. She dipped into a low, graceful curtsy.

"The honor is mine, Lord Rowley."

Opportunity makes fools of us all. The wrong thing at the right time is still wrong.
—Lawrence Sinclair, whose timing has always been a bit off.

Chapter 16

Light blazed from every window of Lord Frampton's town house. Music wafted out the open door. Carriages pulled up, queuing in an unhurried manner that allowed the beautifully dressed guests to disembark and proceed in stately glory through the wrought-iron gate.

Lawrence held back, watching them from the corner. Even now, after walking from Leicester Square to Mayfair in his best new knee britches, waistcoat, and jacket, he couldn't decide if he should actually go in. His Sinclair heritage meant he was on the edge of the aristocracy, but he doubted he'd ever truly belong to this world.

Or with the one person in it who mattered to him.

On the way over, he'd rehearsed in his mind what he'd do when he saw Caroline.

In his favorite imagining, he'd sweep her around the ballroom in a seductive waltz. They only had eyes for each other, and when the music ended, they wouldn't stop dancing. They'd turn and dip right out a pair of double doors that led into a star-spangled garden. Perhaps there'd be a fountain pattering, and faintly, they'd hear music and laughter drifting out from the ball. Night-blooming jasmine would perfume the air and a nightingale would sing. But nothing in the world around them would really matter.

He and Caroline would be as alone as Adam and Eve in the Garden. Then he'd tell her everything. All his failures. All his flaws. He'd lay them bare, and, angel woman she was, she'd say they were nothing. He could be as naked as Adam with her—figuratively, of course—and not be ashamed. She loved him as he was. Past sins, past hurts would no longer signify. The world would be newborn.

Then, in another iteration of the same scene, a much grimmer and more realistic Lawrence was possessed of a will of iron. He'd made the decision to protect her, even from himself. If he happened to come face-to-face with Caroline, he'd be polite but distant. However, when she wasn't aware of it, he'd watch her in hopeless silence, torturing himself while she laughed at another man's jokes. He'd grind his teeth when someone else waltzed her out the door.

But his resolve was steady. He wouldn't interfere. He didn't deserve her, and nothing could change that. The only way to love her truly was to let her go.

"Stow it, Sinclair. You're being a maudlin ass," he told himself gruffly and set off in the direction of Lord Frampton's home.

There was no point in plotting a strategy. He had no idea what he'd do when he saw Caroline. Like the weathercock she'd claimed to be, he, too, was twisting in the wind. Whatever was going to happen would happen.

Maybe nothing.

Maybe everything.

That was the thing about the future. Nothing was written in stone. He did himself no favors by trying to control what was to come. Life was lived one breath at a time.

It felt a little like the morning of a battle. On those days, he'd never known whether he'd live to see the sunset, but he always prayed to live the hours remaining to him the best way he could. He'd been through the smoke and fire and horror of war and somehow survived.

He'd get through this blasted ball, too. He simply had to soldier on. If he was destined to spend an evening watching Caroline laugh and flirt and dance with other men, he'd endure it. He willed himself not to care.

Lawrence squared his shoulders and marched up to Lord Frampton's door, where he was greeted warmly by the host and his gracious lady. They introduced him to Lady Ackworth and a few other matrons lingering near the entrance. Everyone was all smiles and pleasantries.

"I say, Sinclair," a familiar voice called to him. "I was hoping to see you here this evening."

Lawrence turned to see Colonel Boyle, dressed in full kit. The colonel had been Lawrence's commanding officer during his time with the dragoons. He crossed the foyer to join him, and the two men shook hands.

"How are you, sir?"

"In fine fettle. This bit of diversion is just what's wanted before I ship out next month."

"Where are you bound?"

"The gorgeous East, my lad. India." The colonel lowered his voice. "The major who reports to me is ready to sell his commission. I hope to convince you to purchase it."

"I left the service a year ago." If Lawrence had wanted to make a career of the military, he'd have stayed on then.

"I know, and I must say, I regretted not being able to dissuade you at the time. You were the best officer in my command and you'd be perfect for this new assignment."

"I'm sorry to disappoint you, sir, but I've no interest in India."

"You will when I tell you my orders," Colonel Boyle said with confidence. "I'm to raise and train a regiment of native infantry with a cavalry attached. Going to press northward, as I understand it. This company will be garrisoned near Peshawar."

"I'm less familiar with the subcontinent than I should be," Lawrence said. "Where is that?"

"Near the Khyber Pass. At the foot of the Himalayas, my lad. The roof of the world, they call it. In any case, we'll make it a great honor to be accepted into this regiment. Mark my words, we'll even have a few princes clamoring to join up. I hear those fellows ride like the Devil himself. They'll make a splendid cavalry and *you* are just the man to train them."

The idea was appealing. His days would be spent on horseback, training and practicing battle dressage. Lawrence could look forward to being tired in a good way each evening and sleeping like the just.

But he'd be half a world away from Caroline.

"Other interests keep me here, sir."

The colonel shook his head. "Don't make the decision rashly. Say you'll consider it. And remember, lad, this offer is about more than service to king and country. A bright fellow like yourself can make his fortune in the East."

"I'll bear that in mind," Lawrence promised.

"We sail on the twelfth of next month. I'll hold the post for you until then."

Lawrence thanked him but was sure he'd let the opportunity pass. Still, he'd been able to move in the rarified society of Lord Frampton's guests as an equal. If the rest of the evening went as well, this ball would be easier than he'd thought.

However, his resolution not to be vexed by his situation with Caroline faltered when he followed the sound of music into the drawing room.

There she was. While other guests looked on, Caroline floated around the room, light-footed as a hind. Her gestures, the expressions on her heart-shaped face, the precise steps and leaps—they were all exquisite. She was Grace itself, shod in little silver slippers. Lawrence was amazed that she didn't sprout wings. She moved about the room, dancing in a Z-shaped pattern, sometimes alone and sometimes in various holds with her dance partner.

Lucky devil.

Lawrence couldn't tell who it was because the man's face was turned away from him, but he would have given a year in Paradise to change places with the fellow. Not that Lawrence could hope to caper about the room with her like that. It would take years for him to grasp so elaborate a dance.

But just to touch her hand. To watch her turning before him and beside him. So close he could see her individual eyelashes kissing her cheeks. To simply hold her.

He sighed. The wanting was pain and pleasure at once.

Suddenly, Bredon was at his elbow.

"Good to see you here, Sinclair. I half-expected you wouldn't come."

"I wouldn't have but for you," Lawrence said, not taking his eyes from the dancers. "We both know you're the only reason I was invited in the first place."

"Nonsense. You're prime meat on the market, man." Bredon gave him a friendly slap on the back. "Since you came in, you've been noted by no less than half a dozen matrons with daughters of marriageable age."

"Can't imagine why." Lawrence shook his head, only half-listening as he took a step to the right, the better to keep Caroline in his sight. "I'm not seeking a wife."

Just seeking Caroline.

"Doesn't matter. Most of the time, a man's wishes don't figure into it at all," Bredon said amiably. "As a collective, the female of the species consider it their duty to see every eligible gentleman suitably leg-shackled."

"And yet you remain unattached."

"Yes, well, that's the thing about being heir apparent. There's no room for romance in the life of a peer. My parents certainly weren't a love match. Mother came with a dowry that would tempt a prince." Bredon's tone turned a little bit brittle. "When I finally wed—and please God, may that day be in the far-distant future—it will be an arrangement for the betterment of the estate and not much else."

"But you recommend marriage for the likes of me?"

"Absolutely. Of all the fellows I know, you most need a woman in your life. Someone to pull you out of yourself. You may not be the most amiable fellow in the ton, or the most attentive." Bredon waved a hand before Lawrence's face, as if to wake him from a trance. Lawrence grimaced and then turned his gaze back to Caroline's lithe form. "But you make up for those deficiencies with other attributes."

"It certainly isn't my bottomless purse."

Maybe if he were well-heeled, things would be different with Caroline. A lavish income might make up for not having a title when it came to courting an earl's daughter. Lawrence began to wish he hadn't resigned his commission. Plenty of fellows who did a tour of duty in India did come home as rich as maharajas. He'd been frugal and had invested the bulk of his money well enough that he had sufficient funds to purchase the major's rank Colonel Boyle offered him. Would Caroline wait for him to make his fortune? Perhaps if—

Bredon cleared his throat, dragging Lawrence back to the moment.

"Best keep your voice down. Talking about money in public, especially the lack of it, isn't exactly the done thing, old son," Bredon advised. "Wait until you've some privacy and are negotiating a generous dowry. As for what the marriage-minded mamas see in you, plenty of families would relish a connection to the powerful house of Ware."

"If they hope for it through me, it would be a tenuous connection at best."

"The depth of your estrangement from your uncle isn't common knowledge. For all the ton knows, Ware will be providing a spectacular endowment for you and a future bride. And speaking of Lord Ware," Bredon added, leaning toward him and lowering his voice to a whisper, "I think you should know he's here. In the card room."

"Whist was always his game. He can't resist it." Lawrence shrugged. He told himself it didn't matter that the man who'd cast him out was breathing the same perfume-laden air as he. His gut twisted all the same.

"Lord Ware has been paying court to Miss Braithwaite for the last few weeks," Bredon said.

"So I heard."

"I understand she's the oldest of nine siblings—eight of them brothers."

"Hence my uncle's interest in her."

Lawrence caught himself staring at a fixed point on the wall across the room instead of following the dancers. Thoughts of Lord Ware siring an heir on Miss Braithwaite put his dilemma with Caroline in stark perspective. He was one heartbeat from inheriting an earldom, but that was the trouble with being heir presumptive. It was never a sure thing. A son arriving late in Lord Ware's life could knock him out of line for his uncle's title with its first squalling breath.

And without even the hope of succession, Lawrence was out of his depth with a lady like Caroline. Anyone with eyes could see it.

"'A cat may look at a king,'" he murmured as he watched her float like an angel past him, "but that's all he may do."

His feelings for Caroline had clouded his vision. There was no path forward with her. It was foolish to torture himself with wild possibilities. Lawrence raised his voice a bit. "The earl is not seeking a wife. He's looking for breeding stock."

"True, but that sort of blunt observation is best kept to yourself," Bredon said. "Knowing a thing is fine. Saying that same thing is not always the most prudent course of action. Especially when there are so many ears about."

Bredon had brought up the subject of Miss Braithwaite. Lawrence had only carried it to its logical conclusion. London Society and what was permissible within it baffled him sorely.

"I don't understand, Bredon. You say I mustn't speak my mind, but it's fine for a young woman to be traded like cattle so her family can claim relation to a title." Lawrence shook his head and wished his waistcoat wasn't quite so tight. He should have stayed in Leicester Square. It was getting harder to breathe in Lord Frampton's elegant drawing room by the minute. "How do you bear living with all these confounded rules?"

"Habit is everything. I've known from birth what is expected of me. Life is easier if one lets the stream carry one along."

Lawrence had been expected to fail.

But I didn't, he told himself stubbornly.

His uncle had laid down obstacles at every turn, but he'd found a way around them. He might not have been a candidate for Oxford like his friend Bredon, but he'd passed his finals at Harrow with better marks than half the other lads. His uncle had expected him to meet Death in the military, and indeed, Lawrence had been close enough to shake hands with that bony specter on several occasions, but he'd survived.

And here he was in London. Accepted among the ton. Perhaps mostly because of his connection to Bredon, but he was an honored guest of Lord Frampton's nevertheless.

The hope that had been a guttering candle only a few moments before flickered again in his chest. He couldn't give up.

He wouldn't fail now. There must be some way ahead for him with Lady Caroline. He simply couldn't see it yet.

Then the man she was dancing with turned his way and Lawrence got his first clear look at him.

Rowley.

Over the months Lawrence had spent in Bredon and Rowley's company, he'd come to respect the one and despise the other. Lord Rowley was a whoremonger and lotus-eater. He drank to excess. A poor gambler, he reneged on debts of honor, slipping out of town before his creditors could track him down. Once, he had whipped a prostitute till she was covered with welts before Lawrence found him and put a stop to it.

"I paid dearly for the girl," Rowley had complained, telling Bredon he should try it. "Nothing makes a man feel more alive than giving a woman a smart bum."

If Lawrence had known what Rowley was like, he'd have left him to rot in that Italian jail. After the three of them fell in together, Lawrence was glad when Bredon began to pull away from his childhood friend.

"Bredon, you know what Rowley is," Lawrence said, his voice low with menace. "Why do you allow him to dance with your sister?"

"If there's a cobra in the room, I prefer to see it. At least I know where it is," Bredon said, his jaw stiff. "It's only a dance. Rowley can't harm her here."

A red mist settled on Lawrence's vision. He wasn't aware of the exact moment when his fingers balled into fists, but fire burned behind his eyes. If he released the violent part of himself he kept so tightly bottled up, he could happily tear Rowley apart.

It was no exaggeration. Once he unleashed that fury, he might not be able to stop himself before he bashed in Rowley's head on Lady Frampton's gleaming hardwood.

If Lawrence killed a lord on English soil before so many witnesses, he'd certainly swing for it. Lawrence decided it might be worth hanging to keep Rowley's bloody hands off Caroline.

Then, for the first time since he'd started watching her, she saw him. Their gazes locked, and she smiled.

Damn her smiles. They gnawed on his heart.

But then her expression turned to wide-eyed alarm, and that was infinitely worse.

This sort of thing never happens to ladies in Zanzibar. I'd stake my best frock on it.
—from the diary of Lady Caroline Lovell, who wished there were a way to find herself on those exotic shores that very instant.

Chapter 17

Caroline read impending mayhem in Lawrence's dark eyes. Violent intent was scored in the deep line between his brows and the tautness of his jaw.

I take it back. I definitely don't want to see the lion uncaged.

Then Lawrence's gaze shifted to Oliver, and she realized his ill will wasn't directed toward her.

At least not the lion's share of it.

Her heart hammered in a way that had nothing to do with the exertion of dancing.

The music slowed to its stately end as she and Rowley completed their final tableau. Lord and Lady Frampton's guests erupted in applause before the last strains of the string quartet faded. Then, ahead of anyone else who wished to congratulate her and Lord Rowley on a well-executed minuet, Lawrence appeared before them.

"Lady Caroline," he said simply as he bowed to her curtly.

Not trusting her voice, she dipped in a shallow curtsy to acknowledge him. Bredon's account of how Lawrence had laid out four guards unaided ran through her mind in lurid detail. It had been exciting to imagine him beating them senseless when the outcome of the brawl was saving her favorite brother.

Surely Lawrence wouldn't resort to that kind of violence at a ball.

Once, she'd attended an anthropology lecture during which the speaker contended that ancient man often fought for the right to claim a mate. Her imagination quickly conjured up a pair of sweaty, determined males ready to knock each other into next week. For the duration of the lecture, her imaginary brutes kept her well entertained. But according to the expert, they'd finally traded their clubs for plowshares. Caroline had thought it a pity at the time. The idea of men battling for their women had a certain appeal. But that was only in her private musings. Now she was in Lady Frampton's oh-so-proper drawing room. She'd never live it down if Rowley and Lawrence caused a scene, much less came to blows, over her.

Still, her imagination taunted her with the thought that both Lawrence and Oliver might look more than passably intriguing dressed in animal skins and wielding clubs.

"Sinclair, you old stick," Rowley said with every appearance of joviality. Caroline, however, was close enough to note the tic in his jaw. "I haven't seen you out and about of late. Where've you been keeping yourself?"

"I haven't been in hiding, Rowley. Perhaps it's you." The man fairly bristled. "I daresay you avoid your creditors. That may account for me being difficult for you to find."

"That's uncalled for, sir." Rowley narrowed his eyes at the insult, but he didn't deny it as he took a step back. Caroline didn't blame him for moving out of arm's reach. Lawrence's intense glare would have quelled a stouter heart than Oliver's. "Charm has never been your strong suit, Sinclair, but check your bearings. That scowl of yours is likely to scare the ladies."

"It seems to have scared someone."

Nevertheless, Lawrence made an effort to relax his fierce expression. It was not much of an improvement. Caroline couldn't classify it as a smile. It was more as if he bared his teeth at Rowley.

Then Lawrence turned toward her. His body was still tense, but the false smile eased a bit.

"I hope I haven't terrified you, Lady Caroline. That was never my intent," Lawrence said as if Rowley were not still standing by, looking on with a glower to rival Lawrence's previous scowl. "If I have, I beg your pardon. And to show you've forgiven me, perhaps you'll allow me the pleasure of the next dance."

His firm tone made it sound more like a demand than a request. A resounding *no* danced on her tongue.

Both Lawrence and Oliver were behaving like overgrown school boys, and she'd have liked nothing better than to be quit of the pair of them. But thanks to Lady Frampton's belief that her guests should fill in their own dance cards, Caroline didn't have the ready excuse that the next dance was already spoken for. In fact, her card was still blank. She'd been dancing the exhibition minuet with Rowley during the time when other gentlemen might have requested a dance with her later in the evening.

She had no choice. She had to accept Lawrence's invitation.

"Yes, I'll dance with you, Mr. Sinclair," she said stiffly. "It seems the best way to keep you out of trouble."

This time his smile reached up to his dark eyes.

The real smile helped. She felt even better about her decision to dance with Lawrence when she realized her acceptance probably also saved Rowley from a fight he would no doubt lose. A man could bear bruises better than being made to look foolish.

The dance master called for a country dance and the quartet began to play a few introductory bars as the lines of dancers formed up. Lawrence offered her his arm, giving Rowley one final glare as Caroline rested her fingertips lightly on his sleeve.

She was relieved to let him lead her away from Oliver. She was even more thankful that Lawrence remembered Frederica's advice about finding a place at the foot of the pair of lines. It would give him time to find a more amenable frame of mind before he had to dance. And a chance to review the steps by sneaking glances at the other couples' feet.

But while Lawrence seemed to relax during the respite, Caroline grew more annoyed. How could he have put her into such a potentially embarrassing situation?

She took the opportunity to whisper to him when they came together between the two lines. "Just what do you think you are doing?"

"Dancing with you," he whispered back before they separated and returned to their respective places.

The man has a gift for the obvious. She narrowly resisted the urge to give a decidedly unladylike snort.

"You know perfectly well what I meant," she hissed when they danced forward again to circle each other this time. "Why were you trying to quarrel with Rowley?"

"If I wanted to quarrel with him, he'd be on the floor now," Lawrence said softly enough for only her to hear as they continued their circuit. "I gave him a warning, nothing more. That man has no business dancing with a lady."

"Perhaps a lady would like to decide that for herself," she said on the next pass, her voice increasing in volume but still well disguised by the music. Irritation raked her spine. It was beyond frustrating to carry on a conversation with eight or more bars of music stretched between each interaction.

"Perhaps a lady doesn't have sufficient information to make the right determination," he answered before moving back to his line, out of speaking range.

Of all the cheek! She'd never expected Lawrence to be the sort who thought a woman couldn't make decisions for herself. She barely waited until they met palm-to-palm before saying in a normal voice, "Perhaps a gentleman should give a lady such information instead of tiptoeing around with mere innuendo."

What followed this remark was worthy of a Greek tragedy.

The string quartet chose that instant to lift their bows in unison for a half note rest. In the sudden silence, Caroline finished her thought with "Honestly, Lawrence, you are as bad as Lady Ackworth."

The words echoed from the walls and set the chandelier's crystals humming. They were followed by a collective gasp from the rest of Lord Frampton's guests.

Caroline's knees might have buckled if Lawrence hadn't squeezed her hand just then and whispered, "Steady on."

The quartet picked up where they'd left off as if Caroline hadn't committed the faux pas of the decade.

"Concentrate on the steps," Lawrence advised as he waltz-stepped, more or less correctly, back to his place in line.

Against all Caroline's expectations, the wretched dance continued.

Mother must be having a fit of apoplexy.

But Caroline couldn't see Lady Chatham without turning her head and drawing even more attention to herself. Perhaps her mother had excused herself and was hiding in the retiring room, cowering in shame over her ill-behaved daughter.

Lud, I wish I could join her.

When she met Lawrence in the middle of the two lines again, he asked, "How much longer is this dance?"

"Twenty minutes." Perhaps she should feign a fit of vapors. It would at least get her off the dance floor.

"Good," he said. "It will give people time to forget what they think they heard."

"Are you mad? They didn't think it. They heard it and they'll never forget. Lady Ackworth certainly won't."

And again the music called for a half-note rest just as Caroline said the old gossip's name. She couldn't seem to stop the words that came next. They tumbled from her lips of their own accord into the gaping silence. "That woman holds a grudge till it squeals to be let go."

Red-faced, Caroline felt as if she were watching herself from outside her own body. Surely this wasn't really happening. Or if it was, it wasn't really happening to her.

During the next pass, she and Lawrence were supposed to place a hand on each other's cheeks as they circled. He managed to also place his thumb squarely across her mouth.

"Might I suggest you refrain from speaking for the duration of the dance?"

She nodded. Yes, that was exactly what she needed to do. In fact, she might never speak again.

It should have been simple enough. All she need do was keep her feet moving in time to the music. Unfortunately, under the lilting melody of the strings, she heard a buzzing sound, as if a hive had been upturned. When she glanced around the room, careful to flick only her gaze, not turning her head, she saw the word spreading. A quick tête-à-tête behind a fan here, a leaned-in whisper there, Caroline's ill-timed utterances were flying around the room.

If Lady Ackworth hadn't heard what Caroline had said about her firsthand, she'd no doubt receive countless second- and thirdhand versions of it.

There was no way around it. When Lady Ackworth and her minions finished their work, Caroline's social standing would be reduced to rubble. She'd read about unfortunate folk in India who belonged to no caste at all and had no place in society Perhaps she ought to revise her travel plans to include that subcontinent, where she might find some kindred spirits.

No, Zanzibar is still my siren song.

The next time she came together with Lawrence, she couldn't resist a sigh. And a word or two.

"There's never a ship bound for Zanzibar when you need one," she said wistfully, then realized she'd spoken aloud in yet another sudden silence. The lifting of the quartet's bows had caught her again. "Oh, for heaven's sake! How many rests can there be in one dratted piece of music?"

After the short, prescribed rest, the strings continued to drone on.

There was no point in continuing to dance. She couldn't pretend she hadn't been caught acting like a complete ninny again.

The broad double doors at the far end of the drawing room had been propped open to let in fresh night air. They were perfectly lovely doors, Spanish made, with iron studs and carvings of angels and lutes and pear trees. At any other time, Caroline would have been fascinated by the bulky foreignness of the design.

But she wasn't drawn to the Spanish doors. Instead, the dark opening between them called to her.

Not waiting for the music to end abruptly again, Caroline clutched her skirt to lift her hem slightly. Moving quickly, yet trying not to seem hurried, she abandoned Lawrence in line. She pressed through the crowd that ringed the dance floor and made for the way out with as much dignity as she could muster.

Only at the last second did she begin to run.

*None of us can turn back the hands of a clock. But that doesn't stop us
from wishing we could undo the past.*
—Lawrence Sinclair, who would undo several things, given half a chance.

Chapter 18

Lawrence had wanted to be alone with her so badly it bordered on
sickness. He'd imagined several circumstances whereby he might spirit
Caroline out of the ballroom and into Lady Frampton's moonlit garden.

This was not one of them.

He left the line right after she did. It made no sense for him to remain;
he no longer had a dance partner. He felt no sting from the buzz of whispers
around him. Caroline wasn't running from him. She was running from
her own poor luck. He chafed a bit that he couldn't box the gossips' ears
on Caroline's account, but he bridled himself.

He also didn't follow her out into the garden immediately. It would not
serve her reputation for him to trail her like a puppy. So first, he stopped
at the side table where punch was being served and collected a cup for her.
Then he made his way to the open doorway as unobtrusively as possible.
If he drew more attention to her hasty exit, she wouldn't thank him for
joining her in her heliotrope-scented exile.

The last thing Caroline needed was more scandal.

Once through the door, he stopped under the portico and pulled out the
small flask of whiskey he kept in his waistcoat pocket.

And I thought I'd be the one drowning my sorrows this evening.

He took a sip for himself, then poured a generous amount into the cup
of punch. Then he began to search for Caroline in the darkness. The moon
had slipped behind a bank of clouds, so he couldn't locate her by sight.
Instead, he found her by following the soft sound of sobbing.

She'd gone to ground in a secluded corner of Lady Frampton's neatly organized garden. Under a trellis that had not yet been completely covered by a creeper, seated on a stone bench, Caroline was crying her eyes out.

"Come now. There's no need for tears." He handed her the punch. Before he could warn her about the whiskey, she raised it to her lips and downed the whole cup. She came up sputtering and coughing.

"What on earth was in that?" Caroline wheezed.

"Just a wee dram, as my old fencing master used to say. It's meant to do you good, but not if you knock it back like it was Almack's weak lemonade." Lawrence sat down beside her and patted her back. If she'd been a man, he'd have pounded between her shoulder blades to help her get back her wind. After half a minute, her breathing returned to normal and she calmed down. "There now. Feeling better?"

She heaved a sigh. "No. I'm ruined."

"It's not so bad as that. I'm no expert, but I believe ruination involves much more than merely speaking out of turn." He pulled a handkerchief from his pocket and handed it to her.

She blew her nose like a trumpet. "How can you make light of my disgrace?"

"You're not disgraced," he said. "After all, nobody died."

"My dignity has." Caroline balled the soiled handkerchief in her fist. "And my reputation will die, too, once Lady Ackworth has her way with it."

Lawrence shook his head. "You give her too much credit. Besides, was anything you said untrue?"

"No. She *is* the most dreadful old gossip," Caroline said with vehemence. Then her charitable nature, which he loved so much, rose to the surface. "But I suppose it was unkind of me to point it out so publicly. Oh, for pity's sake, my mother was right." She smacked her knee with her fist. "Every time you speak ill of someone, it *is* a prayer to the devil."

Lawrence chuckled. "Then by those lights, Old Nick must be a right busy fellow."

"Evidently not," she countered. "He certainly answered my ill-begotten prayer with lightning speed."

Lawrence laughed aloud at that.

"How kind of you to find merriment in my misery," she said crossly.

He sobered in an instant. "I'm not laughing at you. Just at the whole situation."

She cast him a glare that ought to have rendered him a pile of smoldering ash.

"A situation that, on second thought, is not at all amusing," he amended hastily. "But you must admit the timing could not have been better if you and the strings had practiced together beforehand."

She scoffed, but the corners of her mouth did turn up briefly. "Never let it be said that Lady Caroline Lovell does anything by halves."

"No one would ever say that," he agreed. "You are a force of nature."

She chuckled a little. "A veritable gale; that's me."

"Besides, not everything you had to say was about Lady Ackworth. What was that part about Zanzibar?"

"Just a place I'm longing to see someday," she said. "In fact, I may have to go there sooner rather than later to hide my shame."

From the smile in her voice, he could tell she wasn't feeling nearly as dispirited as when he'd first joined her on the stone bench.

"Why do you want to visit Zanzibar?" he asked.

"Because it calls to me. I know it's there waiting and it's bound to be beautiful beyond belief, and I've never been anywhere really."

"I've done a fair amount of traveling, but in truth, I've never seen anything as fine as the cliffs of Dover. Compared to England, *anywhere* is overrated."

"How can you say that? Everything would be so very much different in Zanzibar," she said. "The flora and fauna, the food, the people—why, even *I* would be a different sort of person."

"I've never been to Zanzibar," he said, "but I expect you'd not be much different there from who you are here."

"Why is that?"

"Because wherever you roam, you take yourself with you. We cannot run from ourselves. Believe me. I've tried," he admitted. "Besides, you've no need to flee London just yet. In the grand scheme of things, the sin you committed this evening is a very small one, Caroline. Trust me, it will pass."

"What would you know about my sins?"

"Nothing," he admitted. "I only know mine, which is heavy enough knowledge."

"Oh! I know a bit about your sins, too," she said, suddenly brightening for some odd reason. "Teddy told me how you and he met. And about how you flattened the jail guards so you could all escape."

She made it seem as if he'd done something grand. She had no idea that he'd unleashed such pent-up fury in that Italian prison; it was only by God's grace that he'd merely rendered those men unconscious.

"Did Bredon tell you how I came to be incarcerated in the first place?"

She shook her head.

Lawrence had imagined confessing his past to her. It seemed he was going to get the chance to see if her reaction was the one he'd imagined as well. "I killed a man."

To his great relief, she didn't flee from him screaming.

"You served in the military, Lawrence," she said gently. "I daresay you've killed a great number of men. But in your defense, they were all trying to kill you as well."

"No," he said. "This was after I resigned from the dragoons and sold my commission."

"Oh." Silence yawned between them for what seemed like ages. Then, finally, she said, "I'm sure you must have had reason."

Lawrence nodded. He'd had too much to drink one night in Rome, and as he staggered back in the direction of his lodgings, he was stopped by a fellow who made him an indecent offer that sobered him in a heartbeat. The man had a pair of children he was selling by the hour.

"*Ragazza o ragazzo?* Girl or boy, your choice, *signore*," the man said, and named a ridiculously low price. Wide-eyed and slight of build, the boy who cowered behind the man reminded Lawrence of his cousin Ralph.

To this day, he couldn't remember taking his first swing at the man. He only came to himself after the *carabinieri* pulled him off the pimp. Lawrence had no clear memory of repeatedly dashing the man's head against the cobblestone street, but the blood spoke for itself.

The children he'd hoped to recue had fled, probably to escape the mad Englishman. They were nowhere to be seen.

"Do you want to tell me why you killed him?" Caroline asked in a whisper.

"No." He couldn't tell Caroline something so ugly. "Only that he needed killing. And at the time, I needed to do it."

She was still as stone for long moments. Then she reached over and laid her hand on his. Her lace-gloved fingertips were cool and soothing. Like a healing balm.

"Then that is all I need to know," she said. "We will speak no more of this."

Over the years, he'd often wished he could weep over his misdeeds, but he'd never been able to squeeze out a single tear. Not even at Ralph's funeral. The sorrow stayed bottled up, seething and writhing. With each passing year, other sins only added to the load.

He'd told Caroline his darkest deed, yet she hadn't rejected him. Something broke inside him then, and without knowing how it happened, he realized his cheeks were suddenly damp.

Caroline reached up and wiped away the tears.

"You're a good man, Lawrence Sinclair," she said. "Anyone who says otherwise will answer to me."

The moon peeped out from behind the clouds at that moment, and Lawrence saw that Caroline's cheeks were shining with tears, too.

"Forgive me. I've made you cry," he said, palming her face.

"It's not you," she said with a tremulous smile. "If anyone weeps in my presence, I can't help but join in. Were I not a lady, and unable to take up an occupation, I might have made a fortune as a professional mourner."

Shaking his head in amazement, he chuckled. How this woman made him smile, even in the midst of the most serious things. It was her greatest gift.

"I would not have you mourn at all. Not ever." He slowly drew his thumb over her bottom lip. "What must I do to make you happy again?"

She met his gaze, her eyes enormous in the moonlight. "Kiss me."

* * * *

In that breathless moment, she still wasn't sure she'd said the words aloud. She only knew they were about to burst out of her heart.

Caroline had never been kissed by any of the fellows who'd courted her during previous Seasons. Not that plenty of them hadn't tried. Caroline had always found a way to avoid such an encounter, even if it meant ducking and fleeing. She'd simply never wanted any of their soppy, slobbering mouths anywhere near hers. A kiss was unwarranted because she didn't feel a thing for any of those gentlemen. Besides, it would surely be an extremely messy enterprise.

Now she ached for Lawrence to cover her lips with his.

He was intensely focused on her, but she didn't feel afraid. She didn't know what she was feeling. The way her insides tingled didn't have a proper name.

His hands, still cupping her cheeks, held her perfectly still while he closed the distance between them. When he stopped a finger's width from her mouth, she nearly wept afresh. Then he leaned the rest of the way and touched his lips to hers.

They were warm and not at all soppy. Then he slanted his mouth over hers and groaned softly. The deep sound made her close her eyes, the better simply to feel. She wanted to open her mouth, to take him in somehow, though she had no idea where that idea came from, or what might happen if she did.

He tasted faintly like the burning liquor he'd put into her punch. She hadn't liked it in the cup, but on his mouth, the taste was intoxicating. The smell of him, all leather and sandalwood with a hint of bergamot, made her breathing come faster and faster. The world began to spin a bit and she wondered if she might faint.

She melted a bit inside. She was becoming part of him. She nearly forgot her own name.

"Caroline!"

Oh, yes, that's it.

But it wasn't Lawrence who'd said it. She'd know that frenzied tone anywhere. She pulled away from him and slid as far as the stone bench allowed.

"It's Horatia," she said, pressing a hand to her cheek, thankful no one could see her blush in the dark garden. "She must be looking for me."

"Could be worse," Lawrence grumbled. "Could be Lady Ackworth."

Caroline was amazed that she could laugh again so soon after her total humiliation. Lawrence had a way of putting everything in perspective. She swept her tongue over her bottom lip.

And a way of setting the world on its ear.

He rose from their secluded arbor and waved a hand to draw her friend's attention. Horatia had been searching frantically for her by the hydrangea, where she'd stumbled across another couple in the dark, but now she dashed to the trellis and bench.

"Oh, Caroline," Horatia said, wringing her hands. "You've got to come quickly."

"Why? What's wrong?"

"It's Freddie. I can't find her anywhere. It's nearly time for the supper dance and you know how excited she was about dancing it with Lord Rowley." Horatia shifted her weight from one foot to the other, clearly agitated. "I can't imagine why she'd disappear just now."

"Is Rowley still in the ballroom?" Lawrence asked gruffly.

Horatia blinked several times, considering. "No. I don't believe so."

"Come then," Lawrence said, taking charge of the situation. He grabbed Caroline's hand and raised her to her feet. "We've no time to lose."

Our vicar tells us we are all capable of change, of being more than the sum of our parts. In theory, I'm inclined to agree. But in practice, are we prepared to do the work required for such a metamorphosis? Ah, there's the rub. Loathe as I am to admit it, Lawrence may be right. We are what we are. Few of us have the will to change our fundamental nature. And that means even a visit to Zanzibar wouldn't change mine.
—from the diary of Lady Caroline Lovell, who would still like to give Zanzibar a try.

Chapter 19

The supper dance had started by the time Lawrence and Caroline followed Horatia back into the drawing room. Couples were gliding around the dance floor in a waltz. He wished he could pull Caroline out onto the gleaming hardwood with him. It would have been a poor substitute for kissing her in the garden, but at least he'd still have been able to hold her.

Frederica had picked the worst possible time to disappear.

"If we split up, we will be able to cover more ground," he said.

"Agreed." Caroline stood on tiptoe, craning her neck to see if her friend was on the dance floor. When her search was fruitless, she settled back down into her flat-soled slippers. "Horatia and I will go to the ladies' retiring room."

"But I've looked there already," Horatia whispered frantically.

"We'll look again, just in case you missed Freddie the first time. If any of us find her, we should bring her back to the drawing room immediately." She shot a meaningful glance at Lawrence. "No matter what we discover, there must be no…unpleasantness."

He nodded, her message received. Very well. No thrashing of Rowley on the premises. But if Oliver was trying to ruin yet another young lady,

Lawrence meant to call him to account, even if it had to be in a different time and place.

After Caroline and Horatia started up the long staircase to the first story, Lawrence made his way to the card room. He hadn't expected to find Frederica playing piquet, but anything was possible.

He did, however, see his uncle and caught the old man's eye for a few uncomfortable moments. Lord Ware glared at him from across the room. Lawrence recognized the expression, and it took him back almost two decades.

Lawrence had reached the spot where Ralph fell first, but Lord Ware had been hard on his heels. His uncle had been frantic, wailing hysterically as he'd knelt beside his son's twisted body, trying hopelessly to straighten his lifeless limbs. When Lord Ware had looked up at Lawrence, the anger and loathing in his eyes had been so palpable, he'd buckled under his uncle's malevolent gaze. Now, no matter how many years had passed, the earl still blamed him for Ralph's accident. The crushing accusation sizzled once more between them, but this time Lawrence didn't look away.

He'd accepted the guilt when he was younger because if his uncle decreed something, it must be so. Time and distance had allowed Lawrence to rethink the events of that terrible day. Now he knew his cousin's death hadn't been his fault.

But Lord Ware's view of the past obviously hadn't changed. Lawrence was responsible for robbing him of his heir.

However, Lawrence didn't have time to settle matters with his uncle at present. He had to find Rowley and Miss Tilbury before someone else did.

Rowley was perfectly capable of ruining Caroline's friend. He used women as if they were nothing. One night and it was blithely on to the next. But Lawrence was even more concerned that Rowley would put Frederica into a compromising position for another selfish purpose. The young viscount was habitually light in the pockets, but word in White's was that now Rowley was deep in Dun territory. He might even have to petition the Crown to allow him to sell off part of his estate to pay back his creditors. That was a downward spiral from which few noble houses ever recovered.

However, Miss Frederica Tilbury's hand came with a princely dowry. Better men than Rowley had married a fortune with feet. Some honored their wealthy wives by using the infusion of cash to settle their debts and reestablish their estates on a firm foundation.

But it was very tempting to spend someone else's money on frivolity and riotous living.

Lawrence had no illusions about which path Rowley would follow. Miss Tilbury's dowry would be squandered and she'd be left with a philandering husband and severely reduced means. Lawrence couldn't allow that to happen to Caroline's friend.

After he'd scoured all the rooms on the ground floor without success, he used the servants' staircase at the back of the house to ascend to the upper stories. Only ladies ventured up the main stairs to the retiring room above. The back staircase was likely the way Rowley had lured Miss Tilbury to a remote part of the town house.

When he stepped through the plain door separating the servants' stairwell from the public part of the home, he was greeted by feminine chatter coming from the far end of the long hallway. The retiring room was no doubt in a parlor with windows facing the street in front of the town house. But there were a number of closed doors between him and that female enclave. If Caroline and Horatia were looking there, he would likely meet them in the middle as he searched the other rooms.

And if they didn't find Frederica on this floor, there were still two more stories above them.

Mostly bedrooms there, Lawrence thought grimly.

The first door he came to was locked.

Likely Lord Frampton's study.

When he came to the next door, he didn't even have to open it to know it was his host's smoking room. The sweet scent of pipe tobacco wafted into the hallway from under the door.

Along with the sound of a stifled cry.

Lawrence shoved the door open. Lit by a couple of wall sconces flanking the small fireplace, the room was paneled with rich mahogany. Its furniture was heavy and masculine. Leather wing chairs flanked a table inlaid with ivory. A chess game in progress was set up atop it. From the stuffed boar's head over the fireplace to the heavy damask curtains at the windows, the space was the picture of masculine civility.

But in the corner, near one of the two tall windows, Rowley had Miss Tilbury pinned to the wall with his body. He was kissing her passionately and, just as passionately, she was pounding his shoulders with her small gloved fists.

"Let her go." Lawrence didn't say it loudly, but his voice was so silky with menace, Rowley released her at once and turned to face him. Frederica seized her chance and skittered away from him.

"Oh, what you must think of me, Mr. Sinclair." Freddie hurried to him. Rowley had pulled the pins from her lovely blond hair, and even to

Lawrence's untrained eye, her carefully styled coiffure was now a jumbled mess. "This is not at all what I wanted…I mean…I didn't intend to let him…please, you must believe me."

"I do."

"You see, Lord Rowley told me there was a secret passage in this house, and rumors of a treasure from long ago, and…well, who can resist a hunt for a hidden treasure?"

"Who indeed?" he said, not taking his gaze from Rowley.

"You won't tell anyone you found us like this?" she said, tears trembling on her lashes.

When he shook his head, he feared Freddie might collapse in relief. At that moment, Caroline and Horatia appeared in the open doorway. Freddie fled into their arms, where she collapsed in earnest.

"Take her someplace quiet where you can fix her hair before the two of you go down for supper," Caroline said quietly to Horatia. "Not the retiring room."

"No indeed. Far too many wagging tongues in there. I'll make sure no one sees her before I've put everything to rights. Come, dear." Putting her arm around Frederica, Horatia led her from the room.

Caroline didn't leave with the other two women, but instead closed the door behind them. "Explain yourself, Oliver."

"What can I say, Caro? I am besotted with Miss Tilbury."

"I love Frederica like a sister," she said, "but I find myself doubting that."

Lawrence was glad Caroline was doing the talking. He was having enough trouble trying to keep from throttling the man.

"If you cared about Freddie," Caroline went on, "you wouldn't have put her into such a compromising position. Her reputation would be in tatters if anyone other than we had discovered the two of you alone here."

"Well, hello, Kettle. This is Pot," Rowley said with a smarmy smile. "Weren't you and Sinclair similarly alone in Lady Frampton's moonlit garden earlier? I saw him follow you out there."

"It's not at all the same thing," she said, color rising in her cheeks. "I was clearly upset by the ill-considered things I said about Lady Ackworth. After I removed myself from the ballroom, he simply followed me out to the garden to console me with a cup of punch."

Rowley scoffed. "If you say so."

"You're in no position to dispute the lady's word, Rowley," Lawrence said, his fingers balling into fists as he took a step toward the viscount.

Caroline raised a warning hand and he stopped advancing. "Mr. Sinclair and I were within easy view of anyone who cared to stroll amid the blooms.

That's very different from being hidden away behind the closed door of Lord Frampton's smoking room."

Rowley splayed his hands before him in entreaty. "Caro, it's not like you to think the worst of someone. You know me."

Her rigid posture said she wasn't so sure she did.

"Honestly, I wouldn't hurt Miss Tilbury for worlds," Rowley protested. "And if by chance we had been discovered by someone other than you and Sinclair, why, I'd have done the honorable thing and married the girl in a thrice. As I said, I'm besotted with her."

"Besotted with her dowry you mean," Lawrence said.

"That's a bit harsh."

"But it's true. And here's another truth." Lawrence didn't let Caroline stop him this time. He crossed the room until he stood nose-to-nose with Rowley. "You are suddenly looking very pale, my friend. I fear you've become quite ill. In fact, you need to take your leave of this house immediately."

Rowley took half a step back, but still shot Lawrence a challenging glare. "Nonsense, Sinclair. I feel fine."

"A man's health can take a sudden turn when he least expects it. Go now while you can." Lawrence didn't move a muscle until Rowley dropped his gaze. "And after you quit this assembly, you should make plans to remove from London. A long rustication at your country estate is in order—say, until the current Season is finished at least. The rest would do you a world of good."

"But I have no need to hide away."

"You're not listening, old friend." He'd promised Caroline there'd be no mayhem, but he hadn't promised not to intimidate Rowley into submission. After all, Oliver knew better than most the kind of violence Lawrence was capable of. "Ignoring a sudden illness can be dangerous. I'd hate to see you catch your death."

"That sounds like a threat," Rowley said, glancing at Caroline for support and finding none. "Caro, you can't let him do this to me."

"I rather think I can."

Lawrence had never loved her more. She not only trusted him to keep the situation and himself under control, she didn't sound the least bit afraid of him either.

"So let us speak plainly," Lawrence said. "Here are the terms for your recuperation from sudden *illness*. You will never seek out Miss Tilbury again. Is that understood?"

Rowley nodded, not meeting his eyes.

"And if I find you are trying to entrap another young lady into a mésalliance, I will visit you when you least expect it. Your affliction will be sudden and devastating."

"Then I'm doomed to bachelorhood on your say-so," Rowley complained.

"No. You're doomed to playing fair. If you wish to honestly court a young woman by approaching her family with your intent, and they approve, I will not intervene," Lawrence said. "But I shall not allow you to ruin another lady or take advantage of one."

"Another?" Caroline said, aghast. Lawrence was so focused on Rowley, he'd forgotten for a moment she was even in the room.

"Pay him no mind," Rowley said to reassure her. "My friend is upset over nothing."

"I'm not your friend." Lawrence itched to wipe that glib smile from Rowley's lips, but he settled for snatching Rowley up by his lapels and slamming him against the wall. He held him there, his toes barely touching the floor. "Gadding about the Continent, leaving a trail of by-blows in your wake, is not nothing. The daughter of the Conte di Vitelli was not nothing. And when she walked into the sea with stones in her pockets because you'd abandoned her and the child she carried, it was not nothing."

Caroline gasped softly behind him. He knew he shouldn't speak of such things with a lady present, but Rowley always seemed to find a way to hide behind a woman's skirts.

Not this time.

Rowley's gaze darted to Caroline nervously. "Sinclair, a bit of discretion, if you please."

"How ironic. The King of Indiscretion can still plead for it," Lawrence said as he lowered Rowley till he could stand on his own. Then he stepped back and motioned toward the door. "Now, make your excuses to our hosts and leave before I haul you down the stairs and throw you out."

Part of him wished Rowley would continue to protest so he'd have an excuse to do it. However, the viscount made a huffing sound and started to stamp from the room.

"One more thing," Lawrence said before he reached the threshold. Rowley stopped but didn't look back at him. "If I hear a whiff of scandal about Miss Tilbury, I shall know whom to blame. And whom to punish."

Rowley flinched slightly, then opened the door and stalked into the dim corridor.

Relieved, Lawrence drew a deep breath. He finally let his fists uncurl. The urge to pummel Rowley had been strong, but he'd mastered it. He was getting better at controlling himself instead of settling things with his fists.

"Well," Caroline said, crossing the room to him. "Strange as it may seem, this sorry situation has made me feel better."

"In heaven's name, why?"

"I no longer feel as if my ill-timed words were the worst scandal of the night," she said lightly. "Of course, no one will ever hear about Rowley and that poor Italian lady, so only my misdeeds are public knowledge, but at least I know I'm not the vilest person present."

"You could never be vile."

"Ah, but I can be tempted to it. A word in the right ear—Lady Ackworth comes to mind—and no wellborn family will let Oliver within twenty leagues of their daughters." She leaned in and placed both her palms on his chest. "Promise me, Lawrence. Before you do Rowley physical harm, let me turn Lady Ackworth loose on him."

"That would be worse, you think?"

"Of course," she said with a laugh. "Bruises fade, but gossip lasts forever."

Lawrence laughed with her. "How do you do that?"

"Do what?"

"Make everything seem lighter." He put his hands on her waist and—*Thank you, God!*—she didn't pull away. "No matter how dire the circumstance, you convince me that things are far better than they are."

"Do I? I don't mean to make light of Freddie's narrow escape, of course." She ran her fingertips along his lapel. "But escape she did, so there's no need to wallow in the drama of it, is there?"

Her nearness made him ache. Every bit of him strained toward her, but he held himself back. The soft pinkness of her mouth was torture. The slight indentation in the middle of her top lip called to him, begging him to nip and suckle it.

"Have you considered," he said, his voice ragged, "that you are in need of an escape of your own, my lady?"

She smiled up at him. Trustingly. Invitingly. "Does that mean you intend to put me into a compromising situation?"

He was as bad as Rowley. He didn't deserve Caroline, just as surely as Rowley didn't deserve someone as sweet and well-dowered as Freddie. Anyone looking from the outside would declare the two pairings similarly ill-advised. Both men were reaching for the moon. The ladies involved were definitely stooping to meet them.

He'd ordered Rowley to play fair, to declare himself, but he hadn't approached Lord Chatham about courting his daughter. He was a hypocrite of the first water. As much a bounder as Rowley.

The only difference was, Lawrence loved Caroline.

The heat of her sweet body so near his made him toss all thoughts of fair play out the window. "This is your last chance to flee."

"I'm not going anywhere."

With that, Caroline melted into his arms.

Her mouth was all sweet wetness and soft yielding. He struggled not to plunder it. Even more than when he'd resisted the urge to thrash Rowley senseless, he fought not to let himself go now. But it wasn't easy with the length of her sweet body pressed up against his.

He wanted more than anything to have this woman, to feel her beneath him, beside him, and on top of him. To be so tangled up with her, they were one, feeling the same desire, thinking the same thoughts, needing the same release. The wanting was so keen, a knife's edge from pain.

But he didn't dare. She was an innocent. Ladies always were, he'd been told. She had no idea this trembling fire was just the start of something much darker and brighter. Something both holy and profane.

Something he ached to share with her.

She tugged on his lapels and her lips parted. He didn't need to be invited twice. His tongue dove into her mouth. It was the best moment of his life.

God help me, I must marry this woman or die.

Life would be much easier if there were no such thing as duty. No drumroll that calls a man to take the field in defense of king, country, and brothers-in-arms. No pressing need to honor one's commitments. No sense of oughtness that drives a man to give up what he loves most.
Easier? Yes, perhaps, but were I to live that life, I'd not be able to look myself in the eye.
—Lawrence Sinclair, who knew full well what he should do but must drag his soul toward it kicking and screaming.

Chapter 20

He was kissing Lady Caroline. His goddess. His love.

The kiss went on and on. It was a merging of breaths, a joining of souls. Lawrence's whole world spiraled down to heat and raging need. Kissing Caroline was earth-shattering, but it would never be enough.

There had to be more. His body demanded it. Judging from the way she pressed herself against him, hers did, too.

But then the door burst open behind them and Lord Ware stormed into the smoking room. He and Caroline sprang apart from each other like a pair of cats who'd been doused with a bucket of water.

Lawrence stepped in front of her to hide her from his uncle's view. He hadn't shamed her. Not yet. But she might feel as if he had, now that they'd been caught in a compromising situation.

Trust Lord Ware to ruin everything.

"There you are, Nephew. Trying to debauch your betters, just as Lord Rowley said." Ware gave a gruff nod to Caroline, who, against Lawrence's hopes, was peeking around from behind him. "My lady, you may leave at once. You have my promise of complete discretion. I would never allow my cur of a nephew to entrap the daughter of Lord Chatham into such a disastrous mésalliance."

Caroline stepped from behind Lawrence, smoothing the front of her gown and lifting her chin. "That is not at all what is happening here, Lord Ware."

"No, Caroline," Lawrence said softly. The last thing he wanted was for her to defend him. Besides, his uncle was right. "You should go. Your friends are probably already concerned that you haven't joined them and—"

"But—"

"My uncle and I have some things to settle that do not concern you."

Caroline opened her mouth as if she were about to object, but then closed it quickly. Then she dipped in the shallowest of curtsies to his uncle and glided softly from the room, closing the door behind her, but not so completely that the latch clicked. Lawrence was grateful beyond words that she had done his bidding.

It surely wouldn't happen often.

He didn't need her to witness the tangled wreckage that was his relationship with his uncle. She wouldn't understand it. Caroline's family was a boisterous bunch, but she and her brothers held each other in obvious warmth. And while she might not be taking the path Lord and Lady Chatham would choose for her, she loved her parents and they her. The house of Lovell was united in loyalty and affection.

His whole life, Lawrence had wondered what that must feel like. But wondering wouldn't change his situation, and even Caroline's touch of lightness, as full of grace as it was, couldn't mend everything.

Sometimes, not even the truth would set one free.

"So, you lived through the war." His uncle's lip curled.

"Against all your hopes, sir."

Lord Ware snorted. "Well, whatever deficiencies you might have had in book learning, at least you read people well enough. Do you want me to admit it? Very well. Yes, I wished a battle death for you, Nephew. After all, it was the best you could ever hope to achieve."

Once his uncle's vicious tongue would have made Lawrence feel low as a worm. Now he straightened his spine.

"I expect to prove you wrong again. It's been my experience that a man can accomplish anything if he's willing to throw his whole heart into it," Lawrence said. "But your heart is too shriveled to be whole any longer. All I read in you now, sir, is pain and bitterness and the desperate need for your woe to be someone else's fault."

"By God, you insolent pup." His uncle's eyes bugged a bit, and the large vein in his forehead grew more pronounced. "I'm a peer of the realm. You will not speak to me so."

"Yes, I will. I should have done it long ago." Lawrence squared his shoulders as he faced his uncle. "You've blamed me for years, but I accept it no longer. I am not responsible for Ralph's death."

Lord Ware swore so vehemently, it was a wonder a lightning bolt didn't cut through the roof and incinerate him on the spot.

The anger that used to terrify Lawrence now struck him as merely sad. And it didn't change the facts.

"When I was a boy, I accepted every word you said as gospel, even when I knew better," Lawrence said. He might have been only a boy, but he would never have encouraged his cousin to saddle that untested Thoroughbred. He'd been aware, far more than his uncle had, of Ralph's limitations as a rider. "You repeated the charge so often, I came to believe my cousin's death was my fault."

"It *was* your fault. You always had to show him up. That's what made him try the impossible."

"No, sir. It was you who goaded Ralph into that jump."

"The devil you say."

"Your son excelled in the classroom, but you never gave him a word of praise. He'd have licked the sole of your boot for a single 'Well done.' Then, the night before his accident, you berated him for being a third-class rider."

In fact, over a particularly contentious supper, Lord Ware had belittled Ralph incessantly for letting Lawrence, "the shiftless know-nothing," outdo him on horseback. Taking that new stallion over the highest fence in the meadow was the only way Ralph felt he could gain his father's favor.

"He'd have dared anything to prove you wrong," Lawrence said.

"That's a lie. I never said any such thing."

"You did, sir." *That and so many other hurtful, poisonous words over the years.*

Caroline was right. Bruises faded. Harsh words sank into a person's heart and twisted themselves into the soul until they became part of who they were. They sucked the life right out of a body.

"You *forced* him to take that jump," Ware said, pounding a fist into his open palm.

Lawrence clasped his hands behind his back to keep from answering his uncle's threatening gestures with one of his own.

"It's true Ralph rode double with me over many jumps, but I was nowhere near the stables when Ralph had that stallion saddled. If I had been, I'd have stopped him."

The more calmly Lawrence spoke, the more agitated his uncle became. He paced like a caged lynx.

"If it's any comfort to you at all, please know that I still grieve for Ralph. He was more than a brother to me."

"As if the likes of you could be a comfort to anyone." His back stiff, his brow low, Lord Ware made a rude, dismissive gesture. "I suppose now that you've altered the past in your head, you think you're good enough to marry Lady Caroline."

"I know better than that. No one's good enough for her," Lawrence said. "But if she'll have me, yes, I want to marry her."

Lawrence thought he heard a small gasp behind him but allowed it might just have been the wind in the fireplace flue.

His uncle stopped pacing and turned to glare at him. "And you expect Lord Chatham will agree to the match because you're supposedly my heir."

"I hope that will not be his sole consideration. The love I bear his daughter must count for something."

Lord Ware cursed again. "Love counts for spit. And don't harbor any hope of succeeding me, boy. No indeed. You may have robbed me of my first heir, but you won't take the next one."

"Sir?"

His uncle folded his hands over his protruding belly. "I'm wedding Miss Penelope Braithwaite by special license on the morrow."

"That's...sudden." Even by London's marriage mart standards. All Lawrence had heard was that he was paying court to the young lady.

"It's necessary," Lord Ware said with an unpleasant smile, "if you take my meaning."

Lawrence must have cast him a puzzled look.

"She's breeding, you bird wit." Ware shook his head at his nephew's denseness. "You don't have to wonder if the old man can sire an heir to supplant you, Lawrence. I already have."

Of course the child would have to be a son. But the limbs of Miss Braithwaite's family tree drooped heavily with male children. She was the only girl amid a gaggle of boys. Lawrence could already see the odds in White's ledger book. Ware would have his son in less than nine months.

"So you see," Lord Ware went on, "you've dropped from heir presumptive to wastrel nephew cut off without a cent. Best you stop dangling that carrot before the ton."

Lawrence had never made much of his position of inheritance. He'd known somehow that nothing would ever come of it.

But sometimes it's deucedly bad to be right.

"As soon as decently possible after the wedding, I'll make sure Lord Chatham and the rest of the ton knows of the impending birth." His uncle chuckled. "If I were you and set on taking a wife, I'd set my sights far lower than the daughter of an earl."

"I've never hidden the fact that I likely wouldn't inherit."

"Really? Then what were you doing trying to seduce Lady Caroline? Did you think to entrap her?"

"Never. My intentions toward her are noble." *If more than a little lustful,* he admitted to himself. "I intend to marry the lady honestly."

"Really? Lady Caroline is used to fine things—houses, carriage rides, 'rings on her fingers and bells on her toes' and all that. Tell me, only because I need a spot of humor, mind, how do you intend to support a lady such as she?"

How indeed?

Colonel Boyle's offer to lead the newly formed native cavalry came back to tempt him. When his old commander had mentioned it earlier, Lawrence had thought he'd have to leave Caroline behind to answer the call of the drum.

But officers were allowed to marry with their commander's permission. And if he and Caroline tied the knot before he purchased the commission, he wouldn't even need Boyle's consent. He wouldn't have to be separated from her.

Now that Lawrence knew Caroline longed to travel, he could take her with him to India. Each regiment had its own brand of society. It wouldn't be as grand as a London Season, but she'd not want for balls and teas and friendships with the other military wives wherever they were stationed. As Lord Chatham's daughter, she'd always be entitled to be known as the Lady Caroline, but Lawrence could bring her a certain regimental status as the wife of a major as well.

Perhaps we could even stop at Zanzibar along the way.

Making just one of her wishes come true would make him feel like a minor god.

"Well, boy? I asked you a question," the earl thundered, his demand dragging Lawrence out of his daydreams. "Are you just going to stand there wool-gathering?"

"No, sir." Lawrence started toward the door. "I'm going to propose to Lady Caroline."

Before he reached it, he heard the quick patter of footsteps skittering on the hardwood on the other side of the portal. They faded away quickly as whoever it had been put some distance between themselves and the smoking room.

"Wait!" Ware bellowed. "Perhaps you'll want to talk to your lady mother before you make that decision."

Hand on the doorknob, Lawrence's conscience stung him. In his haste to confront his uncle about Ralph's death, he hadn't even asked after his mother's welfare. He held no hardness in his heart toward her for not answering any of his letters. Knowing his uncle, she might not even have received them.

"Of course you'd have to catch her on a good day," the earl went on.

"What do you mean?"

"She has consumption. Last stages, I fear," his uncle said. "It's hard for her to breathe, so her mind is a bit muddled from time to time. You've been gone so long, I doubt she'd even know you."

The wind spilling from his sails, Lawrence sank into one of the wing chairs. Granted, his mother had never been openly demonstrative toward him. The earl had been too controlling for that sort of maudlin display in his house.

But there had been snatches of kindness. Small smiles when Lord Ware wasn't looking. A cold tray sent up when the earl had banished him to his room without supper. The morning he left for Harrow for the first time, she had touched his cheek and mouthed *I love you* softly. No one had ever told him that before.

Sometimes, he wondered if he'd imagined it.

Still, she was his mother. He couldn't run off to India with Caroline without first seeing to the welfare of the woman who'd given him birth.

"I shall travel to Ware as soon as possible."

"Good," his uncle said gruffly. "While you're there, see to your mother's removal to the dower house. When I bring home my new countess, I don't want a sick woman cluttering up the manor."

The dower house on the Ware estate had been an unused structure falling into disrepair when Lawrence was a boy. The derelict cottage had a sagging roof, clogged chimneys, and uneven floors back then. He dreaded to imagine the damp and dry rot it must have suffered since.

It was no place for an invalid, unless one wanted to ensure the sick person wouldn't linger. Lawrence couldn't allow his mother to be shuffled off to such a place.

Lord Ware's face lit with a mirthless grin. He'd thrown yet another obstacle into Lawrence's life, and it gave him obvious satisfaction. He seemed to soak up the misery of others as if it were the finest of wines.

But Lawrence wouldn't feed that particular thirst. He schooled his features into something resembling calm.

"By the time you bring your new bride to Ware Hall, neither my mother nor I will be in residence."

"Your absence," Lord Ware said with a grimace, "is the best wedding gift you could offer."

"Then good-bye, Uncle," Lawrence said. "I do not think we shall meet again."

"Not if there's a God in heaven," Ware agreed with a snort.

"Oh, there is. Never doubt it." Lawrence strode from the room. He trusted the One who weighs hearts to settle matters between him and his uncle.

He just didn't think the good Lord would get around to it soon enough to suit him.

Why do good things take their sweet time to make an appearance, while bad things never make one wait?
—Lady Caroline Lovell, for whom patience is not a virtue.

Chapter 21

Lawrence Sinclair is going to propose!

Caroline barely restrained herself from bursting into song over the news, but, as she was a singer of very little talent, putting the words to melody wouldn't have had the desired effect. So she hugged the knowledge to herself instead. Glowing like a candle, she hurried away from the spot just outside the smoking-room door where she'd been shamelessly eavesdropping, and headed down the corridor in search of her friends.

She might not be able to sing about it, but news like this wouldn't keep.

How fortunate that she'd refrained from latching the door. Caroline had even pushed it ajar just a bit, so she could hear Lawrence's conversation with his uncle.

It explained so much.

Now that she knew more about his early family life, and the source of his estrangement from Lord Ware, she understood him better. And cared for him even more deeply. That lump of tenderness that had started out small had grown to fill her entire chest. She was near to bursting with it.

Caroline was saddened by the snippets she heard about Ralph. Lawrence had taken the death of his cousin hard, his voice betraying suppressed emotion with a little raggedness when he spoke of him. Lord Ware only seemed angry and inconvenienced over the loss of his heir.

Well, he's got another one on the way, Caroline thought, raising a hand to her mouth to hush herself. She'd have to guard her lips or she might let that juicy bit of intelligence slip to her friends. They'd learn about it in due course. Miss Braithwaite would soon be unable to fit into those gowns that vexed Horatia so.

Tongues always wagged when a new bride was brought to childbed early in the marriage. Lady Ackworth and her clique would be counting the months after the wedding on their bony fingers.

"It seems the first child can come at any time," Caroline had overheard her saying once. "But the second always requires nine months."

Her minions had tittered at this bit of wit and went on to rip the new mother's reputation to shreds.

Caroline wouldn't give anyone cause to sully Miss Braithwaite's name ahead of time. Lady Ackworth would see to that eventually.

Besides, being married to Lord Ware would be punishment enough for anyone.

By the time Caroline reached the drawing room, supper was over and the guests were forming lines to dance more reels. She spied Horatia and Frederica accepting requests to dance from her brothers Thomas and Benjamin. Freddie's coiffure had been repaired and her smile looked genuine as she accepted Ben's arm. Evidently, she was none the worse for wear, despite her near disaster with Rowley. Freddie had no doubt put the whole debacle out of her mind.

Sometimes a simple heart is a blessing.

If the near ruination had happened to Horatia, she'd still be obsessed with the drama of it all and would bore her friends to tears by rehashing her narrow escape whenever they were alone.

Caroline was relieved not to see Oliver anywhere. Lawrence might not be able to restrain himself otherwise. She wondered if he might even challenge Oliver to a duel. It was illegal, of course, but she doubted Lawrence would feel himself bound by any law that kept him from protecting a lady's honor.

But as pleased as she was not to see Oliver, she was just as disappointed not to see Lawrence rejoining the rout. She'd felt certain his conversation with Lord Ware was winding down as soon as he'd announced his intention to propose to her. Surely the two weren't still locking horns.

Lawrence wouldn't come down the main staircase as she had, so she positioned herself by a potted palm with a clear view of the almost invisible door that led to the servants' part of the house.

She wondered if he'd propose before the ball ended. Perhaps during the last waltz…

Her view of the door from which she expected Lawrence to emerge was suddenly blocked by the slight form of Lord Henley. A spritely and elegant dance partner, he was one of her father's oldest friends. Henley was a courtly soul who made it his mission in life to rescue every wallflower he saw.

To Lord Henley's kindly eye, Caroline must have seemed as wallflowerish as they came. She had to admit she was trying to blend in with the potted shrubbery. Lord Henley had no way of knowing she was quite happy where she was, and she couldn't very well tell him why her gaze was trained on the servants' door like a tabby on a mouse hole. So, for the third time that evening, good manners required her to accept an offer to dance.

As she and Lord Henley took their places near the foot of the lines, Caroline decided Lawrence would just have to wait until after the reel to propose. In fact, a delay might do him good.

She didn't want him thinking she'd swoon into his arms for the asking, even though that was exactly what she wanted to do.

No. I need to be coy. I need to make him want my hand with all his heart and wonder until the last second whether I'll deign to give it. Yes, a bit of waiting is just what the man needs.

As she moved into the first figures with Lord Henley, she cast another glance toward the door.

Could *she* stand a bit of waiting? Ah! That was the question.

* * * *

The string quartet had been rejuvenated by their supper break and now filled the air with a lilting melody. Conversation among the guests who were watching instead of dancing provided a low, rumbling chatter. They sounded like a flock of ducks to Lawrence, nattering away beneath the higher tones of the violins. Everyone's attention was on the dancers, so no one noticed when he slipped back into the drawing room.

He spied Colonel Boyle standing near the open doors that led out to the garden. His old commanding officer was conversing with a young lady dressed in a pallid lavender gown trimmed with black piping. Her jet earrings gleamed darkly, but she wore no other jewelry.

Lawrence wasn't an expert in ladies' fashions, but he recognized half mourning when he saw it. The loss was distant enough for the woman to have put off her widow's weeds, but fresh enough not to return to wearing more than the palest of colors.

He moved along the perimeter of the room to join the colonel and his companion.

Lawrence was ready to commit to purchasing that major's commission this very night. After all, he couldn't very well ask for Caroline's hand without a way to support her. The military was a respectable profession. She'd be marrying down in the eyes of the ton, but as an officer, he'd still be judged a gentleman. Now that he knew she was keen to travel, he was certain the adventure of living in a far-off land would appeal to her. It would be a romantic and exciting way to begin married life.

The more he thought about it, the more he liked his chances.

"I wonder if I might have a word with you, sir," Lawrence said to his old commander.

"Of course, Sinclair. Fine dancing this evening, what? But where are my manners? Allow me to present you to Mrs. Smythe-Marten." Captain Boyle finished the introductions with a listing of the medals for bravery Lawrence had been awarded during his time of service.

He shifted uncomfortably under the colonel's praise. He never felt he deserved those commendations when most of the time, he had little recollection of his actions on the field. When the warrior within burst out of him, he was driven forward on training and instinct alone. His memory of specific events grew fuzzy, which he counted a blessing, all things considered. Sometimes even the details he did recall felt as though they'd happened to someone else.

"Charmed," Lawrence said to Mrs. Smythe-Marten once the colonel finished his accolades. He made a courtly obeisance over the lady's proffered hand and then straightened to his full height. "Smythe-Marten, you say? That name is familiar to me."

"It should be," Colonel Boyle said. "Mrs. Smythe-Marten's husband served under Macdonell. His actions during the Battle of Waterloo will never be forgotten."

Though Lawrence had fought in that battle as well, there were several fronts and he'd only learned how other companies fared after the smoke cleared. The Duke of Wellington had designated the château of Hougoumont as the strategic forward position of the British army. During the battle, Lieutenant Colonel Sir James Macdonell of Glengarry, with only a thousand foot guards, defended the chateau against a force of eighty-five hundred Frenchmen. Captain Smythe-Marten had commanded the company that guarded the gate of the stronghold, which bore the brunt of the assault, but in the end held firm. Wellington himself said the outcome of the whole battle hung on the fact that the chateau had not been taken.

Captain Smythe-Marten, however, was.

"Your husband was a gallant gentleman and a brilliant officer, ma'am."

Lawrence's words were intended to bring comfort. It was what one said to the bereaved when a man gave his life in the service. But when Lawrence looked into the sad eyes of Captain Smythe-Marten's widow, he saw that his words only meant her husband was dead and she was alone in the world.

Lawrence glanced across the room and saw Caroline dancing with an older gentleman. Her eyes were bright, her color high. She was full of promise. Of life.

For a moment, he imagined her clad in a black gown.

What if, after dragging her to some godforsaken outpost at the foot of the Himalayas, he fell in a skirmish?

She'd be half a world away from her family and friends.

Alone.

His dream of a life with Caroline at his side began to crumble. Not even the promise of showing her the Zanzibar of her dreams could hold it together.

"You said you wished to speak to me, Sinclair." Colonel Boyle eyed him shrewdly. "May I hope that means you've decided to take the commission we discussed?"

"I would welcome the chance to serve with you again, sir, but...there are matters that require my immediate attention elsewhere." He glanced at Caroline again, his heart like lead. "I have decided I...I will let you know before your company sails."

She was my goddess, my bright angel. Love burned in me like an inferno.
But I was ever myself, too wary of a misstep to speak. Wordlessly, I adored
her. Hopelessly, I worshipped her. Now only a thin plume of smoke wafts
from the rubble.
"Oh, fiend take it, what rubbish!"
—Lawrence Sinclair, crumpling up the page and tossing it into the fireplace.

Chapter 22

"Is everything packed?" Lawrence asked his valet, looking up from the last of his correspondence. Once these missives were delivered, all his accounts would be settled.

"Yes, sir," Dudley grumbled as he fastened the strap on Lawrence's trunk. "Will there be anything else?"

"Deliver these round to White's, my tailor, and the landlady." Lawrence handed him the sealed letters containing various payments. Then he reached into his pocket for a handful of coins. "Give these to the boy and send him to the coaching inn to buy three tickets for Cumberland. There's a coach leaving London this afternoon, and I intend that we should be on it."

"Billy is like to run off with your money, sir."

"I think not. The boy's never been anywhere. He won't be able to resist a chance to go to the country."

Lawrence stood to go, but Dudley didn't leap immediately to help him into the jacket that had been draped over his chair. He even had to reach into the cupboard to retrieve his own hat.

Good thing I'm not accustomed to having a valet.

Dudley wasn't the best of servants in normal times. Now, he was nearly useless, pining for Alice before he'd even left her.

"Don't know why you're set on taking Billy with us," Dudley said morosely. "The boy scarcely does a thing around here, and besides that, he must have worms, the way he goes through his victuals without putting on a bit of flesh."

Lawrence suspected Billy didn't really eat that much. More than once, he'd caught him squirreling away buns and sausages in his capacious pockets. The boy shared some of his bounty with friends who were still shifting for themselves on the street. Lawrence couldn't fault him for that.

"I have plans for young Mr. Two Toes." Lawrence hoped to arrange for the boy to stay on at Ware as a stable hand. The country air would do him good. "And plans for you as well."

He hadn't told Dudley about India yet. The valet was upset enough over leaving his sweetheart for the wilds of Cumberland. Dudley would be apoplectic over a sea voyage to the most distant outpost of the British Empire. However, Bredon had insisted Lawrence keep Dudley on and was willing to continue paying his salary to make it so; there was no sending him back to Lovell House. It would have seemed ungrateful. Though his friend had fobbed off a problem servant on him, Lawrence wouldn't dismiss the less-than-adequate Dudley. Given time, perhaps he'd warm to his duties. Given the sack, he would be at the mercy of London in short order.

Even as a boy, Lawrence had never been able to resist picking up a stray.

"I shall meet the pair of you at the coaching inn," he said in a tone that brooked no further argument. Then Lawrence left his suite of rooms on Rathbone Street for the final time. He had one loose end to tie up before he left London.

He'd rather have faced a dozen well-armed Frenchmen than settle this final debt, but there was nothing for it.

He owed Caroline a good-bye.

* * * *

Caroline was beyond out of patience with men in general, and with Lawrence Sinclair in particular. It had been three days since Lord Frampton's ball. How could the man announce to his uncle that he intended to marry her and then blithely ignore her?

He'd left the ball without even saying good night.

The next evening, she'd casually inquired at supper if her brothers had encountered him at White's. Evidently, he'd not made an appearance at the exclusively male club because all she heard were grunts of denial from the men around the dinner table.

Surely Lawrence would ask her father's blessing before he proposed. It was the done thing, after all. So she wondered aloud to the earl whether or not Mr. Sinclair had been round to discuss anything with him.

"Anything at all?"

If Caroline had sprouted a second head, the earl could not have shot her a more surprised look.

"I don't believe Mr. Sinclair and I have any points of common interest," her father had said, raising a quizzical brow. "He's Bredon's friend, not mine."

Her brother Teddy studied his dinner plate with absorption. If he was privy to Lawrence's whereabouts, he wasn't telling.

Frederica and Horatia were no help either. They'd been to a flute recital, a dinner party at Lady Eastbrook's, and a lecture on the beauties of mythology at the Society for the Preservation of Our Classical Heritage since Lord Frampton's ball.

"Mr. Sinclair wasn't at the recital or the dinner," Frederica had told her.

"Freddie slept through most of the lecture, so she wouldn't have noticed if Zeus himself had paraded past her," Horatia had confided.

"I wasn't asleep," Frederica insisted. "I was merely resting my eyes."

"Accompanied by a charming little snore." Horatia patted her forearm. "But if Mr. Sinclair had been there, Caro, I promise, I'd have noticed."

No one had seen the elusive Lawrence Sinclair. Caroline's nerves were wound tighter than the longcase clock.

So when Price announced that Mr. Sinclair had come to call, Caroline nearly went to pieces. Hat in hand, Lawrence filled the parlor doorway with his uniquely masculine presence.

This is it. Calm yourself, she ordered herself sternly. The tone she set now might color their entire married life. *Begin as you mean to continue.*

"Lawrence," she said, once Mr. Price left them in the parlor, with the door properly open to ensure propriety was observed, of course. *It's good to see you,* she meant to say, but the words stuck in her throat.

It wasn't just good to see him. All she could do was see him. The rest of the world melted away around him like a chalk drawing in the rain.

So tall, so strong, so dreadfully wounded inside.

She knew now where his hurts were, and she was confident she could heal them if he'd let her.

"Caroline." He, too, seemed unable to make his voice work.

She gave herself an inward shake. "Shall I ring for tea?" Fussing with a teapot would keep her hands from trembling.

"No, thank you," he said with distant politeness. He turned the brim of his hat through his fingers. Evidently, his hands needed something to do, too. "I don't expect I shall be here long enough for tea."

"Then perhaps you should come to the point," she said. An edge of impatience crept into her tone, but she tried to force it down. This moment was something she would remember all her life. She wanted Lawrence's proposal to be a pleasant memory, not one accompanied by the jumble of frustration that churned through her now. So she smiled at him and said lightly, "If you're not quick about it, I'll send for crumpets in any case, so you'll have something to do with your hands besides wear the felt off that hat."

He stopped fiddling with the gray topper, but he didn't lift his gaze from it.

Anticipation made this moment take forever to arrive, but an actual proposal was a very simple matter indeed. They could complete the whole thing in three words.

"Will you?"

"Yes."

Of course, every girl wanted hearts and flowers, poetry and a fellow on bended knee, but Lawrence wasn't that sort of man. Not that he didn't feel things deeply. She knew he did. His proposal would be unadorned. Probably unconventional.

But she was sure it would be heartfelt.

Once she'd given her consent, they'd both have so many things to do in preparation for the wedding, she didn't even mind that he couldn't stay long. They'd have the rest of their lives to take tea together.

Lawrence finally spoke. "I'm leaving London. This afternoon, in fact."

A piece of her heart broke off and crumbled inside her. "Where are you going?"

"You guessed it," he said with a ghost of a smile tugging at his lips. "I'm going to Ware."

"Oh." She smiled back at him, remembering how his confusion over *where* and *Ware* had led to that tortured first conversation in this very parlor.

"My mother—" he began.

"Oh, yes, of course," Caroline interrupted. How could she have been so selfishly stupid? Lawrence had not seen his mother since he and Bredon returned from the Continent. "Naturally, you wish to assure her you're home safe and sound."

"No, it's not that. I mean, it's not only that," he said, finally meeting her gaze. "She's...ill. Consumption. According to my uncle, she's in the final stages. I only just learned of it."

Caroline sank into a nearby chair. "Oh, Lawrence, I'm so sorry. Please, sit." "No, truly, I cannot stay."

"But you may as well sit until you leave," she insisted. "Honestly, why must you be so difficult?"

"My apologies. I don't mean to be a trial. I merely came to say good-bye." She rose and crossed to stand in front of him. "You felt it important to tell me good-bye?"

"You must think it so, my lady," he said with another small smile. "After all, you once followed me across London so you could chide me for neglecting to do so."

She nodded. "Indeed I did. I fear I have some very unladylike tendencies."

"Which only I seem to bring out," he said, taking a step toward her. "Perhaps my leaving is for the best."

No, she wanted to cry. How could parting from each other ever be best? Now she'd have to wait for that proposal until he'd seen to his poor mother's comfort. "When will you return?"

"I don't believe I will. At least not for longer than it takes for me to board a ship at Wapping Dock," he said. "Colonel Boyle has offered me a major's commission."

Taking ship? They could be married by the captain once they put to sea. How refreshingly different. How utterly romantic. Caroline couldn't have arranged matters better herself.

"Where would w—I mean, you be posted?"

"India."

"The Gorgeous East! How marvelous." Caroline's heart pounded with excitement. The love of a good man, adventure, travel—she was only a few words away from everything she'd ever wanted. "Just think on it. You'll be seeing the world, Lawrence."

"But I won't be seeing you."

If this was the man's way of proposing, he was doing an abysmal job of it. She'd have to give him a nudge. "There is a way for you change that, you know."

"I know," he said. "And once I'd dared hope…that perhaps you…"

Out with it! She'd never had to pry the words from her other suitors. Lawrence was singular in so many ways. She just wished this wasn't one of them.

"You are right to dare," she said softly, "because there is always hope."

"No, Caroline. Sometimes there isn't. Trust me when I tell you, this is how things must be. You will not see me again. Good-bye, my lo—" He stopped himself. "Good-bye."

He turned and started toward the door.

He wasn't proposing. He was leaving. Forever.

"Good-bye? Is that all you have for me?" she said in a strangled voice. The sob in her words must have stopped him, for he turned to look at her. His dark eyes were a study in misery.

"Do you not love me?" Tears pressed against the backs of her eyes and found their way down her cheeks. "Even a little?"

Something like hunger was etched on his features. Then, suddenly, he crossed the room in only a few long paces, grabbed her, and pulled her to him, close, so close she could feel his chest expand with each breath. He kissed her mouth, her cheeks, her closed eyes. His hands found her hair and her coiffure faced ruin, but she didn't care. Not as long as he kept kissing her. There was little tenderness in his embrace. In fact, she suspected she'd have more than one bruise from the way he held her so tightly, but she wouldn't have pulled away for worlds.

The low ache inside wouldn't let her. She pressed herself against him, need and desire so mingled, she wasn't sure who was savaging whom.

Sometimes love isn't fine. Sometimes it's fierce. Who'd have guessed?

It was Lawrence who finally broke off their kiss. He palmed the back of her head and pressed her cheek to his lapel, holding her still. The storm had passed. This was the calm that followed when the world was fresh and new and the frenzy of the tempest had worn itself out.

Except the turmoil still roiled within, because his heart thundered beneath her ear.

"Yes, Caroline, yes," he said softly as the great muscle in his chest began to settle. "I loved you."

Her heart leaped, but then she realized he'd said *loved*.

Past tense.

"I loved you from the moment I saw you," he went on, stroking her hair as he spoke. "I worshipped you in hopeless silence. I envied every smile, every nod, every look you ever gave another man. I'd have opened a vein had you asked it of me. I loved you most desperately."

She pulled away just enough to look up at him. "Then why will you not ask me what is in your heart now? I want you to. Most desperately."

He dropped his arms to his sides and took a step back. "Because I no longer love you in that way."

"But, Lawrence—"

"No, Caroline, please. I deceived myself and you with what was only calf-love. I know that now. I must go." He bent to retrieve his hat. The topper had been dropped and trampled upon sometime during their embrace. It would never be the same.

Neither would she.

Then he made for the door without looking back. "Try not to hate me, will you?"

"How could I hate you?" she whispered after him. "I love you."

He didn't stop. After he closed the door behind him, she sagged against it, sure her legs would not support her otherwise.

"I will always love you, Lawrence Sinclair," she said to the empty room.

Then Lady Caroline Lovell—the breaker of dozens of hearts, the seasoned debutante who never suffered fools gladly, the independent-minded miss who had plans for her life that didn't include a man, thank you very much!—sank to her knees and sobbed like a lost child.

* * * *

On the other side of the door, Lawrence stood motionless, one hand fixed on the knob. His feet wouldn't move. He knew he should go, but his heart was still on the other side of the door.

What he'd told her was true, as far as it went. He didn't love her like some soppy, self-involved boy anymore.

He loved her like a man. And as a man, he wanted only the best for his beloved. Even if that meant he had to give her up.

"Good-bye, my darling," he whispered. "I love you still."

*I never thought I'd fall back on my uncle's advice, but he pounded this
saying into my head as a boy. It's the only thing that makes sense now.
"When a man doesn't know what to do, he should do his duty."*
—Lawrence Sinclair, adrift, aimless, and anguished.

Chapter 23

The Lake District was known for its loveliness—deep forests, crystal
waters, and towering peaks. The air was crisp and sweet with the fragrance
of green, growing things. Unlike London, which never really slept, an
early morning here was so quiet a man could hear his own heartbeat. Only
birdcalls and the occasional lowing of a cow ready for milking disturbed
the stillness. The place made a man thank God for fashioning it to be so
unnecessarily beautiful.

Billy Two-Toes's eyes bugged at each fresh vista as he drank in the new
sights and sounds. The street boy obviously thought he'd been caught up
to Heaven. Even the grumpy Dudley found reasons to smile as their coach
rolled along the narrow roads.

The charm of the Lake District was lost on Lawrence.

He was living by rote. He breathed in. He breathed out. He ate only
because Dudley insisted. When they stopped each night, he lay down in
the sagging bed of a wayside inn, staring into the darkness. He couldn't
sleep. His thoughts circled like a dog chasing its own tail. He relived every
moment he'd spent with Caroline, wondering if there was something he
could have done differently. The outcome never changed. When exhaustion
finally claimed him, his sleep was shallow and restless.

From his earliest days, his uncle had drummed a strong sense of duty
into Lawrence's head. A Sinclair honored his debts. He fulfilled his vows.
He did what was expected of him.

Surprisingly enough, those early teachings steadied him. Duty gave him an anchor.

Lawrence was returning to Ware to see to his mother's comfort in her illness. He owed her that. She'd been as oppressed by Lord Ware's heavy hand as he. Perhaps more so, because he'd at least been able to escape to school and the military, though it hadn't seemed like an escape at the time. More like a banishment. But he'd made a place for himself, both at Harrow and in the service. If not for his mother's illness, he'd have already taken that commission to serve under Colonel Boyle.

That, too, was a type of duty.

The regimen of doing what was expected kept him going. He fought to keep Caroline from sneaking into his thoughts during the day. That was the path to madness. His nights were torture enough.

Their coach finally turned down the long drive and rolled to a stop in front of Ware Hall. The manor house was a stone monstrosity built by the first Earl of Ware in the 1500s. Its turrets boasted mullioned windows, and the four-square design enclosed a courtyard large enough to billet that first lord's troop of fighting men.

Lawrence didn't go in immediately. Instead, he sent Dudley and Billy ahead into the imposing manor to let the servants know he'd arrived. Lawrence set out on foot across the meadow to check the condition of the dower house. The small cottage reserved for widowed countesses cowered beneath a towering arbutus near the edge of the forest.

It was in as poor repair as he'd expected. The thatched roof was open to the sky in several places. Most of the floors and interior walls would need replacing. A couple of windows sagged away from their frames.

In a perverse way, Lawrence was pleased. Renovating the cottage would keep him busy. Organizing the workers and laying out plans for repair would occupy him for several days. He wasn't the sort to stand by while the estate's carpenter and his helpers did all the work. Blisters, sore muscles, even a smashed thumb would be a welcome distraction. Manual labor might be the balm his bruised heart needed.

If his body was exhausted by drudgery, his mind wouldn't find time to remind him each night that his life was over. Only breathing in and out was left.

When he returned to the manor, to his surprise, the servants had lined up on either side of the door to greet him. It was something they'd never have done had Lord Ware been in residence. After Lawrence had left home the first time, his occasional returns were treated with as little fanfare as possible.

"His Lordship isna in residence, Master Lawrence, and willna be, like as not, for a month or more. We just received a letter from Lord Ware about his wedding," Angus Holt, the estate steward, told him.

"Then while my uncle is away, it seems a good time to make repairs to the dower house," Lawrence said. "Let's start with a new roof."

Mr. Holt beamed. "I've been telling His Lordship it was penny wise and pound foolish not to keep the cottage in a better state. Aye, lad, we'll get right to it. Er, I mean, sir. Forgive me, Master Lawrence, I still see you as the boy I knew."

Lawrence just smiled. That boy was long gone. And the man who'd taken his place was a hollow husk, but Mr. Holt didn't need to hear about his woes. "Where will I find my mother?"

"In her chambers," Mrs. Bythesee piped up. She was a round little woman with a kind face. She'd served as housekeeper at Ware Hall for as long as Lawrence could remember and always had a soft spot for boys with skinned knees. "Do ye come now and I'll lead ye up."

Lawrence followed Mrs. Bythesee into the plaster and timbered foyer and up the gleaming staircase. Even in the absence of Lord Ware, the Scottish woman kept the manor sparkling clean. When they reached the floor where the family rooms were, Mrs. Bythesee stopped before his mother's door.

"I dinna ken how much ye know of yer mother's illness, but if it's any consolation to ye, she seems to be in no pain."

Lawrence thanked her and slipped into the room. His mother wasn't in bed, for which he was grateful. Sickrooms made him uncomfortable. Someone had helped her dress. She was ensconced in a stuffed armchair with her feet propped on a hassock. The window was open, sunlight streaming in on her when the clouds suddenly parted. She didn't seem ill. She might only have been resting.

Then Lawrence heard her wheezing inhalation.

She must have heard his soft footfalls as well, for she turned her head.

His mother was thinner than he remembered. Paler. But her smile was still sweet. Her lips lifted in one now.

"Oh, Henry, I knew you'd come."

Henry. She thought he was his father. His chest constricted.

"No, Mother. It's Lawrence."

"Are you sure?" A frown crinkled her brow and she drew a raspy breath. "You're so very like my Henry."

Lawrence had been told he favored his father since he was a small boy. Usually, it was by Lord Ware, who derided him for so strongly resembling the wastrel of the family.

As if Lawrence could help the face God had given him.

His mother lifted a thin hand toward him, and he came to kneel beside her chair.

"Oh, yes. Now I see. You are Lawrence after all." She cupped his cheek and leaned to press a soft kiss on his forehead. Then her brows drew together again. "What's wrong, Son?"

"Nothing," he lied. "I'm fine, Mother."

"No, you're not." It was an assessment, not an accusation. "I see...a deep sadness in you. Please don't let it be for me."

"I'm sad that I stayed away so long."

"Don't be," she said softly. "You have your own life to live. I always understood that."

"You didn't answer my letters," he said. *Also not an accusation.*

His mother shrugged. "Lord Ware must have misplaced them, for I never received any."

"That's too charitable by half," Lawrence said. "He purposely kept them from you."

"I suppose it was for the same reason your uncle made sure we didn't have much time together even when you lived here." His mother cast her gaze out the window, but Lawrence wasn't sure she really saw the trees and steep slopes. She was looking backward again. "Lord Ware said spending time with me would make you turn out like your father."

"Was my father that bad?"

Her eyes glazed over, and Lawrence could tell she was lost in her own thoughts. Finally, she said, "Most would say yes, Henry was bad. He hurt me. So many times I lost count."

Then, inexplicably, she smiled. "But he also made me laugh. And every moment he was with me, he made me feel as if I were the most important person in the world." She fingered her bottom lip for a moment. "Unfortunately, Henry wasn't always with me. But the truth is, if he walked in that door right now, I'd forgive him again. I loved Henry Sinclair, the good, the bad, and everything in between."

Lawrence usually only thought of his father as the black sheep of the family, as he'd been taught to do. Now Henry Sinclair seemed like the luckiest man who'd ever lived. "How could you forgive him like that?"

"It's the only way I know to love, Son. All or nothing," she said, sucking in a shuddering breath. "So, you say your sadness isn't for me. I'm glad to know that. I'm dying, but there's nothing for it."

Death was an unforgiving hound that dogged its prey relentlessly. Whether it brought them to ground in a Cumberland manor or on a field of battle near Peshawar, Death always won. Lawrence was caught in a circular trap. He could only support Caroline if he went soldiering again, but he wouldn't risk leaving her a widow in some surely uncivilized, far-flung post.

"Is there anything to be done about why you're sad, Son?"

"No, Mother. Some things cannot be changed."

He took her hand, and they spent a quiet few minutes, looking out the window together. Then her head drooped, and he realized she'd fallen asleep.

Lawrence lifted her from the chair, cradling her in his arms as if she were the child and he the parent. It was heartbreakingly easy. She was so frail. Light as a little girl.

The back of his throat ached as he laid her down on the coverlet of her bed. She didn't wake. Her chest rose and fell in the shallowest of breaths. Lawrence leaned down and kissed her temple just where a tiny blue vein showed through her nearly translucent skin.

When Lawrence walked softly from the chamber and pulled the door closed behind him, he realized his uncle was wrong. A battle death was not the best Lawrence could hope to achieve in his lifetime. Seeing that his mother died in comfort was. He'd make sure the dower house was as snug and safe and pleasant as he could make it.

After that, Lawrence didn't care what happened to him.

Once a lady decides to take responsibility for her own life, she must not expect that every circumstance in which she finds herself will be conducive to happiness. The good news, however, is that she has, within her own will, the means to change her situation.
—from Mrs. Hester Birdwhistle's *Advice to Adventurous Ladies When They Find Themselves in the Slough of Despond*

Chapter 24

In the Lovell House parlor, Caroline pulled the diaphanous curtain aside and watched the carriage traffic rattling past. The Season was winding down. Several families on fashionable St. James Square were already abandoning London. They fled the approaching heat and insalubrious smells that would soon waft from the summertime Thames for the cool comfort of their country estates.

Only I seem to not be going anywhere.

"That doesn't sound quite right." Frederica was perched on one end of the settee, but now she leaned toward Horatia, who was seated on the other. She craned her neck, the better to peer at the pamphlet in her friend's hands. "Are you sure you read it properly?"

"See for yourself." Horatia followed each word with her finger. "It says here, 'She has, within her own will, the means to change her situation.' You're the one who's keen on Mrs. Birdwhistle's philosophy, Caro. What do you make of that one?"

"Sorry." Caroline let the curtain drop and rejoined her friends. "I wasn't attending."

Frederica whisked the pamphlet from Horatia's hand and, in a schoolgirl monotone, reread the passage aloud. "It sounds as if Mrs. Birdwhistle believes we can change our circumstances by simply willing them to be different. That can't be right, can it?"

"I don't know. There's a vaguely scriptural slant to the idea." Horatia tapped her temple. "Only last Sunday, didn't the vicar quote, 'as a man thinketh in his heart, so is he?'"

"The operative word is *man*," Caroline said flatly. In making proposals, as in so much else in life, men always had the final say. What a woman wished counted for nothing in the grand scheme of things. "A man may be able to alter his situation by sheer dint of will, but I see no evidence it would work for one of our gender. Do let's talk about something else."

Caroline crossed her arms, a clear signal the topic was closed.

"London is getting too warm for comfort, don't you think?" Frederica fanned herself, falling back on the tried-and-true subject of the weather. "The Framptons have left for the country already. The Harewoods are leaving, too, but not until the girls give one final wind recital on Tuesday week."

Horatia rolled her eyes. "Please God, my family will be going before then. If I never have to hear another ill-tuned oboe, it will be too soon. Honestly, Miss Harewood's poor instrument sounds like a duck being sat upon half the time."

"Then by those lights, the bassoon must be a gander." Freddie giggled. "Oh, dear. Now I shan't be able to squirm through their last recital without thinking about ducks and geese."

"When is your family leaving, Caro?" Horatia asked.

"Father won't go until the House of Lords calls for a recess."

"But that doesn't mean you have to stay and swelter," Horatia said. "Wouldn't it be lovely if we could all go to the country together?"

"For a house party you mean?" Caroline asked.

"What an excellent idea, Horatia. We've been together nearly every day here in Town. I shall miss being able to see both of you so often," Frederica said. "But if we had a house party to look forward to, I might be able to bear the separation a bit easier."

"Well, my family certainly can't host one," Horatia said grumpily. "Father says he spent far too much this Season and a little rusticating and simplicity will do us a world of good."

Caroline knew it would do her father's purse good at least. Horatia was still smarting over not finding a husband during the weeks her family had spent in London. "Perhaps if you economize in the country, he'll allow more for your wardrobe next Season."

"Perhaps," Horatia said, brightening a bit. "At least I shan't have to worry about Penelope Braithwaite showing up everywhere in the same gown I'm wearing."

"Oh! That reminds me." Frederica suddenly sat forward, balancing on the edge of her seat. "Did you hear? Lady Ackworth's nosiness has finally resulted in something worthwhile."

"Do tell," Horatia said with a skeptical glance at Freddie. It was unusual for her to be the bearer of gossipy tidings. That was Horatia's bailiwick.

"Lady Ackworth uncovered the mystery behind your identical dresses." Frederica's mouth drew up into a smug little bow. Clearly, beating Horatia to fresh gossip was a matter for quiet celebration.

Horatia's frocks were hardly identical to Miss Braithwaite's. They were more like pale copies, Caroline thought but didn't say. It would have been an unnecessary slap. Horatia had suffered enough over Miss Braithwaite's gowns. "What did Lady Ackworth discover?"

"Well, it seems Madame Fournier has not been designing her own gowns for some time. Miss Braithwaite's frocks were made by her apprentice, Mary Woodyard," Freddie said with glee. "She sewed them by night, after she finished her work for her mistress. Honestly, the girl must never have slept. In any case, Madame Fournier caught her at it, took the money she'd made on the side, and decided to use the patterns of Miss Braithwaite's dresses for the ones she sold to Horatia."

How Lady Ackworth had discovered this unusual bit of intelligence was a mystery. If she'd been a man, Caroline had no doubt the lady could have served as an agent for the Crown. But none of the girls doubted the veracity of the story. Whatever Lady Ackworth said, however cruel or cutting it might be, was invariably true.

"Once the matter came to light, did Madame Fournier give Miss Woodyard the sack?" Caroline asked.

"No, the poor girl has another year to serve on her apprenticeship, and Madame will not release her early. She'll be working her fingers to nubbins for at least one more Season," Frederica said with a sigh.

"It will serve Madame Fournier right if Miss Woodyard sets up shop right next to her once she's free," Horatia announced. "I'd certainly give her my custom."

If you can afford her, Caroline thought, but she held her tongue. Lord Frampton's ball had taught her to guard her lips more carefully, even when there wasn't a string quartet around. Besides, Horatia couldn't help that her father either didn't have the money to spend or didn't want to spend it in support of his daughter's appearance on the marriage mart.

Again, men make all the rules, she fumed.

"I suspect a lot of people would support Miss Woodyard if she opens a shop," Frederica went on. "No one likes a thief. And one could argue that Madame Fournier stole her apprentice's creations. But I doubt Mary Woodyard will still be sewing once she's finished her obligation to Madame Fournier."

"Why is that?" Caroline asked.

"As it turns out, Miss Woodyard has been quietly helping a gaggle of street urchins, sewing up their ragged clothes, giving them extra food, things like that. Heaven only knows when the girl found the time!" Frederica explained. "In any case, Lady Ackworth and her clique have taken up Miss Woodyard's cause and are raising funds to start a public school for homeless boys. They'll be taught to read, write, and do sums, all while having a roof over their heads to boot. Once she finishes her apprenticeship, Mary Woodyard is to be their first headmistress."

"Well, I never thought I'd say this, but huzzah for Lady Ackworth." Caroline raised her teacup in salute to the ton's nemesis. Her friends joined her.

"You know," Horatia said, "I believe this proves Mrs. Birdwhistle correct."

"How so?" Caroline asked.

"Mary Woodyard's situation is certainly going to change."

"Yes, but that's Lady Ackworth's doing," Caroline pointed out. "Not because Miss Woodyard *willed* her life to be different."

"Perhaps, but Lady Ackworth wouldn't have discovered Miss Woodyard and her charity cause if she hadn't first sleuthed out the situation about Miss Braithwaite's dresses," Horatia said. "Mary Woodyard *willed* her life to be different by taking matters into her own hands, first by helping those street boys and then by designing more beautiful gowns than her mistress could. Her will led her to take action, which led to a change in her circumstance."

"I believe you're right, Horatia," Frederica said. "Mrs. Birdwhistle's advice is once again proved correct."

Could it be that simple? For all her claims of being an independent woman who sought out adventures, Caroline had been doing nothing but waiting. She hadn't really acted on what she wanted. A devious but brilliant idea burst in her brain with such force, she nearly leapt to her feet.

"I'm sorry to be such a bad hostess," she told her friends, "but I suddenly realize there's something to which I must attend immediately."

"Can we help?" Frederica asked.

"No. This is something I must do for myself."

To her friends' credit, they didn't press her. As soon as Freddie and Horatia left, Caroline practically bounded up the stairs to her chamber.

Heart racing, she drew Lawrence's letter to Teddy from its hiding place in her journal. She reread the simple note in which Lawrence first confessed that he loved her. She drew courage from it.

And strength of will.

Lawrence Sinclair loved her still. She was sure of it. Despite his denials, he wasn't a weathercock sort of man, changing with the slightest puff of wind. He was steady. Dependable. He didn't give his heart freely, but he'd given it to her.

She didn't think he could unlove her that easily.

Now she only had to convince him of it.

Caroline pulled out a fresh sheet of foolscap and sharpened her quill. It would be tricky to recreate the unusual slant of Lawrence's handwriting, but with a little practice, she was sure she could do it.

* * * *

A few nights later, Bredon announced at supper that he'd received a letter from his friend, Lawrence Sinclair.

"Apparently, he wishes us to come to Ware. With his uncle away on his honeymoon, Sinclair has decided to host a house party," Teddy said with a shrug.

"Whom do you mean by *us*?" Lady Chatham asked, casting a curious glance at her firstborn son between spoonfuls of white soup.

"All of us," Teddy said. "You and Father, me, Ben, Thomas, and Charles. Caroline, too. This is Sinclair's way of repaying our hospitality while he was in London."

Lady Chatham made a tsking noise. "That guest list seems a terribly one-sided party. All those gentlemen with only Caroline and me will make for awkward placement around the dinner table."

Caroline was careful not to meet her mother's gaze. She was sure her mother would see her guile if she did. But so much depended on this admittedly underhanded plan, Caroline clutched her napkin in a death grip under the table.

"Surprisingly enough, Lawrence has considered that problem," Teddy said. "Sinclair wants us to bring Caro's friends, Miss Tilbury and Miss Englewood, as well."

"Well, that evens up the table somewhat."

"Hmph," was all Caroline's father said.

"Did Mr. Sinclair say how his mother is?" her mother asked. "I was given to understand she's quite ill."

Oh, no. Caroline had forgotten all about Lawrence's mother. *How could I be so heartless? So selfish? I deserve to go to hell.*

But she wanted more than anything to go to Ware Hall.

"Come to think on it, he didn't mention her in his letter," Teddy said. "Her health must have taken a turn for the better if he's planning a house party."

"Well, that's a mercy, then, isn't it? What do you think, dear?" Lady Chatham asked her husband. "Shall we accept?"

"I can't be haring off to Cumberland as long as the House of Lords is in session," Lord Chatham said. "Those blasted Whigs will—"

"Language, my lord," Lady Chatham said, slanting her gaze toward Caroline, whose tender ears evidently needed protecting.

As if I haven't heard Father say far worse about the Whigs.

Lord Chatham cleared his throat. "The Whigs would love to see every Tory leave London early so they can ram through their rebellious agenda. No, I must stay until the last gavel falls."

"Then I shall stay as well," Lady Chatham said with a sigh. Clearly, Caroline's mother was ready to quit London for the summer.

"But that doesn't mean we must remain," Teddy pointed out.

"No, I suppose not," their mother said. "Of course, Caroline will want to stay in London as long as possible. The Season isn't quite finished, and the Harewood girls are giving their final recital in a few days."

The boys groaned in unison.

"Mother, I'm satisfied the Season is over for me," Caroline said.

"Are you sure, dear?"

The subtext was plain. This was Caroline's third time casting her line into the marriage mart and the third time she'd be leaving Town without reeling in a husband. Despite her better than passable looks, impeccable breeding, and generous dowry, Caroline would be accounted hopelessly on the shelf.

"I'm sure, Mother."

"If Caro goes, you must accompany her and the boys to Ware," Lord Chatham told his wife.

"If you insist," Lady Chatham said. "We'll miss the Harewoods' recital. I shall send our regrets."

This was greeted by cheers all around. Teddy proposed a toast to a summer without wind instruments. Despite the general good mood round the table, Caroline's mother sent her a sad smile.

Lady Chatham clearly feared Caroline would die an old maid. Caroline almost wanted to tell her not to worry. If Mrs. Birdwhistle was right, if a woman could change her circumstance by virtue of her will, Lady Chatham's only daughter would never make a spinster.

"I've not been to Cumberland," Caroline said, trying not to let the triumph she felt show. She'd never been fond of cards, but now she wondered if she ought not to try her hand at games of chance. Forging an invitation from Lawrence was a rash act, but it was the last card she had to play. She'd been lucky. Her boldness was paying off. Teddy was convinced the letter had come from his friend, so she saw no way the invitation could be traced back to her. The game with Lawrence Sinclair was still on. "Tell me, is the Lake District as lovely as everyone says?"

The time we have on earth is finite. The good we might do for those we love in that short span is infinite.
—Lawrence Sinclair, who is trying mightily to make up for lost time.

Chapter 25

Lawrence paused at the edge of the meadow to survey the improvements to the dower house. The plastered wattle-and-daub between dark half timbers gleamed with fresh whitewash. A new thatched roof topped the structure. Glass glinted in every previously broken window. The wooden awnings, which had hung drunkenly over each portal, were now repaired, repainted, and shaded the interior of the cottage, like half-closed eyes. The chimney was being repointed by the estate's mason and his apprentice. Once it was thoroughly cleaned, it would heat the whole cottage. Inside, all the walls had been replastered, the oak floors sanded and restained.

Best of all, his mother was there, seated by the newly planted flowerbed, enjoying the sunshine and watching the workmen at their tasks. Lawrence had ordered a simple chaise to be built so his mother could be carried out by a couple of servants to benefit from the fresh air. It wasn't a perfect solution, but it would do until a Bath chair, specially fitted with four wheels, arrived next week.

"I'd never have thought it possible, Master Lawrence," Mrs. Bythesee said as she came up beside him, "but your mother hasna looked this good in months."

"Your receipt for horehound cough syrup seems to have helped her." With regular doses of Mrs. Bythesee's concoction, his mother coughed less often and less virulently. When she did, she took pains to conceal her bloodstained handkerchief, but Lawrence was too observant for his own comfort. Despite her brave smiles, the disease marched on. Consumption took its victims slowly, like a gentle tide going out, and like a tide, was just as relentless. "I know this new medicine is not a cure."

"Perhaps no'," the housekeeper agreed, "but she feels better, and there's a mercy. Every day is a blessing. Besides, the best medicine for your mother has been for you to come home. For the now, at least."

He couldn't stay. Everyone knew that without saying. Once Lord Ware and his new bride returned to Cumberland, Lawrence would be cordially invited to leave. Probably for good this time. But during this precious time, he was determined to make his mother's brief future at Ware as comfortable as possible.

"A letter has come for you." Mrs. Bythesee handed him a many-folded piece of foolscap. The red blob of sealing wax was embossed with the Chatham crest. The letter had been franked, a privilege of the noble class, so Mrs. Bythesee hadn't been required to pay the carrier for its delivery.

Lawrence's heart raced.

A letter from Lovell House. Caroline?

He thought he'd let it go, but hope sprang up to lodge in his throat. Then, when he tore the letter open, he recognized the masculine scrawl. It was from Bredon.

My dear Sinclair,

Chances are good we shall arrive before this missive does, but in case the post is running faster, or we are running slower—a real possibility when one is traveling with four ladies!—I am writing to let you know we have accepted the invitation to your house party and shall descend upon you shortly.

"What invitation?" Lawrence muttered without reading further.

"I beg your pardon?" Mrs. Bythesee said. "Did ye say something, sir?"

Lawrence shook his head and read on in disbelief. Apparently, he was about to become an unwitting host.

"Somehow, my friend Lord Bredon is under the mistaken notion that I'm throwing a house party here at Ware."

"A house party, aye? Well, that's grand, is that!" Mrs. Bythesee said, skipping right over the *mistaken* part of Lawrence's sentence. "Ware hasna seen enough merriment these past years and that's a fact. How many guests will ye be expecting, then?"

Lawrence shook his head. He'd never even been a guest at a house party. He hadn't the first clue how to host one. "It's a mistake. It must be. I don't know how this could have happened."

"Well, if it be a mistake, 'tis a happy one," Mrs. Bythesee said, cheerful as a cricket. "Guests will liven up the old walls of Ware Hall, indeed they will. How many?"

Clearly, Mrs. Bythesee wouldn't be dissuaded. Lawrence scanned the letter again.

Father insists on staying in London until the House of Lords calls a recess, but my lady mother, my sister, her two friends—though, in truth, I wonder at you for including Horatia and Frederica; a couple of parakeets chatter less than those two—three of my brothers, and yours truly are on our way.

Lawrence did a quick count. "Have we room for eight?"

Mrs. Bythesee laughed. "We've room for eighty. The rooms will want airing and fresh linens, o' course. Some of 'em have been shut up for years. Mercy on us, there's much to be done." She began to tick off the tasks on her bony fingers. "There's a fair fiddle player in the village. Ye'll want him for the dancing, I shouldn't wonder."

"There'll be dancing?"

"If there's lads and lasses about, it follows there'll be dancing," Mrs. Bythesee said. "I'll have Mr. Holt set up archery butts. Like as not there'll be some among your party who'll wish to have a tournament. Let me see. What else?"

"I expect they'll want to ride." Lawrence knew Caroline enjoyed taking a turn on Rotten Row during the fashionable hour for it. If she rode here at Ware, he could show her some of the loveliest places on the estate, the river that cascaded down from the peaks and the overlook with a long view of Conniston Water. Lawrence began to warm to the idea of a house party. It might well be the best mistake of his life.

"Aye, a good suggestion, sir," Mrs. Bythesee said. "The stable hands will make sure we've enough saddles and mounts for your guests to go riding of a morning. Cook will be in fine fettle when I tell her she must do up some special dainties for each night. And I'll have to check do we have supplies enough to feast your guests good and proper."

The housekeeper scrunched up her face and frowned, as if trying to visualize the manor's pantry. "I expect we'll have to slaughter a calf or two to add to the larder. A few chickens willna come amiss either."

"I had no idea so much was involved in hosting a party."

"Of course not. Men never do. But just you leave it to me. I'll see ye through this right enough. It'll do everyone who works here good to have a bit o' purpose again," Mrs. Bythesee said. "When will your guests be arriving?"

The letter was dated three days ago. "Soon."

"Then there's no time to lose." The housekeeper turned and started to scurry away.

"Wait! What about Mother?" Lawrence said. "Won't she be upset by the commotion of having so many people about?"

"Commotion is life, Master Lawrence. Your mother will dearly love watching you enjoy a slice of it. Mark my words, this house party might even put a rose or two back into her cheeks." She took another couple of steps toward the manor, then stopped and turned back to him. "Oh! One more thing. How long will your guests be staying?"

"Lord Bredon doesn't say."

"Undoubtedly, ye must have mentioned a length of time in your invitation, sir," she suggested, as if he were a schoolboy who'd failed to study and must be coaxed to come up with the right answer.

"But I didn't—oh, never mind," he said. Mrs. Bythesee refused to believe Lawrence hadn't actually issued an invitation. He decided not to fight her on it. "Plan on a fortnight. Maybe more."

It was a long way from London to Ware, after all. They must expect to stay a while.

Bredon was playing a joke on him. That's all it was.

Still, the part of his heart he kept tucked away lest it become too painful to bear began to throb afresh.

Caroline is on her way.

* * * *

When the Lovell party, along with the Misses Tilbury and Englewood, arrived around teatime the next day, Lawrence got a rather nasty surprise.

Oliver Rowley had joined them en route.

"We happened upon Rowley in York when the coach stopped to change horses," Bredon explained when he stepped down from his conveyance. His expression said he was sorry, though his good manners forbade him to voice the sentiment. "As Rowley had no pressing business elsewhere, he decided to join us."

Rowley stood there with that smug look of his, daring Lawrence to be rude to him before the Lovells and Caroline's friends. "Isn't it a wonder? I've seen the splendors of the capitals of Europe but never the Lake District. No time like the present, eh, Sinclair?"

Lawrence didn't see a way around it. The only decent thing to do was welcome *all* his guests. After all, he hadn't invited any of them.

That first night, once the gentlemen had finished their after-dinner port, he cornered Rowley as the rest of the men left the dining room to join the ladies in the parlor.

"Not so fast," Lawrence said, his hand heavy on the door through which Rowley intended to follow Bredon. "Why did you come here?"

"Following your advice, Sinclair," Rowley said smoothly. He was one of those few souls who could not be shamed, no matter what he did. "Aren't you the one who told me to leave London for a bit of rusticating in the country?"

"I expected you to retire to your own estate, not descend upon my uncle's."

"Well, there's a bit of a problem with my going back to Rowley End. It's rather the first place my creditors will look for me." He had the grace to hang his head for a heartbeat or two, but his sly expression was anything but penitent.

"So you expect me to shelter you from them."

"Not for long. Perhaps a month or so…"

"That's not possible." Lawrence folded his arms across his chest. Not even he would be allowed to remain at Ware once his uncle returned.

"Come, Sinclair, be reasonable," Rowley said. "Once the House of Lords acts on my petition, I'll be able to sell off the woods and settle everything in one fell swoop."

Until the next time you find yourself in Dun territory, Lawrence thought but didn't say. It wouldn't matter if Rowley owned a hundred thousand acres, a fleet of merchant ships, and married an heiress to boot. He would never have enough to cover his impulsive extravagances.

"Very well; you may stay as long as the Lovells do." Lawrence held up a hand to stop him when Rowley would have started thanking him. "But only so long as you behave yourself. And by that I mean I don't catch you trying to seduce Miss Tilbury again."

"Wouldn't dream of it."

"Being caught or seducing?" Lawrence figured he'd better nail this slippery eel to the floor.

Rowley raised a hand as if taking an oath. "I will not seduce Miss Tilbury."

"Or any other lady."

"You have my word."

Lawrence scoffed. "Or any of the help."

"Be serious, Sinclair."

"I am serious."

"I can't be held to account if one of your serving wenches takes a shine to me." Rowley chuckled. "Besides, what else is a chambermaid for?" "For doing her job without being molested by the likes of you." Lawrence grasped his wrist and squeezed hard enough to make the bones grate against each other. Rowley cowered in pain. "If I catch you putting so much as a toe out of line around *any* woman at Ware—and I don't care if it's the washerwoman or the goose girl—I will thrash you into next week and send you packing. Am I understood?"

Biting his lip, Rowley nodded. Then, once Lawrence released him, he slinked away to join the others in the parlor.

As it happened, Lawrence needn't have worried about Rowley trying to ruin Freddie.

None of the women were ever left alone, which meant Lawrence had no opportunity to speak with Caroline privately either. Not during the heart-stopping moment when she alighted from the coach and the soles of her feet touched Ware for the first time, nor at any time thereafter. Part of the charm of a house party, it seemed, was in keeping the group together for myriad activities punctuated by endless picnics, teas, and meals.

Lawrence would have been hopelessly out of his depth as a host if Mrs. Bythesee hadn't kept the party on schedule. She appeared at his elbow at the most opportune of times, whispering what came next.

And as an added blessing, the housekeeper's prediction about his mother came true. Eleanor Sinclair brightened more each day. She and Lady Chatham clicked like magnets, delighting in each other's company. They were invariably side by side, engaged in companionable embroidery or poring over Lady Chatham's newest edition of *Bell's Court and Fashionable Magazine*. Then, once Eleanor's Bath chair arrived, she was nigh unstoppable. She joined in when the whole group played at cards or listened to Ben play his violin.

His mother passed as happy a time at this unexpected house party as Lawrence could have wished. However, he didn't fool himself into believing this improvement was a turning point in her disease. Consumption often came in sieges, allowing for a respite before it returned to ravage its sufferer. But this was a sweet respite, and if not for the fact that Caroline was just as unreachable as if she were still in London, Lawrence would have been in perfect charity with the world.

He tried seeking Caroline out during the day, but invariably her friends, or her mother, or even *his* mother—drat the luck!—were at her side. After supper, everyone gathered in the large drawing room for games or music or read-alouds. When the whole group was together, Caroline barely met his gaze. Even when the fiddler came so they could dance, Caroline partnered with her brothers instead of him. Every time he screwed up his courage to approach her, she was already being led away on someone else's arm. When the fiddler struck up a waltz, Lawrence ached to hold her, but he knew he didn't deserve to.

Not after he'd left her weeping in London.

After a whole week, Lawrence still didn't know why the Lovells had brought a house party to Ware's door. But he knew why Caroline was there.

She's come to torture me.

The world would be a far better place if a woman could put words into a man's mouth. Heaven knows, I can't find them on my own. Not if I had a map and a compass.

—Lawrence Sinclair, after a particularly trying evening during which he didn't screw up his courage to ask her to dance, no, not once!

Chapter 26

He deserved torture. He was worse than a cur. He'd made the love of his life cry in the Lovell House parlor and hadn't offered her comfort.

Of course, he could scarcely be blamed for that because there was no comfort to be had. Nothing had changed. He still couldn't marry her, drag her off to the back of beyond, and chance making a widow of her in that godforsaken post.

Even so, if he didn't manage to speak to her alone soon, he couldn't guarantee he wouldn't rise from his bed by night and go in search of her. Lawrence knew very well which chamber Mrs. Bythesee had assigned to her. It was located on the family floor, with a bank of windows framing a wide view of the meadow and winding lane. Beyond the woods, the Scottish hills rose in the distance.

If he didn't know better, he'd swear Mrs. Bythesee had known how he felt about Caroline. Her chamber was the best Ware had to offer.

Under the cover of night, Lawrence could find her room without a candle to light his way.

Bad form, Sinclair. You claim to love the lady, yet all you think of is how easy it would be to put her in a compromising situation.

He managed to keep himself from wandering to her chamber by night, but sleep, when it finally came for him, was fitful and full of strange dreams.

In his night phantom, mist rose from the lowlands and then slowly parted to reveal a horse and rider. He recognized his dead cousin. Astride the stallion he'd fallen from, Ralph called out to Lawrence, *"Come ride with me."*

Then the dream Ralph wheeled his mount around and barreled across the heath, bouncing out of rhythm with his horse, but holding on gamely. Just as he had in life.

"No! Ralph, stop!" Lawrence yelled after him. Though he'd no hope of catching the stallion, he tried to run after them. The ground beneath his feet turned boggy and his boots stuck fast.

Clammy sickness crawled over his skin. He was helpless. Ralph was going to die and he couldn't do a thing about it.

Then, to his wonderment, Ralph and his horse easily took the leap that should have killed them both.

"Don't fear to try, Lawrence. If you do, you'll miss everything."

He jerked awake and sat up straight in bed. The dream was so real. From the sound of his cousin's voice to the freckles that peppered Ralph's nose, it felt truer than his memory of actual events.

But Ralph's message to him was all wrong. In life, Ralph had tried the jump and failed. He'd died. He hadn't grown up, or found someone to love, or assumed his proper station in life. He had tried and, as a result, he'd missed everything.

Or had he?

When Ralph had sailed over the barrier for real, before his disastrous landing, Lawrence remembered how he'd cried out in triumph. He'd never sounded so happy in all his life.

Was that momentary joy worth it? Was an unrealized tomorrow worth more than today?

Or is this day, this moment, this breath all any of us ever really has?

Lawrence churned the vision over and over in his mind.

By the time sunrise glinted on the topmost turret of Ware Hall, Lawrence was up and out and headed for the stables. He told himself he wasn't looking for Ralph's shade out on the moor. He wasn't the type to believe in spirits. He just needed a good hard ride to clear his head.

And then, after a blistering hour or so in the saddle, he was determined to speak his piece to Caroline, whether he could find her alone or not.

When he rounded the first bend in the bridle path that led through the woods, he caught a glimpse of another rider in the early morning mist. An invisible fist squeezed his heart.

Caroline.

She was wearing a deep green riding habit with a jaunty hat tilted on her dark hair. She waved to him and then set off at a gallop in the opposite direction. Even riding side-saddle, she coaxed her mount to a breakneck pace. Lawrence leaned forward in the saddle and gave chase.

When they broke free of the forest and raced over the heath, Lawrence finally caught her. Laughing with pleasure, she reined in her mare. The horse danced under her, still ready to run.

"Well, that was quite wonderful," she said breathlessly. Her eyes sparkled, and a thin sheen of perspiration glinted on her brow. Her hat had come unpinned and dangled down her back. The slender ribbon tied at her throat was the only reason it hadn't flown away during their sprint. Her hair, too, had come unbound and framed her face with unruly curls.

She was the most beautiful thing he'd ever seen, and Lawrence wanted her more than his next breath. He dismounted, hurried to her side, and lifted her from the saddle. Her body slid against his all the way down.

She was unbearably soft against his hardness. He didn't release his hold on her narrow waist even once her feet touched the ground. Her breasts rose and fell in shallow breaths.

She waited for him to speak.

His heart might be full, but his throat was tight. No words came to his lips. Lawrence would give his left arm if, just once, he could be charming and glib like Rowley. That blasted fellow always knew what to say to make a girl feel cherished and special, even if he didn't love her in the least.

"Come now, Mr. Sinclair, cat got your tongue?" she said softly.

He wanted to speak, to tell her all he felt, all he needed, but no language could express it. Nothing would explain the depth, the height, the sheer, unbridled, writhing mass of his love for her.

Her brow crinkled in a hurt frown. "We've had our misunderstandings in the past, but surely we can at least have a civilized conversation."

"No, we can't," he said, his voice husky with emotion. "What I want from you is not the least civilized."

He might not be able to speak his heart, but he could act. So, without warning, he took her mouth.

It wasn't a tender kiss. He wished it could have been, but he was incapable of tenderness at that moment. He demanded. He took.

She gave.

God be praised!

When he finally released her, she didn't try to break away from him. Her lips kiss-swollen, she blinked up at him.

"You've been saving up."

"You've no idea."

That made her laugh. He joined her.

"Thank God for your lightness," he whispered. "You lift the darkness from me."

He kissed her again, less savagely this time, but only a little less.

Merciful Lord, she's so sweet.

"I love…you, Caroline." The words were torn from his throat between kisses. "I love…your heart…your mouth…your hair."

He fisted a handful of it and pulled as gently as he could, so her head would tip back, baring her neck. He kissed his way down her neck to the lapel of her riding habit and back up.

"Dear God, your scent…"

His tongue dove between her teeth and then hers followed his back into his mouth. He managed to mumble, "I love your tongue."

"Do you mean you love what I say with it or what I do with it?" she asked when he gave her a second to come up for air.

"Both! I love everything about you, Caroline Lovell."

She kissed along his jawline, feathery light kisses that set his nerves tingling. Then she leaned back a bit to peer up at him. "Would you love me still if I told you I forged your handwriting and invited us all here?"

"I'd love you even more."

She laughed again.

Suddenly, he wasn't quite sure how, they sank down and became all tangled up together there on the lush grass. Her sweet body was under his, but instead of struggling to get away, she was rocking her pelvis slowly against him.

"Marry me, Caroline."

He needed an answer or he'd run mad, but she couldn't give him one because he was kissing her again. His hands brushed the front of her bodice. She was so soft. And she smelled like honeysuckle and warm horse and crushed velvet.

"I'll take a commission under Colonel Boyle and we'll go to India together. I swear you'll never want for anything."

Then he plunged his hand down the front of her habit to cup a breast.

So soft, and yet such a hard little tip.

She put her palms on his chest and pushed. He pulled his hand from that blessed place, but his palm still tingled.

"What has changed?" she asked.

He met her gaze. "What do you mean?"

"You left me in London." Tears threatened, but she blinked them back. "But you meant to ask me to marry you there."

It must have been her footfalls he'd heard in the hallway when he was confronting his uncle in Lord Frampton's smoking room. "I won't ask how you know that."

She blushed. "Perhaps it's best if you don't."

"Clearly a man cannot keep secrets from you."

She cupped his cheek. "Again, it's best if you don't."

"Then here's the truth. I was afraid to try, Caroline. I didn't ask you to be my wife because a soldier's life is uncertain. I feared dying in Peshawar. What if I left you there a widow?"

She pushed against his chest again, and this time he rolled off her. She sat up and peered down at him. "So instead you were willing to leave me in London?"

"I thought it best. But now I know I can't live on *what if*." He pulled her down on top of him and she came willingly. "The joy of now is worth any sorrow that may come."

"But you will try mightily not to bring me sorrow, won't you?"

"With all my strength," he promised. "Caroline, if we don't grab now with both hands, we'll miss *everything*."

"Agreed." She kissed him slowly, her hair tumbling around them like a dark wave. Then she raised herself back up. "But next time you make a decision that affects both of us, you might try asking my opinion first."

"So, you think there will be a next time."

"Plenty of them. I intend to be Mrs. Lawrence Sinclair for a very long time."

She'll have me! God be praised! He brought her knuckles to his lips and kissed them as if they were the crown jewels. "I don't think I can wait for the banns to be read."

"Certainly not," she agreed. "That would take weeks. The ship's captain can marry us once we board for India."

Lawrence shook his head. "I can't wait for the ship either. Gretna Green is only ten miles from here. We can say the words over an anvil and be wed on the spot."

"Well, that's not the wedding every girl dreams of." Caroline smiled wryly. "But then, I'm not every girl. In truth, I didn't imagine I'd ever marry."

"And I never dared imagine it, but Caroline, please, if you've any mercy in your heart, let us fly north." Now that she'd accepted him, he had to marry her straightaway, before she changed her mind. "Right now."

"In a bit, Lawrence." Her eyes took on a hazy, languid glow as she lay back in the grass. "I'm not feeling particularly merciful at the moment."

She lifted an arm in invitation.

He lowered himself to cover her body with his. Then, in a flurry of hastily shoved aside clothing, hot kisses, and urgent pleas, *everything* started to happen.

A button popped here. A hand sought there. The whole world went warm and sweet and dewy. A kind of madness seized him.

But Lawrence clung to a bit of sanity. He was determined for this moment not to descend into mindless rutting. When he finally sank into her, he wanted it to have the rightness of a homecoming, of two halves of a whole finally joined.

With every ounce of will he possessed, he forced himself to roll off her and stand. His breath came in short pants.

"You're about to become my wife," he said, his voice far less steady than he'd hoped.

"Exactly." She sat up, her brow furrowed in frustration. "You can't imagine I'd allow such liberties otherwise."

"Of course not. And that's also why I won't take you now. We're so close to the border, so close to being man and wife, I won't dishonor you by treating you like some milkmaid who's ready for a roll in the hay."

She cast him a sly smile and ran the tip of her pink tongue along her bottom lip. "But what if I *want* a roll in the hay?"

Is she trying to kill me? He started counting backward from one hundred in his mind. In Latin. But he still crowded his trousers so badly, he feared he might disgrace himself.

He held out a hand, praying she'd take it so he could pull her to her feet. "Caroline, once we're married, I will roll you whenever and wherever you'll let me, but please God, help me get you safe to Scotland first."

Even though Mrs. Birdwhistle was a married lady at one time, she was free with her advice on how to arrange one's life without a man. Why, oh why, did she never compose a treatise on how to live with one?
—from Lady Caroline's diary

Chapter 27

Riding was torture. Caroline ached all the way to the border. She'd never wanted so badly, even though she wasn't quite sure where the wanting would lead. She was confident Lawrence knew how to still that ache, and that he'd take care of the confusing sensations still coursing through her body.

Drat the man for his overblown devotion to what was right!

But then, as her body settled a bit, she began to rethink things. She realized she should be grateful for Lawrence's sense of honor. It meant his vow of faithfulness would be worth something.

By the time she spoke the words with him at the first smith's forge they came to once they crossed the border, she thanked God for Lawrence Sinclair. This good man would always care for her, always protect her, always put her needs first. His calm, steady soul was the sea on which she would launch her life.

There was no one like him.

And if I never see Zanzibar, I'll still die a happy woman simply because I loved this man.

Once the quick ceremony was over, Lawrence paid the smith for officiating and asked him if there was an inn nearby.

"The closest lies another ten miles to the north, in the next glen but one," the smith said with a grin. Then he took in Caroline's elegant, albeit grass-stained riding habit. "I canna vouch for its cleanliness, though."

Lawrence glanced upward to measure the sun's progress across the sky. "Can't be much past noon. We can be back at Ware in time for supper." Caroline bit back her disappointment, but she agreed it was the best plan. Her mother would be frantic if she didn't return by nightfall. Bredon would likely organize a search party. He'd scour the hills with a pack of hunting dogs and hire every available villager to beat the bushes.

They rode southward at a more leisurely pace. Once they passed the stone boundary fence that marked the northernmost edge of Ware, Lawrence began pointing out some of the landmarks to her. He had bought a meat pie from the smith's wife so they'd have something to eat on the way. Both of them had skipped breakfast, so they stopped by a rollicking stream, hobbled their horses, and had a rustic picnic.

"Never let it be said I neglect my wife's appetite," he said as he used his boot knife to slice the pie.

"What kind of meat is it?" Caroline asked, eyeing the pie with suspicion.

Lawrence shrugged. "It came from the place that gave the world haggis, so perhaps it's best if we don't inquire too deeply into the ingredients."

But whatever had gone into its making, the pie was delicious. Its crust was light and layered, the filling thick and well-spiced.

"This might just be hunger talking," Caroline said as she licked her fingers, "but that may be the best mysterious meat pie I ever ate."

Lawrence caught one of her hands and brought it to his mouth. Then he sucked a dab of filling off her pinky. His gaze intense, he watched her as he did it. That low ache inside her began again.

"There are other kinds of hunger," he said.

"Never let it be said I neglect my husband's appetite," she said lightly. Then suddenly serious, she leaned toward him and pressed her mouth to his neck, tasting his skin, salty and warm. Beneath her lips, his pulse quickened. "But I don't know what to do. Please, Lawrence. Show me how to love you."

"Just be your sweet self." He gathered her in his arms and she melted into them. His hands slid over her, taking his time. He trailed his broad fingers over the charged surface of her bare wrists. Shivers raced through her.

Then he turned his attention to her bodice, helping her out of her jacket and shirt until she was only in her chemise and stays from the waist up. She mirrored his movements, revealing more of the mysteries of this man as she discarded each article of clothing. She traced circles across his shoulders and then down his chest. She loved the feel of him, hard and hot under her fingertips.

He found her mouth and poured himself into the kiss while his fingers worked the laces on her stays. After she wiggled out of her long, full skirt, he spread it on the ground. The yards of fabric made an admirable blanket. They rolled together on it as he kissed her again, more deeply this time. She helped him pull up her thin chemise, grudgingly breaking off the kiss only for the brief time it took to yank the fabric over her head. He made short work of her pantalettes.

She was suddenly naked as Eve. Yet she felt no shame.

His hot gaze traveled the length of her, from the crown of her head to her curled toes. It was right that he should. She was his, after all. "I'm glad you made us wait."

"I'm not sure how much longer I can," he admitted, love shining in his dark eyes. "But I want this to be good for you."

"I'm with my husband. How could it not be?"

He caressed her bare breasts, his hands warm and strong. Caroline felt as if she'd swallowed a sunburst. Blood sang warmly through her veins. That low ache became a throbbing drumbeat.

She tugged at his trousers and slid them down his hard thighs.

Caroline knew what men looked like. She and Freddie and Horatia had slipped away from old Anna Creassy's watchful eye and sneaked into an exhibit of Greek statuary once. But nothing she'd seen preserved in marble prepared her for the glory of the real thing.

Lawrence was ready for her, but when she touched him, he shuddered and pulled her hand away.

"Not yet." The huskiness of his voice told her he was struggling for control.

Then he rolled toward her, and she found she'd moved off the blanket of her skirt. Her bare back was cushioned by grass. It was cool and soft against her skin, the long blades tickling her. She raised her arms over her head in surrender. Lawrence began exploring her with his mouth, down the side of her neck, grazing her collarbone, and finally suckling her.

She arched into his mouth. She was his, totally and completely. Whatever he wanted, she'd give.

But when he raised his head to meet her eyes, Caroline saw that her new husband did not intend to take. He wanted to give.

And he surely did.

Pleasure washed over her as he touched and teased her in the most surprising of places. He nuzzled her navel. He tongued the soft creases of her knees and elbows. His hands explored the dip of her back. Lawrence led her through an incoming tide of exquisite torment.

"What do you want me to do?" she asked, gasping when his teeth lightly grazed her.

"I'll show you more later," he said hoarsely. "This time is for you."

He moved down her body.

Caroline moaned his name. She writhed under him. She clutched at his shoulders. She begged him to stop.

She feared he might.

When he finally relented and started to enter her, she cried out in relief.

He bit his lip, straining to hold back, but she urged him forward with incoherent little sounds. She couldn't have formed a real word just then if her hope of Heaven depended on it. Then he pushed in with one long thrust. Pain ripped through her.

She didn't care.

Lawrence was hot and hard and strong. The wonder of holding him inside her was such bliss, it far outweighed the quick pain. A tear slid down her cheek.

He saw it and held himself motionless. "Are you all right?"

"I'm better than all right. I'm yours. It's a happy tear."

He began to move, and she answered him. Heart on heart, skin on skin, they were becoming one being. Slowly at first, then with increasing urgency, they strained against each other, surged into each other. Pleasure and pain blurred, but all that mattered was being joined to this man, this frustratingly honorable, this quietly unknowable, this singular man who was now her husband.

Caroline had the strange sensation of standing with her toes hanging off the very edge of a precipice. Then suddenly she plunged over it. All sense of herself burned away in throbbing joy.

She and Lawrence had created something new between them. Whatever happened in the future, wherever she went, she would always carry a piece of Lawrence's soul with her, and he would carry hers. She'd never be alone again.

What a strange thought. She wondered if she'd gone a bit mad.

Then the madness seemed to subside. Lawrence rolled onto his back, pulled the skirt around her to cover her, and snugged her against his side.

"At the risk of starting this marriage off on the wrong foot, I have to tell you, husband, you were right."

"I was?"

"Yes. By waiting until after our vows, what we just did wasn't the least bit wicked," she said. Freddie and Horatia would never guess at some of what passed between a man and a woman in a million years. Not that

Caroline had any intention of enlightening them. This was just for her and Lawrence. "Though I must admit, parts of it were quite surprising."

"I hope that means you approve," he said with a chuckle.

"Oh, I do. And it's not just me. God does, too. All this falls under the creation story, you know, and the Bible tells us He called his creation good."

"I had no idea you were such a theologian," Lawrence said. "Hmm. It's been a while since I was in church, but I seem to recall that God said it was *very* good."

She tugged at his chest hair. "Is that your way of fishing for a compliment?"

"No." He grinned wickedly at her. "Just a repeat performance."

The Spanish claim that God told man to take what he wanted and then pay for it. As long as Caroline is by my side, I have everything a man could wish. I've yet to see a bill, but when it comes, I'll pay happily, considering it a bargain well made.
—Lawrence Sinclair, who was feeling more in charity with the world than ever in his entire life.

Chapter 28

The sun had already dropped beyond the western peaks and the sky was awash in pearl gray by the time Lawrence and Caroline rode back into Ware. He'd hoped to slip in unnoticed, but evidently, they'd been missed.

Billy Two Toes was in the stables, where he'd taken up residence since arriving at Ware. After living rough on the streets of London, he hadn't felt right in one of the servant chambers just under the rafters in the manor house. The haymow, however, suited him just fine, and he'd made himself useful, feeding, watering, and currying the estate's small herd. Now he was quick to come take the reins of Lawrence and Caroline's horses.

But before they could dismount, Dudley came sprinting out to the stables. He'd evidently been watching for their return.

"Oh, thank heaven you're back, sir. Both of you. Safe and sound." The valet had run so hard, he had to suck in a fresh lungful every third word or so. "Lady Chatham is beside herself, and Lord Bredon, he's…well, he's…"

"Upset?" Lawrence supplied.

"Oh, he'd have to climb down several rungs on the ladder to be only upset." Dudley's keen gaze raked them both.

Lawrence realized they looked more than a bit travel worn. Caroline and he were downright disheveled. He reached over and plucked a foxtail from behind Caroline's ear.

"My brother will change his tune once he hears our news," his lovely new wife said, lifting her chin. They'd been well and truly caught, but she was determined to brazen it out. "Shall we go tell them, Mr. Sinclair?" He doffed his hat. "With pleasure, Mrs. Sinclair."

Dudley gasped in surprise while Lawrence gave Caroline his arm. "Then that means Alice and me'll be in the same household again, won't it?"

"As long as your Alice is a good sailor." Lawrence realized suddenly that marriage meant he'd added yet another servant to his small household. He still didn't think Dudley was of much use, but he was stuck with him, especially now that Alice would be coming with Caroline. Of course his wife would need a maid to attend her. He ought to have considered that. He just hadn't considered paying Alice's fare to India, as well as her wages, lodging, and board. The costs of acquiring a wife were probably much greater than he'd imagined. A major's salary was looking smaller all the time.

No matter. He wouldn't undo this day for worlds.

He and Caroline promenaded across the courtyard as if they were about to be presented to the king.

The whole party was assembled in the parlor, and when Lawrence and Caroline came through the door, pandemonium erupted. Everyone began talking at once. His mother and Lady Chatham praised heaven for their safe return, clasping hands with a gentleman in a vicar's collar to whom Lawrence had never been introduced. Caroline's brothers loudly demanded to know where they'd been. Rowley nearly drowned them out in his effort to denounce Lawrence as the worst sort of rake. Frederica and Horatia almost knocked Caroline to the ground in their rush to hug her.

Only Bredon stood in stony silence by the fireplace. He skewered Lawrence with a murderous look. When the general frenzy died down, he said in a low, but no less threatening tone, "I counted you a friend, Sinclair. How could you bring dishonor to my sister?"

"I would never do such a thing. That's why I married her."

The clamor began afresh. Lawrence raised both hands to quiet them back down.

"We were wed in Scotland this morning. It's done and there's an end to it. I intend to take a major's commission, and my wife and I will sail for India in a few weeks."

"I rather think you won't," Bredon said, his former scowl now turning into an enigmatic smile.

Lawrence bristled. "You cannot stop us."

Then the man with the vicar's collar cleared his throat loudly. "I believe I just might."

Ben put a hand on the man's shoulder. "This is Philip Exeter, an old classmate of mine from Oxford. He's recently taken the living at the parish church in the village here. When he was going through the old vicar's desk, he happened upon something that might interest you."

"Yes, well, here it is." Reverend Exeter held out a much-folded piece of foolscap, yellowed with age. A broken piece of wax still clung to it. The seal was embossed with enough of the crest of Ware to show its origin. Someone with access to the official seal of the earldom had written the old letter.

"What is it?" Lawrence asked.

"A letter from your father's mother. It is addressed, if you can credit it, to the Almighty Himself," Reverend Exeter said. "Evidently, it was given to my predecessor for safekeeping. I didn't break the seal. That was done long ago. But I must admit, I did read it."

"That's all right, Philip," Ben said to his friend. "I doubt the good Lord minds."

Lawrence took the letter and turned it over in his hands. "I never knew my grandmother."

"Perhaps not, but she was thinking, if not of you in particular, at least of the welfare of her progeny in general. Lady Ware wrote this shortly before she died. Her last confession, I'd say it was."

"What did she have to confess?"

"Quite a bit, actually," the vicar said. "I understand your father and your uncle were twins."

"Yes." Lawrence stared down at the letter but couldn't seem to make his eyes focus on the small, spidery script. "They didn't favor each other much, but they did share a birthday."

"And therein lies the reason for this letter. Apparently, your grandmother convinced the midwife to collude with her to conceal the truth about which son was born first. She describes Henry, your father, as a seemly child, possessed of a full head of dark hair and a lusty cry. Harcourt, your uncle, was the runt of the litter—her words, not mine—and had the ruddy coloring of her side of the family. The smaller babe seemed so frail, so weak, she wanted to assure his place in the world should he reach adulthood, which she doubted. So your lady grandmother made her midwife swear that Harcourt was the heir, even though Henry was actually her firstborn."

Lawrence swallowed hard. "So my father should have been the earl."

"Not should have been," Bredon said. "Was. Only no one knew it."

"Why didn't your predecessor come forward with this letter sooner?" Caroline asked Reverend Exeter.

The vicar's gaze swept upward. "God knows. Perhaps your grandmother swore him to secrecy as well."

"Or he tried to bring the matter to light and your uncle paid him to conceal it," Ben said.

Lawrence thought it likely. It explained so much. No wonder his uncle had hated him since he was a boy.

"I'm loath to believe a man of the cloth could be bought on such a matter, but avarice afflicts all flesh. It's possible," the vicar said. "But the main thing is, the truth has come to light now. Henry Sinclair was rightwise born the Earl of Ware."

Lawrence drew a deep breath. He was his father's heir. "What's to be done?"

"We show this letter to your uncle and convince him to do the right thing."

"And if he will not?" Caroline asked.

"Then we haul him before the House of Lords with our evidence, and the result will be the same." Bredon pointed to the letter. "Trust me, Sinclair, I have a vested interest in seeing you elevated to the earldom. I'd rather my sister were a countess than a major's wife."

Caroline tucked her hand into the crook of Lawrence's arm. "I don't care which I am, so long as I'm his."

He covered her hand with his. *Just when I thought I couldn't love her more.*

* * * *

Supper turned into a celebration. The rest of the evening was filled with music and dancing and good-natured fun aimed at embarrassing the newly married couple. Lawrence and Caroline were put to bed, supposedly for the first time, by their families and left in peace to consummate their union.

"Quite satisfactory, my lord," Caroline said once they lay spent and gasping on the fresh sheets.

"Only satisfactory? I can do better than that."

"If you can, I'm a dead woman."

Caroline didn't die. But he did make her cry out loud enough for Bredon to tease him over it at breakfast the next morning before any of the ladies joined them. The Lovell brothers slapped his back and cuffed him upside the head as they passed behind him. He'd acquired not just a wife, but a whole quiver of new relations intent on making him part of their big, boisterous family.

Lawrence hadn't felt that sort of acceptance since Ralph died. Ben, Charles, Thomas, and especially Bredon, were his brothers now. Only one masculine face was missing from the table.

"Where's Rowley?" Lawrence helped himself to a heaping plate of coddled eggs and kippers. Cook had outdone herself with the light, fluffy rolls. Lawrence took three.

Married life made a man hungry.

"Probably still abed," Bredon said. "That scoundrel doesn't rise before noon if he can help it."

"Not today, sir," Dudley said as he reheated Bredon's tea. Because Ware wasn't accustomed to so many guests, Dudley had been pressed into service as a footman once more. Lawrence only hoped the fellow wouldn't spill scalding water on Bredon. He'd waited a long time to have a brother. It'd be a shame to ruin one now. "I chanced to see Lord Rowley head for the stables just after sunup."

Bredon frowned. "He rarely shows such industry."

"Unless..." Lawrence left his breakfast and hurried to the earl's study. *His* study now, he reminded himself.

Bredon fell into step behind him. "Where did you put that letter?"

They feared the same thing. "I locked it in the earl's desk."

My desk.

When Lawrence pushed open the door to the study, it was obvious the place had been quietly ransacked. Every drawer was open, and several dozen ledger books lay crack-spined on the floor. Worst of all, the one locked drawer in the large mahogany desk had been pried open.

The letter was gone.

Could a sunrise in Zanzibar be lovelier than the ones here at Ware?
Though I may never settle the question by direct experience, I shall always
believe they could not be.
—from the journal of Mrs. Lawrence Sinclair

Chapter 29

Caroline stood at the window, drinking in the green hills and the blue peaks beyond them. Her throat ached at the beauty of it all. Now that she'd seen Ware, how would she ever bear to leave it? Especially since by rights, it all belonged to her husband. A week had passed since Lord Rowley had disappeared with the letter. Lawrence and her brothers had set off immediately, but no trace of him could be found on the main roads. After a few days, they'd discovered he'd made for Maryport and taken ship. All they could do was wait to see what came of it.

"There is no question of what he's done," Horatia said from her place on the settee. She had draped a skein of yarn around Frederica's outstretched hands and was now winding it into a tight but untidy ball. "Lord Rowley has taken that letter to Lord Ware."

"Don't you mean to Lord Ware's uncle?" Freddie pointed out. "Mr. Sinclair is really the earl, isn't he?"

"Yes, yes, of course. Don't muddle the issue. I'm talking about Lord Rowley," Horatia explained with exaggerated patience. "Honestly, Freddie, and to think you were going to give him the supper dance at Lord and Lady Frampton's ball."

"But in the end I didn't. I do think it's what happens in the end that counts. Isn't that right, Caro?"

"Yes, Freddie," she said, not leaving her place by the window. Sometimes she thought she'd spent the better part of her life by a window, waiting for something, anything, to signal the next change in her life. "What happens in the end is what counts."

But why couldn't the right thing happen?

By all that was holy, Lawrence was the earl. He ought to have been raised in privilege and with pride of place. Instead, he was treated as a poor relation and given only grudging leavings by his noble family. It hurt her heart to think he might be cheated of all he was born to yet again.

Not that Caroline put any store in titles. She wasn't dazzled by the prospect of a countess's coronet. It didn't signify in the slightest because, by virtue of her birth, she'd always be Lady Caroline no matter who she'd married. But Lawrence had been so deeply happy when he'd learned his true heritage.

That was what mattered.

Then she spied a coach approaching, coming down the long, winding lane. No crest gleamed from its side, but she knew, without knowing how, that it must be the old Lord Ware coming back to assert himself. Lawrence must have seen it, too, for she saw him walk outside and then stand, hands fisted at his waist, waiting for the conveyance to stop.

Without a word of explanation to her friends, Caroline flew out of the parlor, into the grand foyer, and out the big double doors to stand beside her husband. By the time she reached him, Lawrence's uncle had already climbed from the coach and was handing down his new wife. Caroline spared a moment of pity for Penelope Braithwaite, who looked rather green about the gills.

Dusty, hot, and bumpy, coach travel was not for everyone. Especially not a woman in the early months of confinement.

Rowley emerged after them, an evil grin on his handsome face.

Caroline could bear it no more. "Oliver, how could you?"

"Rather easily, as it turns out. Before I left London, I happened to hear that Lord Ware and his bride were honeymooning in Bath. Finding His Lordship was only a matter of a short voyage from Maryport, a few discreet inquiries, and—"

"No," Caroline interrupted. "I mean how could you betray us this way?"

"Again, rather easily," Rowley said. "But I prefer not to look on this as a betrayal. It's more of an investment. Am I right, Lord Ware?"

"Rest assured, Rowley," Lawrence's uncle said gruffly, "you will be rewarded."

"So you have the letter," Lawrence said.

"I do," his uncle confirmed. "Without it, you have no claim to the earldom."

He was right. Even if her family, her friends, and she and Lawrence swore on a stack of Bibles that they'd seen the letter and read the earth-shattering revelations it contained, without physical proof of the late Lady Ware's confession, no court in the land would rule against Harcourt Sinclair.

Lawrence and his uncle locked gazes. Her new husband had confided that he had a violent streak, and Caroline had seen it in action in Lord Frampton's smoking room. But surely Lawrence wouldn't set upon his uncle. If he lost control of that "inner warrior," as he called it, he'd never forgive himself for attacking a man so much older than he.

"No, Nephew, you have no claim at all without that letter," Harcourt Sinclair said. "But you do have an uncle who believes in duty. First, last, and always. And a man's ultimate duty is to the truth."

He reached into his waistcoat pocket and withdrew the aged foolscap. Then he held it out to Lawrence.

"Take it and take Ware," his uncle growled. "I give it into your keeping, a strong estate on a sound footing. Try to keep it that way."

Astonished, Lawrence took the letter from Harcourt's hand. "I don't know what to say."

"Hmph. Still don't have a nut in your noggin, eh? Some things never change. Even so, I expect you'll make more of Ware than your wastrel father would have." He turned to go. His bedraggled bride trailed after him.

"Wait. Where will you go, Uncle?"

The former earl rounded on him. "What do you care? I sent you out into the world to fend for yourself. I expect you to do no less to me."

"But I'm not like you. Unless it be with respect to duty," Lawrence said. "As the Earl of Ware, it is my duty to see to the comfort and living of my close relations. We have never seen eye to eye on anything, Uncle, but like it or not, we share Sinclair blood. We are…family."

"I won't take charity from you."

"I wouldn't offer it." Harcourt Sinclair had been left with nothing. Lawrence decided to give the old man a way to accept his help without damaging his pride. "But I will need an adviser as I take my place as the earl. You are uniquely qualified to serve in that capacity."

His uncle squinted at him. "I am, at that. But we've hated each other so long, I don't see how we could abide spending time with each other."

"Perhaps in small doses to start. I've resented you, Uncle. That's true enough," Lawrence admitted. "But I've never hated you."

A muscle jerked in the old man's cheek. "Don't expect me to move into the manor and live under your thumb all day and night."

"No. I was thinking you and your new wife would take residence in the dower house."

Harcourt scoffed. "Now I see your game. You'd love to see me living in squalor, wouldn't you?"

"Actually, Lawrence has just had the dower house completely redone because you said his mother would be moving into it. We'd like to keep her here in the manor with us, so the cottage is yours." Caroline turned her brightest smile on the old curmudgeon. "Trust me, sir. It's a charming place because it was rehabilitated with love."

And perhaps, with love and time, her husband's relationship with his uncle might be rehabilitated as well.

Harcourt glanced at his bride, who smiled weakly back at him. He held out a hand to Lawrence. "Very well. I accept your offer, Nephew."

The men shook hands.

"Wait a moment. What about me?" Rowley whined. "I was promised a reward."

Harcourt cast him a scathing look and then turned back to Lawrence. "I'd like to offer my first piece of advice."

"I'm listening."

"Rowley wants a reward. Give that ninnyhammer what he deserves."

"With pleasure!" Lawrence threw a punch to Rowley's jaw that sent the man sprawling on the pea gravel. He sat up, spitting blood and one of his eyeteeth. Its loss would spoil his looks for life.

"You've ruined me, Sinclair," he wailed.

"You ruined yourself, Rowley. Now get off my land."

Rowley limped away.

Then Lawrence turned to Caroline, clasping both her hands in his. "I won't be taking that commission now."

"I shouldn't think so."

"But I do want to take you to Zanzibar."

"Someday, love. There's ever so much for us to do here."

They'd drawn quite a crowd, with all Caroline's brothers, her mother and Lawrence's, as well as her friends, gathered round. But even with all those onlookers, he pulled her into his arms and bent to touch his forehead to hers.

"Traveling to Zanzibar is your dream," he said softly. "I want to make all your dreams come true."

"You have. You do. Besides, Zanzibar is an island, a fixed place on the map, isn't it?"

"Yes."

"Then it will be there when we're ready for it. Right now, being your wife, living here at Ware, that's enough adventure for me."

"You'll let me know if that changes."

"It may," Caroline said with a smile. She was a weathercock, after all. "Don't be surprised if you find a packed trunk in the foyer someday."

He kissed her long and deeply. "As long as you also pack one for me."

Lord Bredon and the Bachelor's Bible.

Read on for an excerpt from Mia Marlowe's next historical romance!

Prologue

A drizzly Tuesday afternoon in London, 1816

Lady Daly studiously avoided the coffin at the far end of the parlor and concentrated instead on the living mourners milling about the dead man. She leaned toward the woman next to her and whispered, "What did he die of?"

Her friend did not bother to whisper back. "It wasn't of loneliness, of that you may be certain."

No one in polite society would fail to recognize the snide voice of the second speaker. It belonged to Lady Ackworth, the self-appointed arbitress of good behavior and the general terror of the ton. She kept a running account of all the rakes and roués making the rounds of the great houses and delighted in naming and shaming their hapless conquests. She knew who owed whom exorbitant gambling debts and whose credit was no longer welcome at fashionable establishments. It was generally accepted that if Lady Ackworth didn't know of a thing, it couldn't be of much import and, in fact, had probably never happened.

"Sir Erasmus Howard rarely suffered from the lack of feminine companionship," Lady Ackworth went on more softly, "especially when Lady Howard was not in Town."

It was only a whisper, but the unkind accusation seemed to swirl in the air above their heads. However, if the gathered crowd of mourners in Sir Erasmus's London town house heard the gossip's unkind patter, they were too well-bred to show it. Shortly, the entire assembly would form a procession from the Howard residence to the church on the next block, where a brief service would be held, followed by immediate interment in the small churchyard.

It wasn't usual for ladies of quality to complete the entire ritual, a graveside being considered too stark a reality for their delicate constitutions, but Lady Ackworth was not the sort to do anything by halves. She'd see Sir Erasmus firmly in the ground, no matter how soggy the walk to his yawning grave.

How else could she speak with authority on the event in the days to come?

"Sadly, infidelity is not an exceptional failing among gentlemen nowadays." Lady Daly eyed a few peers she suspected of the fault.

"It has always been thus, and frankly, I can't imagine what gentlewoman would have it otherwise. Once one has had children, one needn't be troubled with that marital duty, and good riddance to it, say I." Lady Ackworth made a small moue of distaste. "However, Sir Erasmus would have done well to be more discreet."

Other than that all-too-common fault, the gossips agreed Lady Howard had little room for complaint in her marriage. Sir Erasmus had provided lavishly for her. His young wife never wanted for jewels or a wardrobe cut in the first stare of fashion. If Lady Howard wished to improve one of her husband's many homes, he apparently trusted her judgment on the matter, for he opened his purse wide to let her spend whatever was necessary.

"In many respects," Lady Daly said, "Sir Erasmus Howard was a fine husband."

"Indeed. But was Lady Howard a fine wife?"

"She's managed his funeral well enough." Lady Daly fingered the delicate black gloves tied up with a sprig of rosemary and a long length of ebony ribbon. Quite correctly, she'd been given the mourning token when she arrived, as had Lady Ackworth. The gentlemen assembled had all been presented with black hat bands and handkerchiefs. The house was draped with ebony bunting, and the servants presented appropriately somber expressions while they offered refreshments, which were routinely ignored. No one could fault Lady Howard for not following the prescribed mourning rituals.

At that moment, the widow appeared at the head of the long staircase and made her way sedately down. She seemed to be floating, for her head of raven hair didn't bob a bit and there was a becoming sheen to the whites of her dark eyes, evidence, no doubt, of private grief.

Lady Daly nodded in tacit approval. It was beyond distasteful to express strong emotion in public, but a hint of contained sadness was wholly proper.

The widow didn't smile to acknowledge the presence of the other mourners. At least not by conscious volition. Everyone who knew the lady was aware that, by a trick of musculature, the corners of her mouth naturally turned up ever so slightly.

The effect was reminiscent of the Mona Lisa, of whose enigmatic smile Lady Daly had only heard rumors. She found it charming. Lady Ackworth, on the other hand, always held that the tiny expression revealed a bit of smugness, as if Lady Howard were keeping a delicious secret and the slight smile betrayed her.

"She looks terribly pale, doesn't she?" Lady Daly said.

"Black will do that to a body." Lady Ackworth smoothed the skirt of the bombazine gown she kept at the ready for just such occasions. "It makes everyone appear wan, which equals boring. Look at me. I'm positively peaked."

However, Lady Daly didn't think Lady Howard appeared wan or boring. She looked far lovelier than a widow ought. There was a huge difference between pale and listless, and pale and…mysterious.

"I've heard her new situation means she'll have to come down in the world quite a bit," Lady Daly leaned in to whisper.

"I should say so. Not only is Sir Erasmus's mother still living, which means there will be two dowagers splitting that portion, but her stepson has considerable debts. Now that he's inherited the baronetcy, his creditors will make short work of the estate's assets, so the dowagers' due will be smaller yet." Lady Ackworth made a tsking sound. "This may very well be the last time London Society sees Lady Howard."

Threadbare gentility loomed in the widow's future. For the first time since Lady Daly arrived to join the mourners, real tears of sympathy pressed against the backs of her eyes. Too many gentlewomen were reduced to penury by the untimely demise of their men. Fortunately, her husband—such a clever man—had arranged to die before he could accumulate too much debt. Lord Daly had left their son with a solid estate in Surrey and her with a lavish annuity that was the envy of the ton.

"It's a pity all around. Sir Erasmus was quite a bit older than Lady Howard, but he was certainly no dotard," she said. "Had he been ill long?"

"No. Death came to him suddenly." Lady Ackworth narrowed her eyes at Lady Howard, who was accepting condolences with an air of gracious resignation. "It does seem odd, doesn't it?"

"Was it apoplexy that carried him off?"

"Not that I've heard."

"A weakness of the chest perhaps?" Lady Daly wondered aloud.

"The Howards have always had the constitution of a horse."

A ghastly thought crossed Lady Daly's mind. "You don't suspect... foul play, do you?"

"Did I say so? What a distasteful idea!" Lady Ackworth whipped out the ornate black fan she kept specifically for funerals and beat the air with it. "I'm surprised at you for broaching such a disturbing topic when we are practically at the gentleman's graveside."

Severely chastened, Lady Daly bit her lower lip.

"Still..." Lady Ackworth cocked her head to one side, as she always did when deciding to appropriate someone else's idea and make it her own. "For a gentleman as hale and hearty as Sir Erasmus to be stricken so unexpectedly...it does make one wonder if he was hastened to his death somehow."

Lady Daly glanced across the room at the widow, who was seated near the wide front window, looking out into the deepening twilight. A small frown drew Lady Howard's delicate brows together and, combined with that mysterious smile, hers was a face at war with itself. Less charitable souls might misconstrue the expression entirely.

"I wonder what Lady Howard is thinking."

If she could have peeked into the lady's mind at that moment, she'd have been more than disturbed. Only one thought was singing through Lady Howard's whole being.

I'm finally free.

Meet the Author

Mia Marlowe learned much of what she knows about storytelling from singing. A classically trained soprano, Mia won the District Metropolitan Opera Auditions after graduating summa cum laude from the University of Northern Iowa. She and her family have lived in nine different states, but she now calls the Ozarks home.

Learn more about Mia at www.miamarlowe.com.

Printed in the United States
by Baker & Taylor Publisher Services